Writings on the Walls

Fosseway Writers

ISBN: 9798397558884

Independently published, available as paperback or e-book.

1st edition

www.fossewaywriters.wordpress.com

Cover picture by very kind permission of Vanessa Stone
VanessaStoneArtist.com

Edited by Maria Dziedzan, Linda Cooper and N.K Rowe.
Typesetting by N.K. Rowe

Fosseway Writers

We are a long-established group based in and around Newark, Nottinghamshire (itself situated on the old Roman 'Fosse Way', which is mostly now the route of the modern A46).

The aims of the group are to:

• provide a welcoming and stimulating environment for local writers;

• engage with, support and encourage local people who would like to try writing but don't know where to start;

• help members to improve and develop their writing skills;

...all through meetings, workshops, friendly socials and online interaction.

Contact Fosseway Writers:

• www.fossewaywriters.wordpress.com

• fosseway.writers@mail.com

• Find us on Facebook and Twitter via @FossewayWriters

Other books by the group:

Gobstoppers, Shrimps and Sour Monkeys:
Fosseway Writers Anthology 2018

'This smorgasbord of stories and poems from the talented group of Fosseway Writers is by turns witty, dark and poignant — and deliciously moreish.' Clare Harvey (author of The Gunner Girl, The English Agent, The Night Raid).

Burning Old School Ties

Hercules Clay Comprehensive School is having a reunion to celebrate the 30th anniversary of the Class of '89. We follow eight former pupils as they return to a school they left over two decades ago and none of them are the same as they were. Some have lost their way, some have blossomed, others have reinvented themselves and some are back for revenge. A unique writing project, this is a collaborative novel by members of Fosseway Writers: eight authors, eight voices, eight intertwined tales within one story focused on one night

The Brinwade Chronicles

In a village nestling on a Nottinghamshire hill, hidden by ancient trees, off the beaten track but close to a web of rivers and roads, railways and power lines...there's a crackle of something different, a hint of mystical doorways, tales of unusual inhabitants, the irrepressible force of Nature, the Supernatural and the downright Unnatural. Welcome to Brinwade Catlow, a village like no other. The Chronicles contain twenty-eight stories written by a coven of thirteen authors from Fosseway Writers. Be prepared for Gothic tales which span the years, which surprise and entertain... and which caress your senses with icy fingers of dread.

Blood, Sweat and Typewriters:
Fosseway Writers Anthology 2022

A collection of short stories, flash fiction and poetry from current members of Fosseway Writers. Featuring competition winners and content previously selected for other literary publications, this book also contains a wide variety of genres and styles from eighteen different writers. You will find family dramas, beautiful travelogues, unreliable histories, personal recollections, unexpected twists, quirky tales and a taste of the supernatural. They might not have been written on actual typewriters and the amounts of blood and sweat exuded might have been no more than a paper cut in a warm room, but playing the creative licence card is one of the perks of being a writer.

Contents

Introduction

'I'VE HAD AN idea,' said Clair.

'Oh, yeah?' said Nick.

'For the next book.'

'Oh, okay.' Nick sighed inwardly. They hadn't actually finished the book they were currently working on. What with work and everything he felt like he had too many tabs open and he didn't really have the RAM to think about adding another one.

'We could write stories about, or inspired by, the buildings of Newark.' Clair stared at Nick waiting for a response. She was very persistent.

Thoughts were processed and logged in Nick's CPU. 'Yeah, that could work.' Another tab was opened.

'And then at the next Book Festival,' continued Clair, 'we could have a walking tour around the town between the buildings we've written about, ending at our stall where everyone will buy a copy of the book.'

Blimey, thought Nick, *that's brilliant.*

I'm not sure if we'll get the tour organised, but here's the book. A fair amount of research went on and we're all very grateful to everyone who helped us pull this together. There were a range of reasons for selecting the buildings, from snippets of folklore through to literal kerb appeal. For example, I picked a building I once lived next to and a building I used to work in. Others found curious facts and histories that they wanted to elaborate on. Sam's choice of a modern hotel was sheer bloody-mindedness because everyone else was doing something old.

Bear in mind that although the buildings do really exist, these stories are works of fiction. We hope they help people look at their surroundings with new eyes and perhaps invent a few stories of their own.

Nick Rowe
Chair, Fosseway Writers
May 2023

Hanging Out to Dry

by Linda Cooper

'WELL, IT WAS your idea to move here,' I yell at the door as it slams in my face, the echo resonating down the whole street.

There's no reply from inside and a feeling of dread envelops me like a swirling winter fog. She's threatened many times if I don't alter my ways she'll throw me out and change the locks until I've sorted myself, but I know this time she means it. It may have been her suggestion to move to Newark but I know her intentions were good and I agreed to it, hoping it would improve our lives and we could repair our relationship. Neither of us were very familiar with the town but I know I'm the one with a problem and it's me who has to do something about it. I have to face the fact I need help but can I really force myself to stand up in a room full of strangers and confess?

'My name is Toby and I'm an alcoholic.' Just the thought of it makes me want another drink.

She's been aware of my alcohol abuse for a long time but I've been in denial and played down the idea that it's ruining our life together. Don't get me wrong. I'm not one of those aggressive drunks who beats up anyone and anything in sight; rather one who becomes over generous and does stupid, clumsy things. I spend too much money on booze and not enough time with her and now it's reached crisis point. She won't tolerate my irresponsibility any longer and she's chucked me out with just a bag of basics and told me not to return until I've reformed. But where to start? A pub is the obvious choice for me but I can't face my local, where fellow drinkers know me, and I certainly don't want them to know about what's just happened. Ironically, there are loads of pubs in Newark, though I've rarely frequented many, so for tonight I'll have to go somewhere new to contemplate what I'm going to do, and more urgently where I'm going to sleep.

I head off down Middle Gate and come across a pub I've not noticed before, The Spread Eagle. I promise myself I'll just have a couple of drinks while I process my jumbled thoughts. It looks like a very old building but the interior is pleasant enough, strangely reminiscent of something from the Sixties, when my then underage drinking habit began. Thankfully, it's quiet inside with only one man sitting on a stool at the bar. He nods and smiles as I order a pint and I can feel his eyes on me as I walk to a table in a secluded corner near a window. Two sups later he's standing in front of me.

'Mind if I join you?'

I don't like to be rude and I'm not unsociable normally, especially after a drink or five and besides, I could do with a distraction to avoid drowning in my misery. Drowning in alcohol is a regular occurrence which may not be the answer to anything but for the moment it's all I can manage.

'Not seen you in here before. Local or visiting?'

'Moved here a few months ago after I retired.'

'A wise choice, my friend. Newark is a great place to live. Such a lot of history and fascinating buildings. Have you visited the Civil War Museum?'

'Not yet,' I reply. I don't like to tell him the only building I visit regularly is my local, usually resulting in several trips to the bathroom, followed by falling into a coma in the bedroom.

'Where is it?' I feign interest.

'It's alongside the Palace Theatre on Appleton Gate. You should go to some of the productions there too. They put on some wonderful shows.'

'Maybe I will at some stage, but ...'

'There's so many places you should explore here,' he interrupts. 'All with intriguing histories...'

He then launches into detailed descriptions of places around Newark including the Castle, St Mary's church, the Governor's House, Ossington Palace, the Old Bakery Tea room and the Town Hall. It's a relief in a way to sit quietly and listen, even if I'm preoccupied.

I have to admit he's extremely knowledgeable and interesting and it does help divert my mind away from the urgency of my problems a little.

'And,' he continues, 'I'll tell you something else about all these buildings. They're all haunted.'

He pauses and I start to think it's time to make a sharp exit as I don't want to discuss things I just don't believe in.

'Even the deceased can't bear to leave Newark,' he smirks. 'And I've heard rumours the old Corn Exchange is about to become the new home for some local ghosts, if you're interested.'

'To be honest and no offence intended but I've never believed in all that supernatural stuff.' In truth that's the only excuse I can think of to disguise my deep seated fear of the paranormal, particularly the idea of ghosts.

He says nothing but sits in silence for a moment staring into my eyes in a way I've never experienced before. As if he can see into my soul or something, and it's unsettling. I stand and start putting my coat on, though I have no idea where I'm going once I leave here. He reaches out and gently takes hold of my arm.

'I do know you're troubled, my friend. And I also know you have a drinking problem.' Let me get you a top up and I promise I can help you if you're willing to listen.'

'How do you...?'

'Never mind that.' He taps the side of his nose then flicks my question away with a wave of his arm. 'Just stay there and I promise you'll not regret it.'

He returns from the bar with a fresh pint for me which I must admit I feel like downing in one go.

'So,' he continues. 'First things first. You have nowhere to sleep tonight do you?'

I nod, wondering not just how he knows that but fearing what might be coming next.

'I have a little property on Millgate where you can stay. I won't be needing it this week and can let you stay there until next Saturday. After that you won't need it any longer either.' He reaches into his pocket and presses a key into my hand.

'Number 13 it is, but as you're not superstitious you won't mind that will you?'

I'm a bit lost for words though I manage to mutter a thank you, at the same time feeling anxious as to what he's going to ask for in return.

'I can pay rent,' I blurt out, just in case he's expecting me to pay in kind in some perverted way.

'Not necessary,' he replies. 'Providing you follow my instructions and promise to leave it as you find it. Now, let's get down to the nitty gritty. You won't believe this but a very long time ago I was just like you. Addicted to alcohol, nowhere to go and no hope for the future. But I was lucky enough to find a way out and now I'm always delighted to help others who find themselves in the same position.'

'So what happened?' I ask, inquisitive but sceptical.

'That doesn't matter but I can tell you there's many a success story walking around this area now, thanks to my intervention over the years.'

'How many years is that?' I'm still not convinced and feel suspicious of his motives.

'That's for me to know. If I told you, you wouldn't believe me anyway. Let's just get on with it.' He reaches into his other pocket and brings out a packet of tablets.

'I don't want to swap drinks for drugs.' How can I trust a perfect stranger?

'Don't worry. These are not addictive but believe me, within a week I promise your problems will be history. You'll not find anything like this in a pharmacists or doctor's surgery but trust me, they really are the answer to your situation.'

He pushes the packet into my hand and I must admit despite my many reservations I'm hooked on the idea of a quick fix, easy solution. Who wouldn't be?

'Take one of these in the evening before you set off drinking. If you're not cured within a week just come back here next Saturday and I'll buy you drinks all night. But I guarantee by then you won't want to touch a drop.'

With that he stands and walks out the pub without a backward glance. I don't even know his name. I'm not sure what I'm going to do but I'm feeling exhausted, so for tonight I'll just head to the place on Millgate and take it from there.

I'm surprised the key he's given me really does open the door to the tiny cottage. It's obviously a very old property, two storey with bay windows and shaped gable ends, one of a row facing onto the road but it's warm, well furnished and unoccupied. It doesn't take me long to fall into a dreamless sleep despite all the trauma and peculiarity of the day.

Next day, Monday, I wake feeling surprisingly relaxed yet still anxious about my situation and suspicious of the instructions given to me by a complete stranger. I don't venture out until the evening after deliberating for a long time, then deciding to give the pills a try. I tentatively swallow one before leaving the house and head to the Prince Rupert pub on nearby Lombard Street. I can see it's a very old building with no doubt a long and interesting history but right now I only have the urge to drink on my mind. There are a lot of tiny, dark rooms inside and as I don't want to be involved in any more weird conversations with strangers I order a pint and head upstairs where the rooms are sparsely occupied. The pint quickly disappears and I'm not feeling any different or coming up with any ideas of how to solve my troubles so I head downstairs for another drink. It's a warm summer evening and yet the temperature on the stairs has dropped to near freezing and I shiver as I descend to the bar. I take my second pint and a whisky into the King's Lounge which is busier but where the temperature seems more normal. People are sitting quietly chatting and obviously enjoying an evening out so I'm relieved no one is paying any attention to me. Half way down my drink I witness a man, dressed as a Cavalier materialise from nowhere in a seat in the corner and I gasp out loudly before I can stop myself. All eyes turn on me. I point to the transparent figure in the corner. 'Who the hell is that?'

Heads turn to where I'm pointing but the only expressions I witness are bewildered and confused ones.

'Who? Where?' A burly young man speaks up.

'There. In the corner seat. There's a Cavalier staring at me and I can see right through him.'

At that, the ghostly figure stands, walks towards me then disappears through the wall.

'Oh, he's gone now,' I mutter, embarrassment joining my feeling of terror.

'I reckon you need to be gone as well,' the burly youth continues. 'I suggest you lay off the booze or drugs or whatever you're taking and see a shrink in the morning when you've sobered up.'

Sniggers follow me as I head out the door at speed, make my way hastily back to Millgate while checking in all directions to make sure no one is following me.

I wake the next morning after a bit of a restless night. My mind recalls the row with my wife and the strange man in the pub who gave me the key and the tablets but beyond that I remember nothing. My usual thick head, camel's arse mouth and lethargy are noticeably absent yet I feel sure I must have been drinking somewhere last night. I have a vague recollection of ghostly figures of some kind but I'm sure that's just a dream triggered by the conversation I had with the stranger.

After a quiet day when I feel far more energetic, clear headed and positive than usual, even though I shouldn't, I decide to find a different pub where I can have a drink, though strangely the urge isn't as pressing as it usually is. I decide to continue taking the pills as apart from the weird dream I don't seem to be experiencing any ill effects, quite the opposite in fact.

I take a short stroll through the cobbled yard of The Navigation but it looks rather busy so I continue through several archways and narrow passages until I find myself by the river. A short walk towards the bridge takes me to a modern looking pub called the Swan and Salmon so I decide that will do for tonight. It's attractively furnished inside with views of the river and thankfully fairly quiet. I take my pint to a table in the corner, as far from the few occupants as possible. After a few minutes a pretty, young girl emerges from a staircase I hadn't noticed, catches my eye and takes a seat next to me.

'Good evening, kind sir. I hope you are well. I used to be a barmaid here, so can I get you a drink?'

'Thank you. That's kind of you, though I insist on paying.'

'No need for payment,' she replies. 'You look like a proper gentleman and I could do with some pleasant conversation.' With that she saunters over to the bar, slips behind it and pulls a pint proficiently without anyone seeming to notice.

'So what's your name sir? And do you have a lady friend?'

'My name's Toby and actually I've been married for a long time.'

She sighs but makes no effort to leave. 'I planned on getting married once, but it didn't work out.'

'That's a shame. What was his name?' Best to focus on someone else instead of my own problems and besides, she looks really sad.

'He was called John but everyone knew him as Will. Lovely man he was, tall and handsome, gentle and generous.'

'So what went wrong?'

'I blame myself really. His business took him away a lot and he was always on the road. Even when he was in town he spent most of his time at The Talbot in the Square sharing his spoils with his friends. I guess I was just jealous and a bit angry, especially after he promised to bring me a petticoat when he returned from one of his trips and he never showed up. By the time he did I'd betrayed him.'

'Oh. What did he do for a living?'

'He was a highwayman. A very kind one though and only ever held the rich at gunpoint.'

I try not to flinch but begin to wonder if she's another local weirdo, an actress or just winding me up.

'Well, maybe if you apologise you can get back together.'

'No chance of that I'm afraid, he's dead now.'

'Oh, I'm sorry. Was he ill or did he have an accident?'

'He was hanged in York and is buried there.'

'But...,' I'm stuttering now. 'The last hanging in this country was in 1964.'

'Don't be daft. Will went to the gallows in 1684, just a few years ago.' She gives me a disparaging stare and I'm forced to turn away.

I have no idea what's happening to me but I don't like it. Is it her that's crazy or me? I turn again to tell her I'm leaving but she's disappeared into thin air. I feel the blood draining from my face and ponder if I'm losing the plot. I'm about to leave when a young barman comes over and asks if I'm okay.

'You looked like you were going to pass out there for a minute.'

'What happened? One minute she was here talking about her boyfriend who was hanged in York and the next she just faded away. Did you see her leave?'

'Who?' the barman asks, looking at me with an unidentifiable expression, which only adds to my agitation.

'The girl. She didn't tell me her name but I've been talking to her for the past hour.'

'To be honest sir, we did notice you were mumbling away to yourself but didn't like to interfere. I assure you you've been alone since you came in. You look like you need a drink. Shall I bring one over?'

'It's okay. I think I'll head off now thanks.' That's a first. I can't ever remember refusing a drink. I stumble from the pub and manage to find my way back to Millgate despite the jelly legs and muddled thoughts.

I wake early the next morning feeling decidedly well, fresh and relaxed which hasn't happened in a long time. I remember why I'm sleeping in this strange little cottage but again I have no recollection of the night before. I recall vague memories involving highwaymen, hangings and a young girl in a lacy petticoat and I've no idea where they came from but conclude

I've just had weird dreams again, though I'm not completely convinced. I spend the day reading some of the interesting historical books from the selection in the bookcase. My concentration is tip top and I don't even think about a drink until darkness falls. This is all very weird but I can't allow myself to believe those pills are actually working in a mysterious way. Regardless, I swallow another.

I'm not in my usual rush to start drinking so decide to avoid the town centre as it appears to be very busy and as I'm feeling energised, continue walking down Northgate where I come across The Malt Shovel, another old pub tucked away on a corner. It's a relief when I pop my head round the door to find it's empty. I order a pint and sit quietly, going over the things I remember from the last few days and pondering why I can't recollect others. I feel a little pleased yet embarrassed at the slow rate I'm drinking this pint, aware the landlord is probably thinking I'm just a down and out prolonging my stay to keep warm. After a while I notice a door on the other side of the room open yet there's no one on the other side of it. I think I can hear a distant babble of voices but then am suddenly aware of a misty grey figure in front of me who then proceeds to press his bony hands hard on my chest. I splutter and cry out before a feeling of suffocation takes over, then it stops suddenly and the figure disappears back through the door, which then slams shut.

Shaken, I make my way unsteadily over the room to the same door, scared but wanting to know if I've been hallucinating or not.

'You all right mate?' the landlord calls. 'You look like you've seen a ghost.'

'Just going to the loo,' I mumble, too flustered to explain the real reason. I grab the handle and pull but am met with resistance.

'That door's been locked for years. Out of bounds to everyone, even the staff. Other way.' He points to a door on the opposite side of the room. 'Light bulbs gone so it's a bit dark in there but...'

''It's okay. I'll wait until I get home.' I'm out of the door at speed, leaving my unfinished pint on the table and running all the way back to Millgate. I reckon the last time I ever ran anywhere was at the school sports.

Yet again, I wake with only hazy recollections of what happened the night before. Every time I try to visualise a pub or contemplate a drink anxiety washes over me, yet the improvements in my physical, mental and emotional well being are decidedly noticeable and very welcome. I cook myself a hearty breakfast then settle down to study more of the historical books about Newark. I'm soon totally immersed, finding myself learning so many new things and feeling more inclined to visit these sites rather than pubs. It's all very far from my usual routine, yet still I'm not fully convinced I can go without a drink for the first time in years. I'm pretty sure I don't want to overindulge so decide to stick to the town centre and find a popular pub, as for some reason I can't fathom I don't feel like being alone. I head down Barnby Gate and discover the Rutland Arms, which looks like it's been recently refurbished. Inside it's obvious from things I've been reading that it was once an old coaching inn with original architecture and some stone flagged floors. Now it has large modern television screens, a dining area and posters advertising various lively events posted on all the walls. It's very busy so I scan the room to find a vacant seat. Not feeling desperate for a drink I order a shandy and join a gentleman sitting alone who looks to be about the same age as myself. We soon get chatting and I feel thoroughly relaxed and at ease discussing all sorts of topics I've never really been interested in before when in an alcohol induced stupor. He seems a gentle, pious soul with an amazing amount of knowledge and we've soon moved onto the topic of Newark's history.

'I've read there may be a network of tunnels under this part of the town. Do you know whether there's any truth in that?' I ask him.

'Oh definitely,' he responds. 'Though many deny it and some areas have been blocked with brick walls to prevent too much investigation by the over curious.'

'Why would anyone do that? Surely it's part of the town's remarkable history.'

'That may be so but a lot of bad things have happened in those tunnels through the years and it's best people be kept out for their own sakes.'

'Why? What's gone is gone and the past can't hurt us.'

'You don't believe in ghosts then?'

I hesitate and carefully compose my response.

'Well, I didn't but I do believe I've had some really weird experiences I can't explain over the last few days and...'

'Newark is inundated with ghosts and there's some pretty malicious ones in those underground tunnels so they do all they can to scare off the paranormal investigators who attempt to carry out all night vigils to prove their existence.'

'So, my fear of ghosts is justified then?'

'Not really. Most ghosts are perfectly harmless and many quite friendly. Even in the tunnels there's Fred and Gilbert who are completely respectable spectres...'

'How do you know all this?'

'Because my friend, I'm one of them. I'm Cuthbert, one of the originals who took up residence in the tunnels after The Friary closed. But I do like to stay here in The Rutland ...'

With that he laughs and disappears.

I leave swiftly and as I head back into town, I turn to see a hooded figure at the window of one of the upstairs windows of the pub.

I sleep well, waking early to a beautiful sunrise, feeling hale and hearty and ready to face whatever the day brings. My memories of the previous night are still obscure and foggy yet I'm now pretty sure the strange fragments I do remember aren't dreams.

I'm keen to read more of the books about the history of Newark as my appetite to learn about the many fascinating buildings around town has increased by the day. I trail my finger along the row of books and discover tucked away at the back a book about hauntings in Newark. I hesitate but then bite the bullet and scan through the pages. They're all there, those buildings the stranger had talked of in our initial meeting, and then a chapter devoted to the haunted pubs of Newark. I feel goose bumps and the hair on my neck stands on end as I read about soldiers, barmaids, victims of murder, monks and other poltergeists who have been reportedly sighted in various drinking establishments. I can't put all the sides and corners in place but know there is some connection to my experiences and for whatever reason I don't feel like I need to visit a pub again.

I can hardly believe what's happened and feel determined to persuade the wife to take me back. I've a spring in my step and a smile on my face as I head back to our marital home, praying she'll believe me when I tell her I'm cured. I don't intend to go into detail about the past week but I'm pretty sure she'll see, hear and sense a difference in me and just give me a chance.

**

I wake early the next morning, my eyes and thoughts adjust to my surroundings and a deep sigh of satisfaction escapes involuntarily. I'm here, in my own house, in my own bedroom with my lovely wife sleeping peacefully by my side. I feel content, healthy, optimistic and only in need of a cup of tea. The thought of anything alcoholic is the last thing on my mind. My gratitude cannot be measured and I decide I must find this miracle worker who has resolved my problems and thank him from the heart. I wash and dress quietly then head out to the pub where I first met him. I stroll along Middle Gate but am confused when I can't find a pub of any description. There's a fish restaurant where I thought the pub was but there's no way a pub could disappear and be converted in a week.

I approach a gentleman passing by.

'Excuse me sir, could you direct me to The Spread Eagle pub please? I thought it was here but I must be mistaken.'

The man gives me a curious look and scratches his chin. 'I take it you're not from round here and obviously haven't visited Newark in a long time.'

'Why?' I ask feeling as baffled as he looks.

'The Spread Eagle closed in 1968. I was sad to see it go but times were tough and the fish and chip shop is at least some compensation.'

I'm too gobsmacked to manage a response and too bewildered to contemplate how this could even be possible. Maybe I have my pubs mixed up as I was in a bad place when I first came across the man who helped me but as I've no idea where it could be, I have to think of alternatives.

The house. He must be there. He did say he needed it back on Saturday and he was right to predict I wouldn't be needing it then. I turn and walk swiftly back to Millgate, hoping he's at home and not out somewhere helping another poor soul.

The first few cottages look just as I remember them but as I move forward I can already sense something has changed. There is no number 13 and the space occupied by that house and several others is now occupied by a three storey, modern block of what look like offices or apartments. Completely out of place, but more to the point, impossible to have been built there in the space of a week. I have no explanation at all and no way of finding one. I can only choose to accept something illogical, inexplicable and beyond my understanding has happened and I'm just not meant to figure out what. I feel inside my pockets and find the key and remaining pills, so it's obvious it's not all been a dream, hallucination or my imagination.

I guess I'm wrong and there are things we just can't explain. I somehow doubt I'll ever bump into the man who rescued me from disaster but now I'm not drinking I can at least explore all those interesting historical buildings he talked about. Maybe I'll pluck up the courage to investigate any hauntings I can find out about, though I suspect I'll avoid any pubs. I'm looking forward to this new life and if I need a break while I'm out exploring, well, there's plenty of coffee bars in Newark as well.

The Committee of Adjustment

by Adrian Bean

'**S**AME AGAIN?'

He was aware of her voice but did not look up, his eyes fixed on the small pile of letters sitting on the bar table.

'Same again, duck?'

He looked up. 'Oh, sorry, I – yes, please. Thank you.'

The barmaid leant back on her heels and fixed him with a stare. 'You alright duck?'

He considered. 'Yes. Thank you.'

She held his look for a second, nodded, then turned and walked away. His eyes followed her to the bar, and he noticed a group of young American airmen, apparently refusing to let her pass until she gave them The Password. Despite maintaining a pretence of mild annoyance, she clearly enjoyed the attention of the airmen, each of whom was young enough to be her son.

He looked again at the letters and checked his watch. Gone ten o'clock. He lit a cigarette, noticing that there was only one left in the packet, and inhaled deeply, triggering a spasm of coughing. Reaching into his inside pocket he pulled out a leather case containing a green Bakelite fountain pen and a small dagger-like letter opener. With the practised skill of a surgeon, he inserted it into the envelope. The thin wartime-standard paper slit open neatly and he pulled out three folded pages, ignoring the slight shaking of the paper, the effect of a tremble which had appeared following his recent visit to the MO. He checked the envelope to ensure that it contained nothing else, turning the folded pages over, but nothing fell out.

Somewhere in England!
September 29th, 1943

Dearest Mum and Dad,

Please excuse my handwriting as I'm working by the dim light of a blacked-out train carriage stuck somewhere between Darlington and York - at least that's what the Guard says – he's what Dad would call 'a very officious type' who likes to keep that kind of information to himself just to impress. Needless to say, he didn't impress me – I gave him a flash of the new Air Gunner brevet on my tunic and he soon shut up!

Apparently, there is an air raid alert and so the train has been standing in a tunnel for over an hour now, with no indication of when we might be on the move again, so I thought it would be a good use of my time if I started to write you a letter.

In my last, I told you about the Operational Training Unit I was stationed at up in Scotland, and about the Wimpys we were getting our final training on. Well, the Wimpy is a splendid two-engine bomber, marvellously rugged, and bristling with guns, but according to our instructors (rather terrifying chaps, most of whom have done their tour of thirty 'ops' over Germany) the Wellington is most definitely Yesterday's Thing. All they talk about is the Lancaster, a super new aircraft with four engines and a bomb-bay the size of a cricket pitch! Think of how many bombs we can drop on German factories from one of those. (Don't worry Dad – I'm not revealing any military secrets. The Germans know exactly what a punch the Lancaster packs, as they've been on the receiving end of it for months now).

The whisky glass hit the table with a sharp clunk.

'One double. Sorry about the wait, duck. I got distracted.' Her expression changed, the thin, painted-on eyebrows moving closer together. 'If you don't mind me saying, you look like you could do with it.'

He reached for his wallet, but she stopped him. 'Don't worry duck, I'll put it on the slate. You'll still be here at the end of the week I dare say, unlike some.'

He followed her glance to the group of young airmen, now engaged in turning the pages of a copy of the Advertiser into paper aeroplanes and taking bets on who could fly his the furthest across the bar. There was a roar as one of them managed to land his aeroplane in the fire, and it was consumed in a burst of flames.

'Boys, eh?' The barmaid laughed, and he noticed that her cheeks were slightly flushed, and she seemed a little breathless. He felt suddenly very old. It was a long time since he had affected a woman like those young men did. He reached for his cigarettes.

'I'm almost out,' he said. 'Bring me some over, would you? Ten Piccadilly.'

She raised a single eyebrow. 'What did your last slave die of?', and a sudden stab of emotion caught him in the chest. She meant no harm by it, he knew, it was just a quip, but suddenly he wanted to tell her how unfair it was of her to make jokes after everything that had happened to him today, and yesterday and all the other days; what he had heard, and seen, and done, how it was eating away at his soul and he really didn't know if he could carry on any longer.

But she had already turned on her heel and was threading her way through the gaggle of young men again.

...Anyway, with these grizzled old Instructor types it's 'Lancs this' and 'Lancs that', so I can't tell you how excited I was when I got my orders telling me I was joining a Lancaster squadron for operational duties! Actually, it was when I was chatting to Anne (one of the WAAFS who packs our parachutes) that I learned I was to be flying on Lancasters. I'd mentioned to her the name of the station where I was being posted, and she said that her sister's fiancé was stationed nearby. Anyway, the point of the story is that my new squadron operates Lancasters, and so it looks like my wish will come true!

Well, the train has started up, and it seems we are finally moving. I'll sign off now and post this to you as soon as I can (I'm all out of stamps). I hope you're both well and miss you terribly, but I know that you are as glad that I am doing something worthwhile as I am to be doing it, so that makes the not seeing you easier to bear. When I get home I promise to take Mum for a long walk around Alexandra Park so she can show her brave son off to all the neighbours in his smart blue uniform (you know you want to, Mum!). Give Meg a hug from me (but not too many treats!) and tell her when I see her we'll go for her favourite walk along the canal.

With all best wishes,

Your loving son,

Harry xx

P.S. The old lady sitting opposite has just told me off for straining my eyes in the poor light! Little does she know I have 20/20 night vision.

H x

He sat for a few moments as an image came into his head, of a boy in rolled-up shirtsleeves, a cow lick of hair flopping over his eyes, carefully folding the letter he'd just written and sliding it into the envelope. Except the boy wasn't called Harry, but Philip, and he was sitting in a tent under the blazing North African sun...

'One of your boys?'

She was back, gesturing with the packet of Piccadillys towards the letter in his hand.

'One normally reads these things back in the office, on the Station. Time's so short and one is always in a hurry, it seems...' As he put the letter back into its envelope, he was aware of her watching him. He felt he had to say something.

'I suppose, tonight, I just needed to...'

'It's alright, duck, you don't need to tell me.' She tapped the side of her nose. 'I heard what happened.'

He lit a cigarette, taking a deep, gratifying drag on it. What did she mean by that? He was about to ask her but she was already gone.

Like the first, the second letter was addressed to a Mr and Mrs J Greenhalgh at an address in Oldham, and again, unstamped. He slit the envelope open, repeated the ritual of shaking it out, and began to read.

> *RAF Station Syerston*
> *Nr Newark*
> *Nottinghamshire*
> *September 30th, 1943*
>
> *Dearest Mum and Dad,*
> *Well, I have finally arrived at my new home, after a journey that took over eighteen hours - I could have walked*

it in less time! Apparently, according to one chap in the carriage, we actually went past Newark twice, because of the diversions, before finally arriving there from Leicester, of all places!

Having made our acquaintance on the subject of Night Vision, the dear old lady and I had some interesting conversations during the waits, mostly about her sons, one of whom is a high-up in some cushy War Ministry office in London and the other in a POW camp somewhere in Germany. What a situation for her. Apparently the one in the POW camp was also in the RAF, on Blenheims, and was posted Missing back in 1940, but she only found out that he was alive and being held prisoner six months later! She's had a couple of Red Cross postcards from him since, but they don't say much other than that he is well and uninjured. Poor soul.

Anyway, we said cheerio when I finally got off at Newark and I waved her goodbye. It was four o'clock by now and the Station Master told me I could get a bus 'down the Fosse' that would take me to the gates of Syerston, if I didn't mind waiting (ha ha!), so I thought I would have a cup of tea and a bite to eat but unfortunately the tearoom was shut.

From the railway station you can see the old castle ruins rising above the river, and as the bus wasn't due for half an hour, I thought I would make the most of it and have a quick dekko around the place. Looking up at the ruined towers and thick walls you could almost imagine Roundheads and Cavaliers having a go at each other with pikes and swords hundreds of years ago. Strange that we are still fighting wars after all this time - you'd have thought we'd have learned something by now. Anyway, before I knew it, the church clock was chiming the half hour and I had to hurry back to the train station or I'd miss my bus, so I'm afraid I missed posting your letter. I hope you won't mind waiting an extra day, but I'll wait until I get to the Station and send them both together.

I can't tell you too much about the Station for obvious reasons, but I have to confess to feeling quite a thrill of excitement as I walked through the main gates. I actually think I might have grown an extra inch, feeling like quite the man marching in there, amongst all those other aircrew, knowing that at last I was now One Of Them. I hope you'd have been proud of me, both.

But I soon felt like the new boy at school again: 'Report here', 'Go there', 'Find this' and 'Take that!' Before long, my head was in a whirl as I went from office to hut and back again, collecting a chit from here, drawing an item of kit from there. There is so much bumpf involved in joining a squadron, honestly you wouldn't believe. I tell you, if we bundled up just half a day's paperwork and dropped it on the Germans they'd be suing for peace in no time.

I'm lying on my bed, writing this, in a room with about twenty other beds, each with a metal locker and wooden bedside cabinet, all very neat and tidy, and I am lucky enough to be near a window. Every few minutes I hear the roar of Merlin engines approaching and look round to catch a sight of a Lancaster overhead; I can't tell you how exciting it is to know that I will soon be up in one of those wonderful machines.

As luck would have it, as I finished that last sentence there was an almighty racket in the corridor outside and a couple of fellows stuck their heads in to ask if I was the new Air Gunner and that I should stooge over to the crew room where 'the Skipper' was waiting for me! They didn't hang around for me to follow, so I hope I can find it; I'll end this now and then I'm off to meet my new crew!

Your ever-loving son, (in a rush, as always!)

Harry xx

He uncapped his fountain pen and scored straight thick lines through several lines and paragraphs, eliminating a few names, places, and minor technical references. He took a last drag on his cigarette and was suddenly overwhelmed by a fit of coughing. He'd been to the MO about a fortnight ago, with a nasty cough that just didn't seem to want to go away. After examining him, the MO offered him a cigarette, lit one himself, and said that he was recommending a chest X-Ray.

'Could be nothing. It'll probably all clear up in a matter of days but better safe than sorry.'

He'd put it out of his mind until the call from the MO's Orderly had come yesterday morning, asking him to report to the Station Sick Quarters. He'd gone over straight away, and didn't remember much about the actual conversation, other than the words lung and cancer.

'No doubt, I'm afraid. And it's fairly advanced. I could put you in for surgery, but there are risks associated with that for a chap of your age, and the results aren't always what one would hope for.'

When he finally spoke, his voice sounded weak, strangled.

'How long?'

'Christmas,' said the MO, 'Possibly. You could still be here next spring with a bit of luck, it's hard to make an accurate prediction about these things. Sorry old chap.'

He nodded, his brain numb.

'I dare say you could do with a period of re-adjustment, get things in order. I'll sign you off now if you want, you've done more than enough for the Squadron. You should spend some time at home, let Margaret take care of you.'

He avoided the MO's look. Although they had known each other for years, he realised he hadn't actually ever got round to telling him that Margaret had left last Whitsun Holiday, and that since then she'd been living with her sister in Wrexham.

He'd thought it better not to tell anyone at first, knowing how fast things get round the Station.

The house had felt so empty for the first few weeks, and he nursed the faint hope each evening that he might come home to find her sitting in her armchair by the fire. But she hadn't come back. When the food cupboards ran empty, he took to eating his meals in the Officer's Mess at the Station and started spending his evenings in the Saracen's Head. There was often a fire in one of the smaller bars, and the regular barmaid was rather friendly, always ready with a story to make him laugh. It wasn't long before she had made up a slate for him; not that he needed it, but one evening he had found his wallet empty, and although initially embarrassed about it, soon the fact that he had a slate gave him a new-found sense of permanence. It meant they knew him there. That he belonged. That he would return.

Margaret leaving, he could take. He knew, after all, that he was at least half responsible for the breakdown of the marriage; more, if he was honest. It was the fact that his son had stopped talking to him that was hard to bear. He had become used to Philip's weekly letters from Tunisia, where he was a Flight Commander on Hurricanes. They had never been especially close, emotionally, when Philip was a kid, but war and the distance between them had, if anything, brought them closer together, albeit by letter, and it was something he'd cherished.

All of that had ended when Margaret left. Although Philip had never referred to the separation, the sudden coolness of his letters made it clear he knew, and was taking it badly. And somehow, he couldn't quite find the way to bring the subject up when writing to Philip, so he avoided any reference to Margaret altogether. Eventually he found he was only writing about Station life, as if that was all his life amounted to, which of course, on one level, was true.

After reading Philip's letters he now felt frustrated and full of self-loathing, and in some indefinable way, diminished. He no longer looked forward to reading them. They would sometimes be left on the table for several days until he was in the right mood to handle them, and it took a long time for him to write a reply.

The last one had sat there for three weeks, unopened.

RAF Station Syerston
Nr Newark
Nottinghamshire
September 31st, 1943

Dear Mum and Dad,

Aren't you lucky to be getting all these letters all at once (once I finally get round to posting them, that is). I imagine you both sitting down at the table in the parlour with a large pot of tea and a slice of Mum's fruitcake as you read them together. I am writing this sitting on the grass on the morning of my first flight with my new crew, with our Lancaster providing a dramatic backdrop. Let me introduce them to you:

My pilot Tony, a Sergeant like me, is from Devon. He's rather quiet and unassuming, not at all like the instructors we had at OTU, and certainly not what I expected our Skipper to be. But I like him, and feel confident in his company, and I'm sure he will do his level best to keep us all safe, as well as doing his job to help win the war. He is fond of dogs, and we had a right old time comparing notes about Meg and his collie, who is called Elsie. He has flown four operations over Germany, although he hasn't told me too much about them so far.

Our Bomb Aimer is a Taff, from some place that is all 'L's and 'Y's and completely unpronounceable. I haven't quite got the measure of him, he's a bit moody and keeps himself to himself I feel. Doesn't like dogs, doesn't like fishing, doesn't like anything it seems except dropping bombs on Germans, which is fair enough I suppose, as that's his job!

Merv, our Flight Engineer, is from Australia, where his family have a sheep farm, and he regales anyone who will listen with stories of Life in the Outback and Kangaroos and so on. Hank, our trusty Wireless Op, is also a colonial, this time a Canadian. He worked in insurance in Winnipeg before volunteering.

Arthur, our Navigator, is actually the highest-ranking member of the crew – he's a Flying Officer, but it's accepted that the Skipper, although an NCO like me, is the boss. Arthur's the old man of the crew, being 24, and from Staffordshire. He's also the only married man in the crew, and everyone instinctively looks up to him as 'The Wise One'.

Which leaves only the Rear Gunner, because I am to be the crew's Mid-Upper Gunner! Our Tail-End Charlie is another northerner, but of the White Rose variety, from Rotherham. Don't worry Dad, we had a good laugh immediately, seeming to hit it off despite our rivalry, and we are already firm friends...

So now you've met my crew, and I think you'll agree they're a grand bunch. I didn't need to feel nervous after all, because the fellows were all extremely friendly and welcoming, and we spent the whole of last evening together, exchanging stories and generally getting on famously.

Well, I'd better sign off as there is so much to do today. I PROMISE to post these letters tomorrow and look forward to hearing all your news.

Lots of love,
Harry xxxx

***

After talking to the MO, he had stepped out of the SSQ into the late September sunshine, feeling rather light-headed. The shock, he supposed. Adrenalin.

All around him airmen and ground crew, administrative officers and WAAFs scurried about like ants, each intent on doing his or her bit for the war effort. He saluted passing colleagues automatically, so absorbed was he in his inner dialogue. Perhaps the doc was right, and he should go back into the retirement the RAF had called him out of four years ago. He'd be dead within a matter of months, maybe less, so what was the point of carrying on here? What was the point of any of it, really?

But he knew he couldn't go home to that empty house, not to die. For a while he seriously thought about writing to Margaret and telling her about the diagnosis, but he feared that she would think he was trying to get her to come back, or worse, just feeling sorry for himself. But he would have to tell her that he was dying, in the end, wouldn't he? And Philip deserved to know the truth as well.

The rest of the day passed uneventfully. He found that having work to do stopped him from thinking. At lunch in the Mess, he'd listened to some chaps discussing a show they'd seen in Lincoln, but didn't mention his visit to the MO when somebody remarked that he looked as if he had something on his mind. Hobson, the WAAF who brought him his three o'clock cup of tea, said that the Met Officer had whispered that the forecast looked promising for the next 36 hours, usually code for 'the squadron is on ops tomorrow night'. This meant he would spend the rest of today and tomorrow attending to mountains of paperwork, taking letters or memos from a tray marked 'In' on one side of his desk, and later placing them in a tray marked 'Out' on the other side. Towards six he heard Hobson humming to herself as she typed, and was about to tell her to keep it down a bit when he thought he recognised the tune.

'What's that you're humming, Hobson?' he asked.

'Sorry Sir, I didn't mean to disturb you.'

'No, that's alright. But what is it?'

'The Thingummybob song, I think. Well, that's what I call it anyhow. Gracie Fields sings it. She's the girl that makes the thing that drills the ...something that somethings something that's going to win the war.' She laughed. 'I've a frightful memory, Sir.'

He didn't say anything, and after a while Hobson got on with her work. She glanced over at him a few times, and saw that he hadn't moved, still staring into space. She almost jumped when he scraped back the chair and stood, saying he was going out.

'When will you back, Sir?' she asked.

But he had already gone.

***

'The usual, duck?'

The barmaid had seen him as he came into the bar and was already holding a bottle of his preferred whisky.

'You know me too well, Connie,' he said, and leant against the bar, one foot resting on the polished brass foot-rail running around the perimeter.

'Well, that's a turn up for the book,' she said, measuring the amber liquid.

'What is?'

'You've never called me Connie before.'

'Haven't I? Well, I've heard one or two of the other chaps and um...' He paused. 'I hope you don't mind me calling you Connie.'

'Course not, duck. It's me name, in't it?'

She brought the glass over and set it on the bar in front of him.

'So?' she said.

'So what?'

'So what's your name? I can't just call you Squadron Leader, can I?' She leant in, mischievously. 'Or is it an Official Secret?'

He stared at her for a moment, before smiling. 'Squadron Leader Ronald Emerson, Retired. But my friends call me Ronnie.'

'Thank you, Ronnie.'

He raised the glass and knocked the whisky back in one, grimaced, and started coughing.

'Not getting any better, is it?' she said.

'Another please, Connie,' he wheezed. 'Make it a double.'

'A double – at the double, Sir!" she laughed at her own joke and went back to the spirits.

He paid for the drinks and inwardly relaxed, the confusing thoughts that had been whirling around in his head seeming to calm and settle now he was in the familiar, safe surroundings of the pub.

'Bad day?' she asked, gently. He smiled and shook his head. 'I'm fine, thanks.'

'This place feels a bit more like home, eh duck? Bit o' company and a nice warm fire.'

'Yes, something like that.'

'Chance to get away from the wife too, I wouldn't wonder.'

After a few moments during which the silence hung awkwardly over them, Connie moved off. He knew that although respectful of the social distance between them and not wanting to overstep the boundaries of her profession, she had been encouraging him to talk. But there was no way on God's earth that he was ever going to discuss personal matters with a barmaid. He just wasn't that sort of chap. Getting On With It had been drilled into him since school. Once, he'd actually broken his wrist in a cricket match and batted on until he passed out from the pain, and for a time he'd been the hero of the Second Xi. And besides, pleasant and professional as Connie seemed, could he really trust her not to blab all his intimate secrets around town?

He was still standing at the bar, deep in his own thoughts, when they came in; a bunch of airmen, quite likely a crew from the Station, although he didn't recognise any of them. Hardly surprising, given the numbers who passed through the squadron these days. One of the lads, an Air Gunner, was evidently a new member of the crew. They introduced him to Connie, who told him not to believe anything they said about her, and his laugh sounded a little too forced. A couple of glances from the other members of the crew confirmed that they had seen him at the far end of the bar, and almost imperceptibly they shifted their positions so that none except the new boy was looking in his direction. Something else he had become used to, these days. Absorbed in his private thoughts, he returned to staring at his glass and slowly swirled the amber liquid around.

This much at least he knew: he didn't fear death, that was something he had become all too familiar with in recent months. But he was afraid of dying alone. Until recently it had never been something he'd even considered; now he worried that one day they would kick the door down and find him dead in his bed, after he had failed to turn up for morning briefing two or three days on the trot. Or he feared that his condition would worsen so much that he would be carted into a hospital to die, alone, and unmissed...

'Excuse me, Sir... Sir?'

He looked up and saw a young airman, pint glass in hand.

'Me and the lads are having a few drinks in memory of... well, we're having a bit of a celebration if you like, and I wondered if I could buy you a drink, Sir, as you seem to be alone?'

It was the boy who'd come in earlier with his crew. He glanced over the boy's shoulder, to the group of airmen standing at the bar, pints and cigarettes in hand, ruddy faced, Brylcreemed, glaring at him with undisguised contempt.

'Thank you, Sergeant,' he said. 'That's a very kind offer, but I think your friends might have other ideas.'

The boy's expression changed. 'Are you sure you're alright, Sir?'

He looked at the boy for a moment, remembering Philip, probably no more than two years older than this one, and was about to speak when a hand appeared on the boy's shoulder and a Sergeant Pilot interrupted: 'I'm sorry, Sir, he's new to the squadron, and doesn't know the form. I'm sure the Chairman of the Committee wouldn't want to dirty his hands by drinking with us flying types. Come on, Bumfluff.'

The Pilot tried to pull the boy away, but he resisted, standing his ground.

'I beg your pardon, Sir. I didn't mean to be rude. I just thought you looked like you could do with a bit of company, that's all. Sorry, Sir.'

And before he could say anything, the two airmen had re-joined the group, and stood with their backs to him.

His cheeks burned. Eyes stinging, he took a minute to compose himself, downed what was left of his whisky, grabbed his greatcoat and cap, said 'Night Connie,' and walked out of the bar and into the market square. He almost collided with a group of airmen, who had formed a short pyramid with one drunken soul on top, reaching up to tie a scarf around the head of the Saracen, which already sported a pair of flying goggles. An airman apologised, another swore and the pyramid collapsed, and he turned the corner, navigating his way through the dark, narrow backstreets towards Lombard Street.

Usually, he would catch a bus from the station by the Beaumond Cross, but tonight he just carried on walking down Portland into Victoria Street, his hands thrust deep into his greatcoat pocket, collar pulled up against the chill of the clear, starry night. As he passed through the outskirts of the blacked-out town, his footsteps echoing in the silence, the road was illuminated brilliantly by the moon, almost full, hanging high in the starry blackness of the night. He walked a slightly zig-zag path, the effects of the whisky thankfully anaesthetising the desperation that was steadily consuming him.

The walk home took over an hour, and he didn't meet a soul, barely even aware of the last bus from Newark as it sped past him. As he lifted the latch on the garden gate, he stopped and looked at the cottage, still and dark. He seemed to be seeing it for the first time, which in a sense he was, having never stood in the moonlight gazing at it as he did now. How had he never done that? he wondered. What a waste. It was such a beautiful little house, and he'd never really appreciated it. He thought he heard the distant drone of aircraft engines, and standing half-way up the path he looked up into the black, starry sky, craning his neck back until he could look no higher. Mouth open, his breath rising in clouds, he stood there, looking for something, and seeing nothing.

***

The next morning, half an hour before dawn rose over Syerston airfield, the silence was broken by the metallic grinding of the great hangar doors being pushed open. A tractor coughed, spluttered and slowly pulled P-Popsie, like some enormous black prehistoric bird, out onto the concrete.

'Chiefy' Bennett had kept the ground crew working on her through the night, in anticipation of this evening's operation; the Station Commander, keen not to antagonise Group without good reason, expected all aircraft to be serviceable for what was going to be a big show. The Fitters had been crawling all over her, repairing damage from the night fighter attack that had necessitated the replacement of the Mid-Upper Gunner a few nights ago: replacing shattered Perspex turret panels, tracing and fixing sheared cables, repatching aluminium skin, and generally working to get the Lancaster On The Top Line. Now he needed P-Popsie out on her dispersal pan, so his team could do the final repairs on the engines, at least one of which had sustained cannon-fire damage during the attack.

Despite not having fallen into bed much before one o'clock, the crew of P-Popsie were woken around the same early hour by a Service Policeman, doing his rounds with a clipboard and torch, and after going through the motions of washing and dressing they stumbled their bleary way to breakfast. Wherever they were going tonight, the crews knew that they had a full day's work ahead of them. Checks, briefings and night flying tests all before lunch, then there would be the Grand Reveal of the target for tonight, followed by more briefings, more checks, before take-off in the early evening. If all went well and they returned, there would be de-briefings and their throbbing heads probably wouldn't hit the pillow until three or four o'clock in the morning.

After breakfast, during which little was said and copious amounts of tea were drunk, and still nursing a thick head, Harry Greenhalgh strolled across the airfield, surprised to see the tremendous amount of activity already taking place. He asked a passing Erk if he knew where to find P-Popsie, and followed the man's grunted directions, heading to a dispersal pan out on the perimeter where he eventually found a Lancaster surrounded by bicycles, stepladders and toolboxes. Engine cowling panels lay on the ground, and Fitters crawled over her upper surfaces, reaching into her inner recesses, straining and swearing as they tried to finish the job before the canteen closed. Moving closer, he could make out the large dark red squadron codes and the letter P, indicating his aircraft. He nodded shyly at the Erks as they clocked him, walking under the great bird's wings, until he was standing below the Mid-Upper turret, where a couple of Corporals were discussing the finer points of football as they fed long belts of .303 ammunition into trays.

This would be his office tonight.

***

Later that morning, fully kitted up, the crew of P-Popsie sprawled on the grass a few yards from their Lancaster, waiting for 'Chiefy' to pronounce her serviceable and ready to fly.

Not much was said. Someone read a copy of the Daily Mirror, a couple played cards, and another lay on his back, hands behind his head, looking up into the sky, watching the clouds change shape and imagining what his new baby daughter must look like now. 'Chiefy' approached from the Lancaster, Form A700 in hand, pronouncing P-Popsie fit and healthy for her night flying test. As the crew rose up from the grass, Harry was about to put the letter he'd been writing into his pocket when he had a thought; he called a Fitter over, asking if he wouldn't mind taking the letter back to his billet and leaving it by his bed, ready for posting later. The Fitter promised he would and hurried on to catch up with his mates.

The crew climbed into the aircraft and prepared to put P-Popsie through her paces. In the Mid-Upper turret, Harry dug deep into his flying suit pocket and found his lucky rabbit's foot keyring, relieved that he hadn't left it in his room. Shortly after eleven, the Skipper started up the Merlins, ran them for a few minutes to check for mag drop, and when he was satisfied the Lancaster rolled forward, turned onto the runway and took off into the air.

The bomber lifted easily into the sky, and whilst still climbing, the Skipper started a sharp banking turn to the left. Behind his guns, Harry couldn't help smiling as the horizon tilted at a crazy angle and he saw the silver ribbon of the Trent thread its way through the Nottinghamshire landscape opening up below him. He watched a green toy bus move slowly along a straight road and pass a row of small cottages. The Lancaster was still low enough for him to see a figure emerging from the front door of one of the houses, and look up.

From his position two hundred feet beneath the bomber, Ronnie Emerson couldn't see Harry. He was looking at a stream of oily, black smoke pouring from the Lancaster's starboard outer engine, hearing the loud and distinct bangs as first one, and then another propellor stuttered and stopped.

The huge black aircraft suddenly dipped, as if caught by a powerful hand that flipped it over and hurled it downwards. The remaining two Merlins screamed as the Lancaster arrowed vertically towards the earth, and disappeared behind a wood. There was an awful crump; a shower of spinning fragments flew up and a huge orange fireball erupted as the fuel tanks on P-Popsie exploded, followed by a mushroom of black smoke, billowing into the sky.

It was all over in seconds.

He would find it hard to remember the exact sequence of events following the crash, but vivid images and details of what happened over the next two hours burned themselves indelibly into his brain. Running along the road towards the burning wreck, the searing pain in his lungs, finding a gate (locked – damn!) climbing over it and running across the corn stubble towards the burning Lancaster; the sudden, unexpected heat of the flames, smoke stinging his eyes, the acrid smell of fuel and burning metal and flesh, the alarm bell of the fire tender hurtling up the Fosse.

It all ran through his brain like jump-cut images in a nightmarish film: the roar of flames, the slowly-emerging skeleton of the Lancaster as the fire ate away at its metal skin; the crack of ammunition going off in the heat; men shouting as they dragged fire extinguishers and hoses across the field; the sudden quiet as the flames were smothered by high-pressure foam so that he became aware of the chatter of people, pouring out of the green bus; a red-faced Service Policeman drawing his revolver and yelling at the people to get back; the hacking at metal and perspex with axes, the pulling of bodies, largely unrecogniseable as such, from the smoking wreckage, to be placed on stretchers or tarpaulins and carried to the blood wagon. And later, once all the locals and dogs had been cleared away, the issuing of sacks and cricket-stump length poles with nails in the end, and the sight of Erks wandering the field in lines, collecting small body parts; a man in overalls, sitting at the edge of the field, his head in his hands, wiping away tears; identity tags collected and laid on the bonnet of the Station Commander's staff car; serial numbers matched and ticked off a list. Somebody saying 'Seven. That's the lot then.'

Within a few hours the carcass of the Lancaster had been winched aboard a Queen Mary Trailer and carried away. The LDV posted sentries, watching for children on the look-out for ammunition. The staff cars and trucks pulled away. There would be no investigation, no inquiry. It was an accident, just one of those things that happen in wartime.

On the large wall-sized blackboard in the Watch Office, the line containing the details of P-Popsie and her crew was wiped clean by a WAAF, and a back-up aircraft and scratch crew was quickly thrown together in order to ensure the squadron maintained its strength for the night's big effort over Germany. And although every crew on the Station was aware of the incident, there was no time to dwell on it. They attended briefings, groaned and swore as the target for tonight was revealed, went over routes and weather reports, and checked fuel and bombloads; flying kits were donned, last cigarettes smoked, letters written and bladders emptied. At 6.46pm the first of the Lancasters took off, and eighteen minutes later both A and B Flights were in the air.

That was when the Committee's work began.

As 'Chairman' it was Squadron Leader Emerson's job to assemble the members of the Committee of Adjustment in his office: the Station Warrant Officer, the Padre, a Sergeant Clerk from the Pay Office, two trusted orderlies, and himself, were given a list of the names of the seven airmen killed in the accident.

A truck pulled up outside the barracks, and the men of the Committee went through the rooms, identifying beds. Quickly and quietly, they stripped the beds of their linen, piled it into bags for the Station Laundry and placed neatly folded fresh sheets and blankets on the bare mattresses. They emptied lockers and cabinets of personal belongings, examining every pocket and wallet for photographs or any other evidence that might betray an affair, and searching toilet bags for prophylactics. Anything that might prove embarrassing, tokens of sexual conquests such as stockings or garters, along with rubbish like books and magazines, were thrown away or left for the surviving crews to divvy up; the rest was packed into boxes for return to the dead men's families. Flying kit and uniforms were returned to the stores to be re-issued.

Little was said during the process, other than the occasional response to a short question: 'Yes? No?' Often a shake of the head or a shrug would do. The members of the Committee carried out their tasks dispassionately, and largely without emotion. The letter left on Harry's bed by a Fitter that morning was thrown casually into a cardboard box along with the other letters, his pen, shaving kit, cufflinks and a handful of photographs.

When everything of interest had been removed, the Squadron Leader ran an expert eye over the beds, lockers, cabinets and surrounding walls. If all was clear, the Committee could move onto the next billet and the whole process was repeated. This operation was carried out after almost every raid; as soon as it was known which crews had failed to return, even as the exhausted surviving crews were sleeping in nearby beds, the Committee would go to work. If they did their job well, by the time the crews woke the next day, no trace of their former comrades' existence would remain, and replacement crews would never suspect that they were sleeping in dead men's beds.

By mid-evening, with the operation over Germany still in progress, the Committee of Adjustment broke up, keen to get back to other jobs, or to the NAAFI in time for a sandwich, a mug of tea and a smoke. For some it would also be an opportunity to catch up on any Station gossip and speculate on the possible cause of the crash.

***

He always reserved the task of vetting personal letters for himself. It wasn't a job that could be rushed or delayed; it demanded concentration and sensitivity if it was to be done properly. He saw it as his duty to ensure that, where humanly possible, any letters that would provide comfort to the bereaved, and not cause distress, or reveal military or romantic secrets, should be returned to the family. But he also understood that not everyone could read a letter, appreciating the subtle nuances, the sub-texts and the tricks that could betray a clue, a feeling, or a secret. It took a writer of letters to be a reader of them, and, at least until recently, he had considered himself more than up to the task.

When the Committee had dispersed, he settled himself in his office to read through the small pile of letters which had been left behind by the crew of P-Popsie. At first glance they did not seem to have been a particularly literary bunch. The Sergeant Pilot had left just a single letter, a communication from his brother Reg, who bemoaned the war's curtailment of his beloved pigeon racing. Harmless. He put it to one side for forwarding. More interesting were the half a dozen or so postcards that were in the Bomb Aimer's box. Evidently, he had a habit of instigating and maintaining intimate relationships with women in various parts of the country, each of whom appeared to believe that they were the sole objects of the man's affections. These went into the bin. The Navigator had a small bundle of letters, all extremely short, from his wife, all variations on the 'Dear Arthur, Thank you for your letter, I am glad that you are well, the baby is well, I am doing well, all things considered...' theme. Nothing of interest or concern there, safe to be returned. The Rear Gunner, Wireless Operator and Flight Engineer had left no letters. He had long ago stopped wondering how this could be so.

He lit a cigarette and stretched, exhausted by the events of the day, his nerves already shredded. In front of him sat the small pile of rather thick-looking envelopes, sealed and addressed letters which the Mid-Upper Gunner had written but not posted.

He picked one up and turned it over between his fingers, feeling its thickness and weight. The lad must have had a lot to write home about. They would take some time to go through if he was going to do the job properly.

He dropped the letter and was rubbing the tiredness out of his eyes and trying to hold off a rising swell of despair that seemed determined to overwhelm him, when he stopped; through the open window, probably from the radio on the NAAFI van, came the sound of the popular song that Hobson had been singing yesterday.

Hearing the song properly for the first time he smiled, appreciating the cleverness of the lyric. War was like a machine, that was a cliché, but the song took the cliché to another level, laughing at the absurdities of Total War, at the same time acting as a Recruiting Sergeant to get more workers into the factories. It occurred to him for the first time that this was what war amounted to, when it came down to it: it wasn't the men firing bullets at each other from trenches or raining phosphorous bombs on women and children from a great height. It was about which side had the capability to organise and pay for and execute the biggest and most expensive military operation. Dockets, warrants, invoices and orders, queried, approved, stamped and signed, In/Out. This was what Goebbels meant by Total War.

In his mind's eye he saw himself from above, sitting like some deranged clerk at a huge desk, surrounded by the flotsam and jetsam of young men's lives, poring over letters containing their most personal, intimate thoughts and expressions, each item to be forwarded on to a loved one if considered useful to the War Effort, or incinerated if not, much like the young men themselves. War was a machine, pure and simple, and he, it had suddenly become clear, was as much a cog in that machine as the factory girl in the song and the boys climbing into their Lancasters every night.

The well of despair that he had been holding back finally rose up to engulf him. Fearful of being heard or seen in this state, he fought to hold back the sobs, covering his mouth with the back of his hand, but it was no good. Soon he collapsed in a fit of uncontrollable coughing and tears.

After several minutes, he wiped his eyes, exhausted, and realised that his outburst had gone unnoticed in the adjoining offices. He looked at the letters, and for a moment actually considered the possibility of burning them and walking away. After all, who would know? He flicked open his lighter, and then closed it again. He knew he couldn't destroy them arbitrarily; the lad had written them, they had to be read. But he couldn't do it here.

He put the envelopes into his pocket, switched off the desk lamp and headed out. If he was quick, he'd catch the next bus into Newark.

***

In the bar room of The Saracen's Head he had found a table in the corner, and sat down to read Sgt Greenhalgh's letters. Connie, bless her, had interrupted him a few times, but she meant well, and soon he had read the first three, written to the boy's parents; the first covering his train journey from Scotland to Newark, and the others describing in some detail life on the Station. The letters were warm, simple and honest; well-written and engaging. There were admittedly some unfortunate references to names and places which he was easily able to redact with his pen, but all in all he couldn't see how they would bring anything but comfort to the lad's parents.

He slit open the last envelope, addressed to a WAAF at a Station in Scotland, and clearly, unlike the others, written in haste.

RAF Station Syerston.
A million miles away from you.

My darling Anne,
It's gone two in the morning, I can't sleep, and am writing this on my knee in the ablutions so as not to wake the other fellows. I have to confess to getting filthy drunk this evening so this letter probably won't make much sense and will probably come across all gushing and Over The Top, but you know you really are the most important person in the world to me, and I need to tell you these things, if only because I hope you may understand just a little bit of what I am trying to say. Please don't screw this up. Not yet anyway.

It seems like it took days to get to Newark on the train (air raids, diversions and what-not) and all the time me thinking about our precious night together, and the damnable argument that happened the next morning. As I looked miserably out of the window on the bus which took me the last few miles to Syerston, I noticed the most beautiful little cottages dotted along the road, and I couldn't help thinking that maybe one day when this is all over (or perhaps even before then?) we might be able to find a little cottage to rent, where we could be happy in each other's company, sitting beside a roaring fire in the winter, tending the garden in the spring and summer, or just sharing a bed, just the two of us, alone together, to live as we want to, without a care in the world, NO WAR and with nothing but a happy future together to occupy our thoughts.

And it suddenly hit me that although I always thought being able to fly was the most important thing to me, I realised that there is one thing more important, and that is you, darling Anne, and the love I have for you. If only we can forget the hateful things that were said, and which I am sure neither of us truly meant, we can find a way out of this awful mess.

Do I sound like I've had too much to drink? I hope not. Please don't think this is just the beer talking. It's just that although I am happy beyond words to be finally in a place where I can do my bit in the war, I am going to be so far away from you. I can honestly say that suddenly having all this distance between us for the first time I now see clearly how much you mean to me (please PLEASE don't throw this away, I beg you!)

The rest of the letter was written in a neater, less rambling hand, and was separated from the first section by the underlined words:

Half an hour later.

Anne, I realised I was sounding like Leslie Howard on a bad day, and made myself a VERY STRONG mug of coffee, and smoked two cigarettes outside, which has helped clear my head somewhat. I did a fair bit of thinking too, and shall endeavour to ensure that the remainder of this letter reads like it has been written by a man of sound mind, low blood-alcohol level, and a Happy Heart.

Syerston is a splendid place, all very new and comfortable, and VERY BIG! After I'd drawn my kit etc and found a billet I was feeling a bit lonely, wondering when I would meet my crew, and I was half-way through writing a letter to my parents when I was scooped up (literally) by two Hairy Colonials and frog-marched off to the Crew Room, where I found my new crew, lounging about in their armchairs.

'Here's the sprog,' said Hank, one of the Hairy Colonials, and I was suddenly aware of six pairs of eyes, all looking me

over, taking the measure of me. It was rather unnerving, I must say. I felt like a beast at market, pushed into the auction ring and forced to parade up and down under the scrutiny of cold, experienced eyes. Would I be good enough for this crew, would I fit in?

'About time,' announced one fellow, throwing down his newspaper. 'We thought you were lost. Good job you're not our new bloody Navigator.' (General laughter). Without getting up he introduced himself as 'The Skipper' and told me that 'P-Popsie was in urgent need of a new Mid-Upper Gunner, owing to the last one not being as alive as he used to be, thanks to a scrap with a night fighter over Essen a couple of nights ago.'

I was a little surprised, not realising that I was to be a replacement for a dead man. I suppose I had just assumed that I was to be part of a new crew. Registering my confusion, the Skipper told me not to worry, the turret had been hosed out and wiped down by the Erks and was spick and span, so you'd never know.

He said this with an absolutely straight face, and there was a deathly silence as I took it in. I half-expected the crew to burst out laughing at the joke, but no-one moved. They all looked awkward, as if no-one knew what to say. 'I'm sorry to hear that,' I said, finally. 'You must miss him terribly.'

'Of course,' said the Skipper. 'Old Wilko was a bloody good bloke.' (Nodding in agreement). 'More importantly though, he had the foresight to pay me back the five quid he owed me before we took off, and he said that on no account must I use the money for anything other than getting the lads thoroughly drunk if he didn't come back.' Several of the crew smiled at this. 'And on that happy note,' he continued, rising to his full height, 'seeing as it looks like we'll be on ops *tomorrow night, we are all going into Newark to get well and truly plastered. Bus leaves in ten minutes.'*

At one point the bus passed through a small village named East Stoke, which I remembered from my history lessons as the site of a major battle of the Wars of the Roses. I mentioned this to the Wireless Op, telling him that as far as I remembered, it was thought to have cost the lives of as many as six or seven thousand men. 'Can you imagine?' I continued, 'All those men killed in one day?'

'I don't have to imagine,' he said. 'That's how many we kill every night when we hit those German towns.'

I have to say I was stunned by what he said, and equally by the way he said it; as if he were describing something casual, routine.

'There's a difference though,' Tail End Charlie piped up, from his seat behind us. 'We're burning women and children, not just men.' And he went back to his paper.

Do you think that could be true, Anne? Or was it just another one of this crew's very dark jokes? I couldn't get the thought out of my mind, at least until we hit the Saracen's.

The Saracen's Head is a rather large affair, an old coaching inn located slap bang in the middle of Newark's market place, and it gets a very favourable mention in Sir Walter Scott's novel 'The Heart of Midlothian', apparently. There are plenty of pubs to choose from in the town, but the lads seem to like this one, with its rather imposing statue of a bearded Saracen above the door.

The Skipper slapped the five-pound note on the bar and told the barmaid to 'Keep the beers coming while there's a man still standing,' and the drinking began. I was a little surprised that nobody made any kind of a speech about Old Wilko, the fellow who was paying for the beer and who I am replacing, and kept expecting the speeches to come with each round, but somehow they never did. I think though, that the crew were all remembering him in their hearts, and were maybe just a bit embarrassed to make a show of their feelings.

Half-way through the evening I noticed a rather elderly officer (a Squadron Leader, I think) who was drinking alone. He looked rather preoccupied and weighed down by his thoughts. Now my parents always brought me up to treat everyone I meet as my equal (or at least no better than me!), and so although I know it's not entirely the done thing for an NCO to talk to an officer, I headed over and asked if we could buy him a drink, in memory of 'Old Wilko'. Suddenly everything was silent and rather awkward, and the old chap looked at me as if he'd seen a ghost. The fellows glared at him like he was Blind Pugh – the way they acted, I half expected him to hand one of them the Black Spot. The Skipper quickly intervened, saying that 'the Chairman of the Committee wouldn't want to drink with the likes of us flying types.' With that the Skipper turned his back on the poor old Squadron Leader, rather rudely I thought, and I last saw him heading out of the pub looking like his world had collapsed around him.

The letter continued for another couple of pages, mostly romantic stuff about how much the boy was missing his girl, who it appeared was several years older than him, and more hero-worship of his new crew. When he had finished reading it, he folded the pages, slid them back into the envelope, and threw it into the fire. He watched the flames lick around the edges of the envelope before finally consuming it, and when he was satisfied that the contents were completely burnt, he put on his greatcoat and cap and went out into the night.

***

Sitting on the bus as it headed down the Fosse, he looked out of the window, mentally listing the jobs that he would have to do that night. First, he would gather and pack all the personal effects and letters from P-Popsie's crew that were suitable for return to the families and forward them, with personal letters expressing his sympathy for their loss. This would include the unposted letters written by the Air Gunner to his parents. After that he would grab some food and wait for the return of the squadron's Lancasters from Germany, and if required, the Committee of Adjustment would begin its work again.

All this would be easy; he had done it a hundred times.

It would be harder to go back to the dark, empty cottage when these jobs were done, but he would do it. And once inside, he would open one last letter, and sitting at the table with a pot of tea, he would read it, before taking his pen and writing a reply.

The Almshouses, Northgate

by Maria Dziedzan

Circa 1870

H E FORCES THE breath out of his chest. Did it even reach his lungs? He raises his head to see if there is indeed some incubus sitting on his sternum...but, no, there is nothing there. The blockage must be inside him then. He tries another shallow breath, listening for how far it penetrates. Not far. He can't lift the weight off his chest. He lets the breath out on a sigh. It's the dust. He might as well admit it. It can only be the dust.

He thinks back over the unbroken years of levelling the barley on the floor of the maltings, taking pride in how smooth a layer he could achieve. He can almost feel the moist barley beneath his bare feet as he prepares to let it steep and sprout. The last of the dust floats golden in the air, backlit by the sunlight pouring in through the vents. He only ever sees the barley in this harvested state, turning it daily for several days on its journey to becoming malt. Not for him the visions of green fields, the barley swaying in the breeze, wave upon wave, the soft beards resting against one another until a light touch of air sets them dancing again.

He sighs as this vision presents itself. He was imprisoned in the maltings from May to September, from Monday till Sunday, turning load after load of barley. No wonder the iron weight on his chest will not let him take a deep breath. But he had always been in work and so had been rewarded with this cottage, gifted to "a deserving married couple to reside in in old age".

He hears her stepping into the kitchen, slamming the washing basket onto the deal table. He hears the wicker shift as she announces her martyrdom in washing his spare shirt.

'What do you need a clean shirt for?' she had demanded.

'You know Mr Shoal is calling in to see me.'

'Why he wants to see you, I don't know. You only shifted the barley after all. It's no good giving yourself airs, you know.'

He doesn't reply. Fighting for breath in a charity bed does not feel like giving himself airs. And he knows that, in truth, she is proud enough to want both him and their cottage to be presentable to the foreman who, for so many years presided over Ned's fate. He knows also that she has her reputation to keep up. A regular churchgoer, apologising to the vicar for her husband's lack of attendance, for working on the Sabbath. Although he knows she had enjoyed having much of her time to herself, cooking his meals and making his wages stretch far enough, especially in the winter months when he took whatever work he could, holding her head up in the market, all without the nuisance of a man under her feet.

There is a tapping at the window. He looks up and wiggles his fingers to the enormous tabby, looking in solicitously. He lifts the blanket and rolls on to his side. It is easier to get out of bed this way. The incubus on his chest will not let him get up otherwise. He steps across to the window, his bare, skinny legs feeling the cold. He opens the window and the cat jumps down into the room as lightly as it can. They both know she'll be in with the broom if she suspects the interloper is here.

Ned rolls back into bed and the cat leaps up lightly, circles twice and settles himself by Ned's side. Ned strokes the cat's broad head.

'You old rogue. I know you only care for the milk I give you.'

The cat purrs. As a maltings cat, he has always had his milk allowance, on the understanding that he does his job, catching the rats and mice which burrow into the sacks. But the tabby has decided that if Ned has retired to his bed, he should too.

Needless to say, Ellen resents them both and the broom serves to keep them in check. It's true, she only catches Ned with the broom handle where the bruises won't show, but she will catch the cat anywhere she can. She no longer fears the foreman's protection of the maltings' cats. She won't be sacked for mistreating the wretched animal.

Ned tries to ignore his other aches and pains and closes his eyes to take a nap. But the image of her grin as he stumbles over the broom stretched across the doorway insists on presenting itself to his mind's eye. He had fallen heavily against the corner of the table that time.

'Oh, have you hurt yourself?' she had asked loudly enough for the neighbour to hear, should she be listening. They might have the end house on the row of six almshouses, but she still has to be careful that her abuse is not overheard.

She hadn't always been like this, but when he was pensioned off, she had made it clear that his continued presence,

'Get out of my way,'

and his coughing,

'Can't you do that outside?'

had tried her limited patience.

He hears the clang of the pot on top of the stove and pulls the thin blanket over the cat's bulk, curling himself around the warm body. The cat knows better than to purr.

She flings the bedroom door open. 'What's happened with that window?' she says as she slams it closed. 'Are you trying to die on me?'

He says nothing. They both know his death would render her homeless.

'Do you want some broth?'

He shakes his head. 'Is there any milk?'

'Oh yes,' she sneers, 'and white bread too.'

'Nothing, then,' he says and closes his eyes.

He hears her step in the only other room of the cottage and the chink of a bottle against a mug.

'Here,' she says, handing him the mug.

He takes it from her. 'I'll drink it in a minute.'

'Well, I haven't got time to stand here all day waiting on you,' she says and stomps out of the bedroom, slamming the door behind her.

'Here you are, puss,' he says, lifting the blanket and tipping the mug so that the tabby can lap up the milk.

Ned has been doing this for some weeks now. He can't remember when he last ate something solid and he drinks little. A life of struggling to breathe and of trying to ignore the aches and pains of the bruises seems like no life at all. And who could he tell? He would only be derided for his lack of manhood. So a quiet diminution has been his decision. She doesn't notice, preferring not to minister to him too closely.

The cat finishes the milk and Ned places the mug on the floor beside the bed. He pulls the blanket over himself and the cat settles against Ned's shoulder, purring into Ned's ear. The tabby's whiskers tickle Ned's face...and then they don't. The cat gives Ned's unshaven cheek a valedictory lick with its rough tongue and turns to face the door. He sits with his paws tucked into his chest, waiting for the mistress of the house to make her entrance. He might be old but he has beautifully sharp teeth and claws, strong enough to rip out a rat's throat.

The Guardians

by C.L. Peache

In the beginning...

I HAVE BEEN MANY things to many different people. I have cried and laughed, been scared and happy, and I have loved and lost. I know some people would not believe a building can feel. That the very essence of why the human created it could, would, should, seep into the wood, glass, bricks and mortar. That the very purpose they created me for would determine who I was. They would scoff at me having a soul. But...

I was born but unlike humans I don't really have a birthday and I have taken many forms. I have after all, been chopped, reimagined, created, moulded, chiselled and transformed throughout my time. Only I hold the secret and knowledge of my beginnings, unsurprising as the land I sit on changes as the moles and worms dig, as the trees grow and shift, as the weather seeps and shifts through the air, shaping and changing the ground and everything above.

History would tell you I have been here for over a thousand years but I am made up of so many elements from so many places, created by so many people, that it would be impossible to tell my story in full with any accuracy, much to the disappointment of the historians I'm sure.

I love the events which bring people in, each one bringing their own energy. The Christmas tree festival is full of light and happiness and it's with a rare sadness I feel the solitude when the lights go out. My soul, my batteries, my light and hope for my future swell as the humans whisper as they wander in on their day trips. They wonder what will happen to the churches when religion is no longer here. I feel the church guardian's sorrow as the number of believers dwindle. Sometimes I feel melancholy at the passing of time, my youth has long since been lost and built the way for maturity and knowledge. New hope has come today and once again I feel happy and secure. This new guardian explodes with positivity and love. I can feel it from her loving caress and in every gaze. Hers is a rare and positive soul. I hope she stays... I need someone to help me and a mystery is a good place to start, don't you think?

***

It had been a long day and the latest vicar of St Mary Magdalene's church was tired. Ophelia wandered the church on the now familiar routine of 'putting the place to bed'. It was funny, her mother had always used that phrase when she'd closed down the parish house they'd lived in until her father died. She often imagined his shock as her father would never have expected his daughter to be a member of the clergy. Who would have dreamed such a thing possible back then? But her brother had shown no interest in the calling, much to her father's often voiced disappointment. Ophelia loved churches, she loved God. It was hard to explain to people why she believed in God, especially when faced with a parent who had lost a child too soon. Life was a test and she didn't profess to have all the answers. She could only describe the peace she felt that someone was with her, the voice and feeling which guided and comforted her. If she lost God she would feel as if she had lost a part of herself.

She turned the key and smiled, she always felt she could hear the building sigh a deep breath of relief. It had been another busy day. The café was doing well and she didn't mind if the 'non-believers' as Mrs Penderton called them *in her loudest whisper voice,* only came in for the company and cheap refreshments. It certainly wasn't for the heating, which was temperamental on the best of days. As far as Ophelia was concerned, everyone was welcome. God to her wasn't just about believing in a higher power. If others didn't have faith, then she hoped hers was enough to embrace them and bring them comfort. She always had a smile and a keen and patient ear if they needed it. They were here and God would love them through her.

She groaned as she knelt on the stool, yet couldn't help but smile thinking about Marjory who'd asked her if she 'joined' the church, then would God be able to help with her arthritic hands, which she needed in working order for the many times she threatened to strangle her husband of forty years on a daily basis. If only, but she supposed God did help; as when she finished her day here in meditation and prayer, she never felt the ills of the body. Ophelia liked to think God was giving her a little break for all the years of service. She tied up her long chestnut hair with its flicks of silver into a bun. Paul always maintained he married her because of her hair, it reminded him of a dog he'd had as a child. He'd also said he'd had a massive crush on Meryl Streep but she hadn't returned his calls, so she was the next best thing. She smiled thinking on her unchristian response to both of those statements.

Tonight, the air felt different. There was an expectation as she closed her eyes. More than ever, she felt a great presence. The confessional or prayer was often the most difficult but also the most rewarding part of her life. She liked helping people. A problem shared was a problem halved, was also another of her mother's sayings. Her mother had sprinkled them in conversations, like a baker dusting icing on a cake.

She jumped as a loud noise shattered the silence. She was only just getting used to the sounds and smells of this place she would love to call home. It hadn't been confirmed that this would be her full-time parish but she was hopeful. Sometimes she'd smelt the faint hint of what she thought could be cannon smoke when she was in the church. Her mother had told her as a young child that she had connections to people in time which couldn't be explained but also, that she had a vivid imagination which was as likely to wander as to stay fixed on its intent for any great length of time.

Ophelia finally rose. Her parents had long since passed and she enjoyed the memories which brought them into her mind. She walked slowly down the nave in search of the noise. She wondered if it was the squirrel again. As much as she loved animals, she knew they were liable to cause damage to the church and it was always a race against time to preserve what they had. She had secretly named the squirrel, Freddie but not in the hearing of Marcus, the church warden.

Climbing the steps, leading to the area which closeted the choir she quickly found the source of the noise. One of the seats in the choir stall had fallen down. She frowned as she walked over to them and bending slightly, she flicked the seat back into its resting position. These cinema style seats, as she thought of them, often rested in the upright position. Her husband had informed her they were called Misericord or a mercy seat, he was ever the fount of knowledge when it came to the architecture and history of a building. The wood often changed shape with the weather so it wasn't unusual for them to creak and groan. She shivered and turned to move, it was time for home and the roast dinner her husband had promised her. She stopped and put her hand on the worn head of one of the wooden carvings and bending down again, she noticed something out of place on the rear pew. There were many names and shapes, including a windmill which had been gouged into the wood by bored choir children over the centuries. The so called 'graffiti' went back untold years. Children never changed but she hadn't noticed this one before. It was a set of numbers rather than an image, which is why it had caught her eye. She traced her finger over the numbers which looked like they had been freshly cut: 942.524.

Pondering what she had seen, she made a mental note on her to do list tomorrow to ask Marcus, the Church Warden. Somewhere the sequence of the numbers was trying to strike a chord but her brain was full and tired. She chuckled at her own joke and left the church to its slumbers to be guided home by a red sky. She murmured to herself as she turned left and wandered through the cobbled marketplace, which was devoid of traders and visitors for a change. The new fake looking Christmas tree in the centre of the market square created a welcome glow.

***

The vicar jumped and her gentle laugh dissipated into the space above her. Ophelia pushed herself off the uncomfortable pew. She knew these had probably been built purposely uncomfortable, maybe so the devout parishioners stayed awake and the church resonated with the sound of prayer, scripture, and music, rather the sounds of Mr or Mrs Penderton's snoring. She chuckled to herself thinking of the very active church couple snoring next to each other on the previous Sunday. The Facebook group had been alive with the news, but they had to be careful. No-one wanted to suffer the wrath of Mrs Penderton.

They were lucky Mrs Penderton thought Facebook was the work of the devil.

Ophelia had been meaning to speak to the warden all day but today hadn't been the day for a cup of tea and conversation. Freddie had been particularly active and Ophelia was beginning to suspect one of the parishioners was purposely ignoring the warning posters the warden had pinned, with force, onto the noticeboard to warn people about feeding the vermin or letting it into the church. She was sure his faith would be tested if he found out the squirrel had an ally in her.

She shuffled along the aisle and couldn't supress the smile at the view before her. One hundred and fifty Christmas trees had been delivered that morning and pine scent permeated the air. She could see the cleaner rolling her eyes as the pine needles announced their trailing presence, just like the married couples covered in confetti she thought. Ophelia loved weddings. She said a prayer every night for her 'long suffering husband' as he called it. He knew most days his needs were maybe third on the list after God and her parishioners. She always nullified him by saying he was number one in her heart. He would give her that look as he knew God shared that particular organ with him as well.

As she finally made her way into the office, she saw the cause of the noise. A very large book lay on the floor. She frowned, the church book cleaning group had been earlier that day. It was unlike them to leave a book out, as they were old and precious and kept under lock and key in the church library. She'd been impressed by the Bishop White Library when she'd read about him when she'd found out Newark was to be her temporary patch. A previous vicar, Dr Bishop White had bequeathed his large collection of books to the church in his will in 1698. Paul admired the way Dr White had insisted that the books be brought to the library and bookcases erected within one month.

He must have been used to getting his own way in real life, Ophelia surmised. Also, and her husband had laughed at this, the Vicar was to *'hold the key'* and the mayor and Alderman of Newark should never embezzle the books or take, or lend them at any a point. He must have been turning in his grave when in 1854 they discovered that three works had gone missing and they hadn't been found since. Paul had been delighted to find one of the works was by a poet Edmund Spenser and she'd lost her husband to research for the rest of the week.

Ophelia picked up the large leather-bound book carefully, hoping it wouldn't be damaged. The volunteers took such care to maintain the collection. They really needed a book specialist to come in and digitalise the titles so they could be used by research students across the world. She was all for preservation but not at the cost of some gem being lost to the past. Her hand shot out and she managed to catch the piece of yellow paper which had dropped out of the book. She placed the book firmly on the solid oak desk, and on inspection, it was a modern post-it note which had been folded, rather than one of the yellowed ancient pages of the book.

She unfolded the note and after scanning it, she nearly dropped it again. She'd heard the story from many different people involved in the church, especially from past Vicars and here was real evidence and not just whisperings. A thrill of excitement ran through her. She wondered if she really would be the person to solve the mystery of the missing books and suddenly, she realised that the numbers on the bench might actually have meaning. Surely it was a co-incidence. She knew a clue when she saw one!

***

It had been with much difficulty that Ophelia put the mystery of the note and the numbers to one side. Of course she was very good at keeping secrets and confidences, it came with the calling, but a good mystery set her heart racing. She had to confess a love of the Agatha Christie novels at her last book group and she'd recently started reading the books by Sophie Hannah, who she found to be a worthy successor of the mystery tales. She had surprised her husband by taking to the Kindle he had purchased for her last Christmas; as she found often her hands ached at the end of the day and pressing a screen was so much easier than holding a paperback, even if it wasn't quite the same. Her book group friends had been aghast when she had produced it with a flare but she caught more than one shift their interested gaze in her direction when the book group boss or mafia boss, Simon showed his displeasure at her confession.

Today was the start of the Christmas tree decorations and there was much to be done. Marcus wandered off to open the large carved wooden doors as Ophelia turned, catching a flicker of movement from the corner of her eye. Freddie was perched on the end of one of the pews, staring at her.

"Well, hello, Freddie. Do you mind me calling you Freddie?" she whispered, hoping the warden wouldn't hear her or catch her, more to the point.

Freddie turned his head as if he was considering her suggestion. She smiled, and she would have sworn in her prayers that he nodded his head.

"I'm Ophelia, it's nice to meet you formally." She held out her hand, feeling very silly. She could only imagine what Paul would say and Mrs Penderton would probably write a letter to the highest authority and have her thrown out, and Marcus, well, Marcus would send her to Coventry at the very least. There would be no more offers of cups of tea for her for the foreseeable future.

Freddie surprised her by reaching out his dirty paw and touching the top of her hand. Ophelia felt an overwhelming rush of love and it quite surprised her. Footsteps and the clang of keys announced the impending arrival of the squirrel's arch nemesis and the sound of excited chatter as the first Christmas tree decorators carried their treasure down the aisle. Ophelia turned to hurry Freddie on his way but he had wisely disappeared. On the pew a perfect acorn was perched, a little gift perhaps. She quickly put it in her apron pocket and brushed off the little bit of soil he'd left on her hand before heading to greet everyone. She loved Christmas and was delighted to be involved in her first Christmas tree event.

***

"Well, Marcus. That went well don't you think?"

They were in the office enjoying a well-earned cup of tea. Her feet were aching and she was looking forward to the luxurious long bath later, knowing the next few days would be the same and she doubted she would get much rest now until the new year. Her jaw ached from talking and laughing. She felt the church swell at the hustle and bustle of chatter as people delightedly perfected the decoration of their trees ready for the start of the festival. She felt like the old building had come to life.

"It did. Apart from that blasted squirrel turning up every time I turned around. I'm going to have to call pest control in soon," Marcus said ominously.

Ophelia stayed silent as Marcus complained about the squirrel. She had seen Freddie a few times and throughout the day she'd fiddled with the acorn in her pocket, enjoying the smooth texture and feeling special that Freddie had left it for her. It kept the note company and throughout the day she wondered about where to look for the next clue. She had to start with the local library. It was the only place to try and solve this mystery.

Marcus's moan brought her back into the room, "Also, I've lost count of the amount of people who haven't had their lights PAT tested. Every year it's the same people who pretend they've forgotten. One year I'm going to ban lights! We've told them about the risk of fire I don't know how many times. God, forbid we suffer a fire like we nearly did in July 1903! The storm shattered so many windows and it was lucky my namesake was as dedicated as I am and came to check the church, as someone had left one of the candles burning. I ask you!"

Ophelia didn't add that it was probably the warden's job to check the candles were extinguished. She raised her cup to her lips to hide her smile. Marcus was great at referencing moments from history, it was why he and Paul got on so well. Despite his gruff manner she had seen him giving some of the little children a treat to keep them quiet as the trees were decorated. Marcus was as much a part of the church as she now was. The place couldn't run without him and she hoped it wouldn't be able to run without her.

Marcus got up and made his way back into the church. Ophelia treated herself to a couple more minutes of silence and relaxation whilst she contemplated the note and the number. She took out the acorn and note from her apron pocket and unfolded the post it note. In tiny writing it read; *The mystery of the missing book: Hosts walked & fog greens.* It sent another shiver of excitement through her and she looked at the number again. 942.524 for the life of her she knew the numbers meant something. It seemed a very odd title for a book though. The numbers were not a date of birth or a significate date. It didn't tally with any particular day or month. The numbers were familiar though. Also, why only one book and not the three which had reportedly gone missing.

"Hello, Ophelia? Are you in there, Marcus... oh, there you are, just as he said."

The upright form of Ms Kenny marched into the room. Marched described perfectly the way Ms Kenny moved around in life. She did everything with a purpose and woe betide anyone who got in her way. An ex-Librarian, she could silence the church with one raised of an eyebrow. A feat which had been employed only last week when the children were practising their hymns with a little bit too much enthusiasm. Usually, Ms Kenny was in charge of the Bishop White Library but she volunteered where she was needed. She and the many volunteers were the reason this church was still thriving.

"Hello, Ms Kenny. What can I do for you on this wonderful afternoon?" Ophelia felt suddenly guilty for having her first break of the day. She wasn't sure what powered Ms Kenny but she had never seen her eat or drink anything in the months she'd been here.

Ms Kenny tucked a stray grey hair behind her ear, which had dared to escape across her face before she answered, "I wanted to see how you are fixed for tomorrow? I have the pleasure of my grandchildren and you know they are of an age where they need to be entertained otherwise, they will likely get up to all sorts..."

Ophelia interrupted her, knowing she was about to receive the well delivered lecture about children today. How they behaved or didn't behave. How back in Ms Kenny's day children were seen and rarely heard and how she had brought her daughter up to be respectful and it was her feckless husband's fault the grandchildren were so pampered.

"Yes. The more the merrier, Ms Kenny. You know that. You and your family are always welcome. I'm sure we can find some hard labour for the children." She had meant this as a joke but the approval on Ms Kenny's face made her realise her statement had been taken literally.

The words were out of her mouth before she realised she was going to ask. "I wonder if you could make sense of this number Ms Kenny?"

Ophelia wrote down the numbers on a piece of paper. She didn't want to reveal her mysterious note just yet. Ms Kenny took one look and a smile crossed her face.

"Are you trying to test me to check if I have the required credentials to run the Bishop White Library Vicar? Tut tut." Ms Kenny actually wagged her finger in the air.

Ophelia was about the protest, when what could only be described as smug look passed Ms Kenny's face.

"Nine. Four. Two. 'point'," Ms Kenny's finger already poised mid-air, stabbed at an invisible spot in the air, "Five. Two. Four." Ophelia was mesmerised by her finger, like a conductor with a symphony, "is the Dewey Decimal number for books classified in England and Wales, and that specific, Five, Two, Four," again with the figure pointing, "relates to local history. Specifically, Newark-On-Trent, our wonderful town may I add."

Ophelia started clapping. "Ms Kenny, you should go on Mastermind with that level of incredible knowledge."

Ms Kenny stood even straighter at the compliment.

"If a Librarian does not know her Dewey, then she shouldn't be allowed anywhere near the classification of books."

With that, Ms Kenny did her best Mary Poppins salute and without asking why Ophelia wanted to know, turned on her heels and marched from the room, her head held slightly higher to God.

"Of course," Ophelia said to the empty room, "Dewey! How could I have forgotten the Dewey Decimal System."

Ophelia secured her scarf as the darkness and cold air descended in the early afternoon as she made her way to Newark Library, leaving the rest of the preparations in the safe hands of Marcus and Ms Kenny. She felt guilty that she had not been a regular of the library, only visiting once on her first tour of Newark as getting to know the church had taken up so much of her time. She made a promise to God to change this in the new year. She strolled past the beautiful garden which had been transformed following a protest to turn it into another car park of all things. The protest had happened before her time but she would have been at the forefront if she'd been here. Her husband said it was best not to get her started on such topics. She vowed to pop along and help come springtime. Maybe she could talk some of the parishioners into helping with some weeding.

She walked through the doors and waved at some of the locals she recognised. They did a double take, as people do when they see someone 'out of place'. She often did it herself, embarrassingly she had once spoken to an old schoolteacher for twenty minutes in Waitrose carpark before realising who they were.

Walking up to the information desk she returned the warm smile and asked to be pointed in the direction of the intriguing Dewey number she was seeking. She was efficiently taken to the books at the back of the library and offered help 'should it be required' before the librarian returned to their desk. Ophelia stared at the shelves hoping for some inspiration. An hour later she was making no progress. She'd found all the books relating to the church but she had no idea what she was looking for, and as suspected, none of the books had the strange title attached to them. Maybe there was a spelling error she mused.

"Can I help?"

Ophelia peered up at the young face staring down at her. She thought she'd seen her before at the local College when she'd popped in to visit them during one of the open days.

"Well, maybe you can. I'm looking for a book but I'm not sure which one it is and I don't exactly know the title."

The girl looked understandably confused.

"Let me explain. I have these numbers and this, which I think refers to a book on Newark but I'm lost as to which one. It's such a strange title."

Ophelia handed the note to the girl, Layla she thought her name was. The girl scanned it and handed it back. "Well, that's easy. It's an anagram, Mis..." Layla faltered as she no doubt worried what to call the vicar.

"Ophelia will do fine." She smiled, encouraging the girl to continue.

Layla smiled widely. "Like I said, it's an anagram. It's from a book by Rosemary Robb; Ghosts and Legends of Newark, Mis... I mean Ophelia." Layla blushed as she handed the note back.

"Well and how did you work that out so quickly may I ask?" Ophelia stood up and smiled gratefully at Layla.

Layla blushed, "I'm very good at anagrams and we were researching local history books for a project and I love ghosts..." The blush deepened, she obviously didn't think ghosts should be spoken about with a vicar.

"I've got to go now miss, my mum's waiting for me."

And people couldn't see God's hand in coincidences. What were the chances that this very girl would be in here at the same time and she would know the book Ophelia wanted.

"Thank you." Ophelia called to the departing girl. She hadn't seen that particular book on the shelf. It was time to employ an expert and she called for the librarian.

***

"Hi Marcus, sorry. Time ran away with me. Everything okay?" Ophelia enquired, as she clung to her bag containing the Ghosts and Legends of Newark by Rosemary Robb, Dewey number 942.524 ROB. She though Ms Kenny would be proud.

"Yes, everyone has left now. Just a few more tomorrow to set up and then it's all ready. I've swept up some of the mess. I will never know why I clean up before Marion comes in."

Ophelia put her gloved hand on his shoulder. "Because you're a very kind man Marcus that's why, and like most of us, you appreciate a quiet life."

Marcus laughed and locked the door to visitors so they could put the building to bed. The church was full of joy and happiness everywhere they looked. It would be beautiful when all the lights were shining. It lifted her heart to see the church so vibrant.

Later that evening after Marcus had left and she was about to settle herself to her prayers before home time, she found Freddie was waiting for her on the carved figure at the end of the pew.

"Well, little Freddie. I wonder how you got in here? I hope you've not found a hole into the church. That would not do at all. We don't have the funds to repair another problem."

Freddie stopped his grooming and if a squirrel could look smug, then he held an air of smugness.

Ophelia grinned as she took her place on the cushions. She still preferred what she would call the traditional seat of prayer, even if her knees protested.

"What do you think of all this then, Freddie? Doesn't the church look wonderful?"

Freddie raised his tiny grey head and looked around at the array of trees as if he knew exactly what she had asked him. To her delight Freddie turned back and nodded his small head.

"Right, just give me a few minutes and then it's time for us both to go home. It's been a very long but fruitful day. I've solved a clue, with the help of friends I hasten to add."

Ophelia closed her eyes and felt the warmth of God's presence soothe away the day. There was so much joy to take from life but society felt as if it was at a turning point. The effects of Covid, wars, climate change, the government and every other worry was a melting pot of stress and the future was so unclear and unsteady, she knew her community was struggling. She was determined this would be the best ever Christmas tree festival. She couldn't take away people's problems but maybe she could help them forget it for just a little while.

She collected her coat, scarf, hat and bag from the office and wrapped herself up before heading to the side door.

"Come on then, Freddie. Time for you to go home. If I leave you in here Marcus will never speak to me again."

Dutifully, Freddie jumped off the pew and bounded out of the door as instructed. On a last-minute whim, she decided to double check the numbers she'd seen to make sure they really did match the book she'd borrowed. She couldn't think why they would be important or what they were leading her to. She walked swiftly down the church and as she pulled down the seat she frowned, there was the amazing picture of the bears but she was sure the numbers had been on this one. She moved across to check the other seats. Closing the last one, she shivered. The numbers which had been so clearly etched into the wood, had disappeared.

***

Ophelia sighed as she laid back in bed and opened the book, 'Ghosts & Legends of Newark' which she had borrowed from the library.

"What is this?" her husband Paul asked, popping her night-time hot chocolate onto the bedside cabinet. "Since when did you believe in ghosts, Vicar?"

"One must always be prepared to broaden one's horizons, husband."

Paul snorted. He'd quoted that to her when she'd spotted him reading a book about Star Signs and him being a scientist and historian.

She proceeded to tell him all about the clues she'd found and about the missing numbers.

"Intriguing. Maybe they are playing a trick on the new girl? Perhaps Ms Kenny or Mrs Penderton are really devout practical jokers."

Ophelia ignored him, although it made her smile to think of Ms Kenny crouched down scoring the numbers into the wood and Mrs Penderton hiding the note in the book. Like some kind of test. Well, in the very unlikely event it was them, she was up to the challenge. She just had to find the next clue and find out exactly where the missing book was. Also, it didn't explain the now missing numbers. She was pushing the boundaries of fiction even further thinking Ms Kenny had erased them with an electric powered sander.

On page 24 she read about The Ghost of St. Mary Magdalene's. In the war the choirboys were 'volunteered' to fire watch the church. She could just imagine the children of today loving being locked in the church and exploring the crypt, which was now the church Treasury. How scary and exciting. The story went that they'd heard thunderous knocking on the vestry door and it was moving. The next day they found the back of the door had been torn off and was covered in scratch marks. A past vicar had stated that they had seen a figure praying but this didn't explain why they would damage the door. Maybe this was a clue? She would look at the door tomorrow, just in case.

"Solved the mystery?" Paul asked, looking over his glasses. She could tell he was desperate to be involved.

"Not yet. I'm not even sure there is a mystery to solve."

"Once you remove the impossible, what is left, is probable." Paul touched his nose in a knowing way.

"Please don't quote Sir Arthur Conan Doyle if you cannot quote it properly."

Paul shrugged and smiled. She knew he was waiting for her to ask for his help. Well, she wouldn't. Her mother said she was also the most stubborn child when she set her mind to it.

Ophelia finally nodded off and dreamed of people trying to get into the church and meeting the immovable forms of Ms Kenny armed with a sander and Mrs Penderton with a look.

***

The next day she walked around the whole of the church. She hadn't really taken in the beauty and workmanship of some of the doors. She ran her hands over the aged wood and wondered if these were made from the trees in Sherwood Forest. Paul had found some records which stated that the six oaks from Sherwood Forest were donated to the building by Henry III. She'd seen the enormous keys of course but in their way the doors were as stunning as the beautiful stained-glass windows. She recalled one Marcus had mentioned the other day, something about them all being blown out by a freak storm in 1903 on the north side of the building and nearly 4,000 individual panes had to be replaced and Paul had said the spire was damaged in a lightning strike in May 1894. The church was certainly a beacon for the weather.

Ophelia looked closer, spotting something in a split in the wood. As she squinted and moved closer a loud bang on the other side of the door made her say a very bad word. A gasp from the other side confirmed they had heard her expletive.

Ophelia's face burned brighter than the sunrise that morning. The large door opened tentatively and Paul peered around the door with a massive grin on his face.

"You!" She swung her bag at him.

"Now, now Vicar. Please set an example to your parishioners, if not with your words, with your actions."

Ophelia was just about to reply when Mrs Penderton arrived. As she spotted Paul, a rare smile crossed her face. Marcus had once observed in a most unchristian like way, that an upturn of Mrs Penderton's lips into a smile was as unbelievable as the devil delivering an act of kindness.

"Vicar," Mrs Penderton said, with a tone which suggested she might have also heard her colourful language. Mrs Penderton turned to her husband, "Paul."

Ophelia choked back a snort of laughter as she avoided Paul's eye – she would dissolve altogether and lose any thread of respect Mrs Penderton had for her. His name was said with such intent that it would make even the most forward person blush. From the moment they had met, Mrs Penderton was a different woman in Paul's presence and he milked it for all it was worth. With a thought for her, Paul steered Mrs Penderton away and Ophelia went back to looking at the door. She finally found the little crack she had found underneath the locking mechanism. She peered in, sure she could see something there. Excitement bubbled inside her. There was definitely something there.

"Could I help a damsel in distress?" Paul was back looking smug. She lifted her bag threateningly and he laughed, raising his hands as if to say it wasn't his fault he was God's gift.

"Look," she pointed to the crack in the door, "I'm sure there is something in there but I cannot get it out. We will be opening any moment for the festival and there will be no chance to check again until later."

Paul peered in and took his Swiss army knife out of his pocket. As a historian and scientist, he was never without it. He found the implement he required and like a determined surgeon playing the game 'operation', he pulled out his prize.

"Voila," he declared triumphantly. Ophelia clapped and took the thin piece of wood from him. Turning it over she could see a cat delicately carved into the wood.

"Well, I'll be damned!" Paul crossed himself and looked up to the roof. Ophelia smiled and added a mental note to ask for forgiveness for them both later.

"What is it?" she said in a whisper.

"That's a symbol the suffragettes used. The game is afoot Watson."

Ophelia didn't have time to say that actually, out of the two of them, she was Sherlock and he was Watson, when the familiar jangling sound of Marcus echoed down the church. It was time to open to the public. The mystery would have to wait.

***

"Well?" Ophelia stretched out her toes under the covers. Her feet were burning and her mouth was aching but what a day it had been. They'd had record numbers of people through the door and the place had felt alive. At the end of the day, she'd said her quick prayer and she could feel the energy and joy of the building. God's house was happy.

Paul had popped in during the busy day to say he was going to investigate the mystery of the cat symbol. She'd been fascinated when he said it was linked to the suffragettes but had had no time to think about it.

Paul consulted his notebook, his glasses perched on the end of his long but regal looking nose. Apparently, he had perfect vision and only wore them for effect. She'd told him God punished liars but he said 'They' had an understanding. She sipped her drink as Paul started to read out what he had found with his usual enthusiasm. Unlike her, he loved research.

"The cat was definitely one of the symbols used by the Suffragettes and after talking to your very helpful Marcus I found a fascinating detail about the windows which were restored in 1957 in the Holy Spirit Chapel at the back on the church."

Ophelia nodded encouragement as she welcomed the warming sensation of the hot chocolate.

"They were restored by a Miss Joan Howson in 1957 and you will never guess who she was?"

"A suffragette?"

Paul turned, a look of disappointment on his face that his moment had been stolen away.

"How did you know?"

"Elementary, my dear Watson."

After they'd both stopped giggling he continued.

"Joan Howson was a member of the Suffragettes," Paul said pointedly. Ophelia stifled a laugh and let him continue. "I cannot see much evidence of her being a key player but she was definitely involved and the fact that she rearranged the glass in the stained-glass window in the church cannot be a coincidence."

"It's very exciting. Thank goodness for Marcus."

Paul coughed and Ophelia added, "And for you knowing exactly who to talk too. My very clever husband."

Paul sat up straighter, a little mollified but not sure if she was playing with him.

"I tried to have a proper look at the window but it was so busy today and there are blasted trees in the way," Paul stated.

"Do you think the next clue is there then?" Ophelia was excited. It would be amazing to find one of the missing books. She was sure she would be made the permanent Vicar and if she was Ms Kenny's favourite then no member of the church, right up to the highest order, would question Ms Kenny's recommendation.

***

It was with an excited air about them that Ophelia and Paul held hands as they practically skipped their way to the church as the birds chirped their morning greetings. Even the market traders hadn't arrived onto the cobbled square to start selling their wares. It was a bitterly cold, dark morning and she felt sympathy for them standing out in the cold all day. She made a mental note to take them all a cuppa. It was the least she could do.

Neither of them had slept very well, the excitement of Paul's finds and what they might discover in the window had dominated the evening's conversation and eventually, their limited sleep. They needed to get into the church before the visitors arrived for the Christmas tree festival viewings.

It felt a little naughty as they opened the church and wandered inside. Usually, Marcus was the gate keeper and Marion usually followed suit to clean up to start a fresh new day. The morning light was just starting to stream through the beautiful stained-glass windows but the light still didn't reach the corners. Paul switched on his torch. They didn't want to put the main lights on and alert anyone to their presence.

Walking down the south choir aisle, they passed the panels depicting The Dance of the Death paintings on the side of the Markham Chapel which always made Ophelia cross herself. She wasn't normally bothered by scenes and paintings. There were some hideous pictures and carvings in churches. Some of the carvings on the church roof were questionable in their taste but this one gave her the creeps, plain and simple.

They arrived at the window in the far-right corner of the church, the one which Joan Howson had restored using the glass from the other windows. They very carefully moved around the Christmas tree which had been decorated by one of the local schools and began their search.

Ophelia moved her head from side to side trying to whittle out the stiff knots. Staring up at the window for the last hour had produced nothing but a lot of oh, maybe, oh no, maybe nots, as they didn't know what they were looking for as they didn't really have a clue what was relevant and what was not. They were so engrossed they'd lost track of time until a well-placed cough behind them made them both jump. Ophelia managed to curb her exclamation this time and Paul just managed to hold onto the tree as he jumped at the sound.

"Sorry to startle you," Marcus said. "Everything okay?"

"Erm, yes. Thank you, Marcus. Just erm checking for damage. Bit windy in the night you know," Paul said.

Ophelia had long since decided her husband would probably go to hell and that was another lie to add to the list of his misdemeanours. He thought he was safe marrying a vicar as his sins would be absolved but she wasn't so sure and if she remained silent, she would be pushing her luck as well.

"Was it? I hadn't noticed myself. I'm popping the kettle on. Would you both like a drink?"

"Thank you, Marcus, that would be lovely. We will be with you in a minute."

Marcus turned and walked into their office. Paul grimaced as he tried to disentangle himself from the tree.

"Well, that was a waste of time. I will have a cuppa with you and then I'm off to the library to see if I can find anything else which may help."

Just as they were about to turn, a shaft of light lasered through the glass.

"What the..." Ophelia gripped his arm to stop the next word he was about to utter. God had limits.

Paul rushed over to the wall where the light had highlighted some initials gouged into the wall. Ophelia joined him as she finished tracing the L and G, the light faded.

"If that isn't a sign, I don't know what is! Perhaps there really is something to your God after all."

Ophelia nudged him in the ribs. "I wonder who LG is or was?" There were many initials and names gouged into the walls of the church if you looked for them. At the top of the stairs leading to the roof people had scrawled their names into the walls over the centuries. Maybe they thought it would keep them forever with God or maybe they wanted someone to wonder who they were long after they were gone. Maybe it was more primeval than that. But the light had shone directly on these initials. Why?

"Tea's ready," Marcus called.

"Come on. Let's get a drink, I'm so thirsty. We can look at this later." Paul took out his phone and took a photo. Since the numbers had disappeared, it made sense to have a permanent record, just in case.

***

It had been a challenging day. A dog had torn loose from its owner and created havoc as it chased Freddie up and down the pews. The animals seemed to be the only ones enjoying the game as cups of lukewarm tea went flying during the coffee morning and visitors to the Christmas tree festival tried to squeeze out of the way. The sound of a few things breaking heralded the news that some of the decorations hadn't survived this particular event.

Marcus, as a consequence, was in a foul mood by the end of the day. Most of the visitors had found it highly amusing and the very red-faced owner of the dog had made a very generous donation to the church for the inconvenience. Since the church faced a five hundred pound a day running cost, not mentioning the roof work that needed tending too, it somewhat nullified the joint wrath of Mrs Pendleton and Ms Kenny, as one word from them both brought both the dog and Freddie to their senses. With the dog returning to its grateful owner, Freddie had leapt over a very excited child and exited, at what Ophelia would have called, a teenage saunter.

It was with relief that she'd put the church to bed and she and Marcus had left, with much grumblings about the trees. Ophelia decided she would treat them to a nice pastry tomorrow – they always cheered Marcus up. Yes, it was just what he needed.

Crossing the market square, she waved as she saw Layla walking out of Chain Lane. Out of all the streets this one reminded Ophelia so much of the ginnels and cobbled streets of York where she has spent much of her youth.

Layla waved back and despite her tiredness, Ophelia enthusiastically walked over to say hello. She hadn't seen the family in church before, and it didn't hurt to try to make new friends.

"Hello, Layla. This must be your mum. You look so alike. How are you both?"

"Hi Ophelia. This is my mum, Wendy."

Ophelia held her hand out to Wendy who seemed a little surprised, maybe because of the revelation her daughter knew the local vicar on a first name basis, then shook her hand.

"We met at the library. Your daughter helped me find a book."

Ophelia thought it would be good to give her mum context and Wendy nodded her head knowingly.

"Layla loves the library. She gets that from me. Bookworm from a young age."

"Me too. I love reading. Such a wonderful treat to be able to be submerged into another world. Have you read the latest Sophie Hannah?"

Wendy's eyebrows raised, maybe she didn't think that a vicar would be reading a murder mystery.

"They are brilliant. We've just received the latest copy in the library. You will have to pop in and borrow it."

Ophelia recognised that her mum must also work there and that libraries were probably in the same situation as religion. So many other options in the world. They were both up against it when it came to dwindling numbers.

"You've got a deal. Thank you." Ophelia turned to Layla, "I'm glad I've seen you again. I wanted to ask a favour, if your mother agrees of course." Ophelia turned her smile to Wendy before looking back to Layla.

"We are in desperate need of someone to come and help with the cataloguing of our book collection in the..." Ophelia lowered her voice, "the secret library."

Layla looked interested.

"I thought that you might be the perfect person for the job. If you could spare the time of course?"

Layla looked a little shocked at the knowledge. It wasn't exactly a secret but it was surprising how many of the local people of Newark didn't know about the library hidden away up the stone spiral staircase in the church.

"That would be brilliant, Vicar. Layla needs to do some work experience for her college course and I'm sure she would love it. Wouldn't you love?" Wendy prompted.

Layla nodded, suddenly shy.

"Why don't you pop and see me in the new year and we will see what we can sort out?"

Layla nodded again. Wendy muttered something about teenagers and Ophelia met Layla's eye and rolled hers, making Layla smile.

Pleased with herself, Ophelia said her goodbyes and made for home. Another one hopefully converted to the cult, Paul would say. He definitely deserved his hour of judgement. She hoped she would be there when God and Paul met. She would pay money to watch him squirm.

***

Ophelia kicked off her shoes and slipped her aching feet into her slippers. There was a divine smell coming from the kitchen and she retracted her thoughts about her husband's judgement day. She said a prayer to keep him safe and asked God to forgive him his sins.

"What's cooking, good looking," she called, as she made her way into the kitchen.

Paul smirked as she noticed too late that Ms Kenny was seated at the breakfast bar.

"Ms Kenny. How lovely to see you. Paul, you should have let me know that we had company."

Paul raised his glass of red wine. "And spoil the surprise. You know I just love surprising you darling." He never called her darling. She mentally reversed her prayer.

"Come, have a drink. We are celebrating."

"Why what's happened?" Ophelia accepted the wine gratefully as she seated herself opposite their guest at the large kitchen island. She saw even Ms Kenny had succumbed to Paul's charms as she also had a small glass of wine.

Paul turned and stirred the pasta before turning back to them.

"Ms Kenny is a genius." The woman in question actually blushed. Her husband had an even better way with people than her. It helped that he had a winning smile and could give Idris Elba a run for his money in the looks and charm department.

"Well, I know that," Ophelia said, hoping to score some points back.

"I'd been doing some research and hidden myself away in your wonderful 'secret library' but Ms Kenny discovered my hiding place." He actually winked at Ms Kenny. He was too much.

"I obviously had to confess what I was doing and Ms Kenny has solved the mystery of the initials."

Ophelia forgot all about her husband, "You have? That's amazing. Who is it?"

"Not who," Paul said with a waft of the pasta stirrer. She noticed a blob landed on the tiled wall. She wondered how many wines he had had, "but where, my dear Watson!"

"Where? As in, LG is a place?"

"Yes. Ms Kenny told me that there is a place in The Crypt which has these very same initials scored into the wall. It has to be a clue."

"Oh well done Ms Kenny," Ophelia said and raised her glass. Ms Kenny did the same and they clinked glasses.

The crypt housed the Treasury and now Ophelia thought about it, she remembered one of the parishioners mentioned secret tunnels which many locals believed ran under the town. How exciting. Ophelia felt as if she was acting out the life of a character in one of those mystery novels she so enjoyed.

"We didn't go and check because we wanted to wait for you and you had your hands full with a dog and squirrel when we came to find you."

Ms Kenny actually tittered at this. Ophelia took another large drink of her wine as Paul turned. She could see he was trying not to laugh. Eventually they settled into conversation until Paul served up a delicious meal. Afterwards, he insisted on walking Ms Kenny home so Ophelia had a few minutes to herself, a rare treat. She ran a bath and luxuriated in the warmth as she wondered what they were going to find tomorrow. The game was afoot!

***

Ms Kenny, Paul and Ophelia met inside the church. Once again, they were up before the traders but not before Marcus and Mrs Penderton, who to their surprise were waiting for them in the café area. There was a freshly brewed cafetiere and a large teapot adorned with a crocheted stripey cover sitting alongside five cups.

Ophelia felt like a naughty girl and it brought back an old memory of being summoned to the headmaster. Vicars were not always vicars. Sometimes they were children, with the devil inside them. Or so the teachers said. Ophelia dared not look at Paul as she knew he would be absolutely revelling in this moment. This would be a story to be added to his repertoire of 'stuff my wife has got me into' to be told at every opportunity. There was never a dull moment with Paul, she had to admit.

There was absolute silence as they all seated themselves and Mrs Penderton did the honours of pouring the drinks.

"Right," she announced when she had finished.

"What is all this sneaking around all about? If we have some 'kind'," she actually raised her hands and made quotations. "of cult. Then 'we'.". At this Mrs Penderton looked up to God and not to Marcus. Ophelia bit the inside of her lip. She would not smile. Paul grabbed her knee under the table and she nearly spilt her drink. "Need to know about it. Isn't that right, Marcus?"

Marcus nodded. The only sensible action to take. This was Mrs Penderton's moment and she was milking it for all it was worth. Ophelia looked at Ms Kenny. She was surprised she was taking this quietly. They all shared a love of the church but the rivalry between the two women was legendary, or so she'd been told.

Ophelia cleared her throat, "I'm afraid you have it all wrong." She could feel the self-righteous smile adorn Ms Kenny's lips in the reflection of the stony face of Mrs Penderton's. As she pulled her shoulders back to protest, Ophelia hastily added, "The only cult we are in, is the church."

Paul spluttered out his tea and started coughing. Ophelia knew she shouldn't have said it. It was that devil in her. Ms Kenny held up a napkin to Paul but before anyone could say anything, Marcus gasped. They all turned to the strange sound coming from behind them. Ms Kenny's mouth dropped open at the sight of Freddie, perched on top of one of the carved pews, making what Ophelia could only deduce as, squirrel laugher.

Ophelia dissolved into giggles as Marcus grabbed the nearest item, which happened to be a feather duster and chased after the squirrel. Through blurred eyes Ophelia got up to try and save Freddie as the others joined her. She thought she would die right there in her beloved church when Paul started humming the theme tune to Benny Hill as they raced around the church. The sight of the five of them behaving in such a manner would be laid down in history as one of the greatest comedy gold moments; once the CCTV was mysteriously shared on social media.

Freddie led them on a merry chase until they reached the Crypt, where he promptly disappeared down the steps and into the darkness. Marcus threw down the feather duster which he seemed surprised was in his hand, switched on the light and raced down the steps in pursuit. Poor Freddie, Ophelia thought, he was for it now. She looked at Ms Kenny who also had tears streaming down her face and such a look of happiness it quite transformed her.

"Where are you, you vermin? Not so clever now, are you?" Marcus shouted with glee.

"Now, now, Marcus," Mrs Penderton said, "even a squirrel is one of God's creatures."

"He's the devil reincarnated and I will not have him in my blasted church!" Marcus shouted as Mrs Penderton flinched. Ophelia thought he would be in for a world of trouble later, Mrs Penderton did not tolerate blasphemy. If Marcus did kill the squirrel, then he would be following its fate. Ophelia looked up and held her hands together in apology. Even thoughts were subject to scrutiny.

"Look, Freddie has gone in there," Paul said, grinning at her as they all joined Marcus in the crypt.

Ophelia nudged him hard in the ribs. If Marcus knew she had named him she would never leave the crypt.

They all watched in fascination as Freddie's tail disappeared into the wall.

"What the hell?" Ms Kenny blurted out. From the look and gasp from Mrs Penderton, Ophelia was surprised Ms Kenny didn't burst into flames. She hoped God was in a forgiving mood tonight when they said their prayers.

Marcus ignored her, or didn't hear what Ms Kenny had said and made for the hole which looked like it had been gouged out with teeth into the wooden stand which housed the church treasure in the glass case above.

"Well, I never," exclaimed Paul, "Watson, it looks like we have ourselves a secret tunnel."

Ophelia hoped the others hadn't acknowledged this. At this rate she would never be allowed to stay here permanently. She had to take charge and calm it down. She stood straight and brought the group to order.

"Right." At that word, everyone stopped and stood to attention, even her husband. Impressive.

"This is all getting out of hand. For the record, 'we' are not a cult. I found a clue to the mystery of one of the missing books and to cut a long story short, this led us to coming to the church to see if we could find the final clue."

Ophelia took a deep breath to continue but Mrs Penderton interrupted, "How marvellous. I love a good mystery. There are five of us now so Sherlock and Watson are out." They all stared at Mrs Penderton. Even Marcus had stopped peering into the hole.

"I've got it." Mrs Penderton actually clapped. "Scooby-Doo!"

Ophelia decided that actually this must all be a dream or she had just heard Mrs Penderton shout Scooby-Doo in the church Treasury at day break. It really was too much.

"Scooby-Doo had four adults and two dogs though," Paul said, as if this was a serious conversation about what they were naming themselves. As if they were trying to come up with a pub quiz name. It really was too much and just as Ophelia was about to lose her mind, Freddie helpfully popped his head out of the hole again and mayhem ensued.

***

It was another week before they managed to get back into the crypt to look at the markings Ms Kenny had originally identified. They'd had to wait until the Christmas tree festival was over and then surveyors and various other experts arrived to look at the hole Freddie had revealed. On the day of the discovery Marcus had shone a torch down it to reveal a much larger space.

It was with excitement that they all waited at the top of the steps to see what would be revealed. They did find a hidden space behind but it was decided that it was possibly the original entrance to the crypt and sadly, no tunnels were found. It didn't stop the increase in visitors over the coming year as people came to visit and Marcus was frequently caught whistling as they exceeded their daily funds and the new swipe machine they had installed proved a success for the church funds.

Ophelia even caught Marcus leaving some nuts out for Freddie. She said nothing and pretended not to notice.

Sadly, and with much disappointment, the letters 'LG' engraved in the crypt hadn't turned up another clue to the mystery of the missing book. Despite spending hours looking around they simply couldn't find either a book or a clue.

It was some months later when Ophelia had been enjoying a lovely walk in the church grounds. It was too early for the spring bulbs but at this time of year she loved to scour the grounds and look for shoots of hope. She thought about the clever plants striving to get out of the ground and find the light. It was often an analogy she used with her parishioners when they were struggling with depression. One day, she told them. You will push through the dark soil and into the light. It was cheesy but there was also a lot of truth in it.

A squirrel came bounding across the green. She wasn't sure if it was Freddie as many of his friends lived in the church grounds but when he dropped an acorn at her feet, she knew it was him.

"Hello, little Freddie. How are you doing?" Ophelia bent down and delightedly took the little paw. It left a trace of soil again as he quickly pulled his paw away and grabbing the acorn, he raced off.

Ophelia laughed. A game of chase with a squirrel. Whatever next. She followed as quickly as decorum allowed. She had a meeting next week about Newark becoming her permanent residence. She didn't want to get her hopes up but with footfall increasing, she hoped and prayed they would stay. Paul had fallen in love with the historic town and it would really feel like they were leaving family behind if they had to move again.

Freddie stopped at the base of a huge oak tree and started digging before dropping the acorn into the hole. It made a loud noise as it hit something solid. Frowning, Ophelia knelt on the ground, heedless of dirtying her clothes. Freddie looked at her and again the look of smugness crossed his cute face.

Using her hands, she tried to widen the hole. There was definitely a hollow underneath. It took a bit more effort but finally she managed to get her arm into the hole. She could feel the corner of something, as well as things, like worms she didn't want to think about. She loved all God's creatures but liked to keep some of them out of direct contact and admire them from afar.

Ophelia pulled out her arm, took out her phone and called the Scooby-Doo team. It was what Paul had taken to calling them and now they had an actual dog to add to the mix. When Mrs Penderton turned up with her sister's dog, the name had stuck.

Paul lifted out the box. The air fizzed with expectation as with a grunt he set it on the ground. By now, they had a bit of audience. It's not everyday the Vicar was caught digging up the church grounds. Ophelia spotted the photographer from the local paper. Oh Lord, she thought!

The metal box was old and the hinges had rusted through, so it made it easy for Paul to open it. Inside was another metal box which had fared better over time. Paul had also found a fair few of Freddie's nuts. That one had earned a bark of laughter from both Ms Kenny and Mrs Penderton. The hairs on Ophelia's arms stood on end though as Paul carefully opened the box and revealed the contents.

***

At the end...

I've felt such joy since Ophelia was finally made my guardian. I only wished I had the power to give long life. I would keep her and her friends forever. They breathed a new life and soul into me and I'm grateful for it.

Throughout the last few months, the carpenters, stonemasons and builders have been working their own magic on me. I have a new lease of life and I know I will be here and stronger for many more generations to come.

A new display cabinet was proudly opened by the local mayor and inside 'Edmund Spenser's Faery Queen, the Shepheard's Calendar and other works, London, 1611' was displayed with pride. Layla had been delighted when she'd been able to place the book on the stand. I like her, she has a good soul and her laughter and youthful enthusiasm is a welcome sound. I hope she stays.

As I watch everyone go about their day, I give thanks that my little plan worked out. The mystery of one of the missing books has been solved and I know Paul will not let it lie. His search for the other two continues and as for the secret tunnels underneath Newark... well that is for me to know...

A Visit to The Navigation

by N.K. Rowe

E LIZABETH MILLER SLIPPED inside the building, her long brown skirt briefly snagging on a bolt fixture before she swished it free and pulled the door closed. There were still several men in the courtyard engaged in loading a cart with goods brought to Newark via the Trent and she didn't want them to see her sneaking about. Despite the late afternoon sunshine outside there was little illumination coming through the low windows. Down at the wharf-end of the building a boat was just completing its unloading and the crew would be looking forward to a well-earned pint. She had watched and waited until now to act.

She scanned the gloomy room and noticed that a single gas lamp, turned down low, burned softly some dozen yards away from her. She twitched her pursed lips in thought. He would be towards the top of the building so she needed to climb some stairs, if she could find them amongst the gloom, sacks and wooden crates. Elizabeth headed towards the lamp, guessing correctly that it was placed near the foot of a staircase. She placed her hand on the bannister, wood both damaged and worn smooth through years of use, and took a deep breath. The air was full of rich smells of the goods that were stored and transported through the building: grain and hops, linseed oil, ropes and canvas. Her fingers gripped the handrail and she pulled herself up the steep wooden steps, her boots loudly announcing her progress despite trying to ascend as lightly and quietly as possible.

Elizabeth's heart was hammering by the time she reached the next floor. More stored goods nestled within the iron, brick and wooden structure of the building, waiting to be bought and despatched to businesses in and around the town. She glanced down at a sack that had fallen over near the next flight of stairs. Perhaps these were local goods heading further afield. There were crates of beer bottles in the corner, nailed closed to prevent stock losses to thirsty workers. She pushed thoughts of warehouse business from her mind and concentrated on the task ahead.

Stepping up towards the second floor she paused as a figure moved across the landing, a sack on his shoulders. The man weaved between stacked crates and iron pillars and disappeared further down the building. His footsteps on the wooden floorboards faded away and Elizabeth could only hear the clop of hooves on cobbles from the courtyard below as a horse was harnessed up to a cart. She moved forward to the next flight of stairs and crept up towards her destination: the third floor of the Trent Navigation Wharf and Warehouse building.

Dust hung in the air, twinkling softly in the light streaming through the loading bay that overlooked the waterway below. As she stepped around some stacked crates and sacks she could see the ropes of the pulley block that was attached to the overhanging gantry. Wilf had described his workplace to her many times and although she had seen it from the other bank this was her first sight of it from inside. The silhouetted rope swayed very slightly in the breeze.

Seth was sitting on a crate, puffing on a pipe and staring out across to the trees beyond the canalside work sheds of the opposite bank. She watched him reach down and lift a bottle of beer secreted near his ankle and take a deep swig.

"Hello, Seth."

Startled, he coughed and spluttered, dropping his pipe and moving the bottle out of sight. He wiped his mouth and grinned. "Lizzie, what yer doin' up here? You shouldn't be in here, the gaffer'll have your guts fer garters if he finds out. Mine too." He stood up and wiped his hands on his worn brown trousers. He removed his cap and clutched it in front of him, softly squeezing it with rough rope-worked fingers.

She stepped slowly towards him, peering at the walls, the ceiling, the floorboards, as well as the assorted goods waiting for loading or onward travel into town. "I wanted to see where he worked. I need to see what he saw every day he was here."

"Aye, well, it ain't much but it did us grand. Wilf were a good worker and it's a crying shame what happened."

Elizabeth stared out of the loading bay window before looking up at Seth's face. His moustache needed a trim and she could detect the tobacco and beer over the smells of the warehouse.

"Thank you for coming to the service."

"It were the least I could do. Not find another worker as good as Wilf."

"Mmm." She looked out of the window once more.

Seth shuffled his weight from foot to foot and wrung at his cap. "Well, this is about the sum of it all. I suppose you'll be getting on your way now."

"Tell me how it happened." Her eyes hadn't left the window.

"Oh, now Lizzie, I can't be doin' with making you upset. There's no need to go through the grisly details."

"Tell me." She turned and stared into his eyes. "I need to know."

He shrugged and took a step backwards. "Well, it were a simple accident. I didn't really see it very clearly meself. One second he were there and the next he weren't. I'm not even sure I heard him hit the water."

"And he didn't say anything, cry out?"

"Not that I heard. Not enough time between falling out and going under to draw breath, never mind shout out."

"Hmm."

Seth rubbed the back of his neck with his cap. "Perhaps it were the beer."

"What beer?"

"Well, we're not supposed to have a drink up here but this is thirsty work. And Wilf did like to partake. He could get through a few bottles up here. I told him to be careful but he was his own man."

"Seth, are you telling me that Wilf was drunk?"

"No, Lizzie, not drunk, definitely not. But maybe a little... impaired. Easy to trip and bang yer 'ead."

"My Wilf was not drunk."

"Now, begging yer pardon, but you were only sweethearts who saw each other for a few hours a week. I worked with the man every day from sun-up to sun-down and I'd wager I knew him the better."

"You'd wager, would you?"

He stood up straighter. "Aye, I would."

"Seth, I don't think you knew anything about Wilf at all. Did you know that we went to church together every Sunday?"

"I, um, thought that you might do."

"Did you know that Wilf had also forsworn alcohol and was attending Lady Ossington's new temperance tavern with his brother?"

"The Ossington?" Seth frowned. "He never mentioned that to me."

"No, I can imagine he didn't. He told me how you liked a bottle or five, though."

Seth chuckled nervously. "As did Wilf."

Elizabeth cocked her head to one side. "Seth, I have a keen sense of smell. Beer is not something I could ever detect on my fiancé."

"Your what?"

"Yes. Another thing you didn't know. We were engaged a month ago."

He took a deep breath. "I see. Well, you have my condolences, Lizzie."

She stepped towards the loading bay window. "So, you say he might have tripped and banged his head and fell into the Trent where he drowned?"

"Aye. Like I say, I didn't see meself but that's what I told the gaffer."

She remained silent for a while, looking down at the water. "The doctor said he did have a wound on his head."

Seth swallowed. "The doctor?"

"Yes. Doctor Evans is a friend of the family and I asked if he could take a look at Wilf's body. A post-mortem examination, he called it. My poor boy did die from drowning but this was because he was likely rendered unconscious by a blow to the back of the head."

Seth said nothing.

"Wilf mentioned that you were a jealous man, Seth. Jealous of Wilf's rise in the eyes of the manager. Jealous of his cleanliness and Godliness. And although he didn't speak of it, I could read between the lines that you were jealous of Wilf's relationship with me." She could feel him stepping closer to the window; he was just behind her right shoulder. "I've seen you looking at me, Seth. I've seen your demons."

She could hear his breathing over her hammering heart.

She looked down and exclaimed in shock: "Oh my goodness, what is that woman doing without her clothes?"

She stepped backwards in perfect synchronicity with Seth as he stepped forward to peer over the edge of the loading bay, drawn by yet another of his demons. It only took a small push and he was over-balanced, arms flailing, fingers grasping for the rope that was just too far away, and then he was gone. Elizabeth considered that Seth was right about one thing: there was no time to cry out. But there had been a clear thud as Seth hit the boat moored some twenty five feet below.

She took a tentative look over the edge. Seth's body was in the water and already sinking below the surface, presumably much as her beloved had done. Elizabeth reviewed the likely fall trajectory, Seth falling head-first to his doom. She had probably over-done the push and he'd only just hit the deserted boat before sliding into the water. For a spur-of-the-moment plan, it had gone surprisingly well.

No doubt, she thought to herself, this would haunt her for the rest of her life. Murder is a cruel, evil sin. But sometimes if you need an avenging angel you just have to look in the mirror.

She straightened her clothing and walked briskly down the stairs as the sun shone brightly into the silent warehouse through the gaping loading bay window.

The Corn Exchange

by Mark Smith

THOMAS RUSHED THROUGH the wall. 'There might be a vacancy at The Corn Exchange,' he announced.

'The Corn Exchange?' replied Sir Everard.

'Yes. I was speaking to some maiden from Doncaster who knows this Lord from Leeds who bumped into this headless fool from nowhere whose head, which he carries around with him everywhere, is friends with this other head, which before it was disembodied used to hang around with someone at the estate agents, and who overheard someone saying that the Corn Exchange is empty and has been for some time.'

'Isn't that the building that keeps changing its name? A bit common if you ask me.' Thus spoke The Lady In Green. 'Any place worth its bricks should stand by the name it was given.'

However, there was some agreement through muttering and the angling of knees, shoulders and elbows that this was possibly the most exciting thing that had happened for a hundred years, and then that had only been the arrival of Smock Boy. So probably the best thing for well over a hundred years.

Their current abode was the derelict officers' mess at Syerston airfield. This was an abandoned building full of debris from chipped walls, decaying wood and unnecessary graffiti. It had been their home for quite a while now and was, by any description, an awfully pointless place, but then marginally better than the crumbling farmhouse that had been home for the previous two hundred years. Who they were was Sir Guy Saucimere, Sir Everard Bevercotes, Elizabeth Palmer, Thomas Footitt, The Lady In Green and a boy wearing a smock who had no name by virtue of not being able to remember his name (if he had ever had one) and who they unaffectionately called Smock Boy.

'Common,' continued The Lady In Green. 'Common,' she repeated, 'but it would have to do. I dare not even ask what they call it now.'

'It used to be Time And Diva,' said Elizabeth. She had died of the plague and they kept her at a small distance on account of not being sure if they could still be infected in any way. That and the smell. Well, probably the smell mostly. And the boils, which were unsightly and numerous. She also seemed to expel air rather too frequently and this was a crowded place which again made the Corn Exchange an exciting proposition.

'Oh dear,' concluded The Lady In Green.

'Well, I too am used to certain standards,' said Sir Guy, joining the debate.

'That was hundreds of years ago. You can't still be used to it now after this place.' Sir Everard often challenged Sir Guy on account of having been murdered by him over their pursuit of the same lady. Such things didn't help relationships, and it had only been six hundred years ago. Sir Guy had begged the Lord for forgiveness and eventually lived out a life of penitence, but murder is murder after all, and Sir Everard couldn't care how nice Sir Guy had been post his death. All that mattered to him was pre his death and particularly the moment of his death when Sir Guy's sword had become a significant part of his body, accompanied by blood and foul language on both their parts. It had all left Lady Catherine not too impressed with either of them, alive or dead.

'I still don't know why we can't be considered for the theatre.' This was one that Sir Guy could never let go of.

'Because we need to be somewhere that people can't see us,' said Thomas.

'What's the point of that?'

'We're not supposed to be seen.'

'But if anyone saw us there, they might just think we are part of whatever they are putting on, especially if we wore gowns.'

'Why gowns?' asked The Lady In Green.

'Because that's what actors wear.'

'I'm not wearing a gown.' Although The Lady In Green did consider the advantage of this, especially if there was a colour choice.

'Me neither.' Sir Everard had to consider that gowns had never been in fashion. Not in the way he saw them as long, black robes billowing behind a walking master. In six hundred years he had seen the rise of quilted petticoats, knee breeches, curly wigs, liberty bodices and flares but gowns had never got past the school gates.

'We are not moving to the theatre. We don't want to be seen...' and The Lady In Green stopped for emphasis, '... by anyone. I can't be seen like this.' It was all about the green dress.

'I thought the whole purpose of this was to be seen occasionally,' said Sir Guy. 'I didn't sign up to not being seen. What is the point otherwise? The only real fun we can have is sitting on the edge of some child's bed or sending someone hysterical by walking through a wall.'

'None of us signed up for this. It just happened,' said Thomas.

'Lady Ossington gets away with it.' The Lady In Green was concerned by the elevated status of Lady Ossington and aware that it might all have been vastly different had Lady Ossington too been wearing green when she had died.

'I haven't signed anything,' said Elizabeth.

'I'm not sure you could,' said Thomas. 'With those fingers.' He had a point. Eight on one hand and only two on the other. There was more to Elizabeth than just the plague.

'I quite like the idea of haunting a theatre,' said Elizabeth. 'I had an uncle once, hundreds of years ago, and he used to haunt one of the dressing rooms. Probably not that long ago. He might still be dead now, but I've just not heard from him. Anyway, he said you got to see all the shows for free. And you heard what was going on backstage which was usually a lot better than most of the shows.'

'Not for me. A place like that,' said The Lady In Green.

'On account of your dress is it?' said Sir Everard. The Lady In Green could so easily have been The Lady In White or The Lady In Black, but it doesn't matter how many white or black dresses you have, you are what you die in. That and the colour of the lake water she had drowned in had made a not at all pleasant puce colour, and it had been all The Lady In Green could do to get them to agree on green rather than puce. Never, never, never, would she concede to being The Lady In Puce. Nevertheless, Sir Everard had enjoyed centuries of teasing her. He was taking the sort of pleasures in death that had been denied him in his short life. And this time around he very much had time on his side, and little else to do.

The thing about being a ghost is that that is all there is to it. You watch the world go by taking no part in it. A bit like sitting through endless repeats of the local news without alcohol or drugs. And without sleep. And that's the bit that really gets to you. In effect, watching for the two hundred and fiftieth time some story about a local man seeing the face of Karl Marx in his coffee and you can never nod off to get through it. If you are a ghost you are there all the time, just watching the same old world go by.

'But The Corn Exchange has been abandoned for years,' said Thomas. 'It would be much nicer there. I bet they've got curtains and carpets. And we would be in the centre of Newark.' He felt the need to move everyone on and get something done.

'Can I come?' asked Smock Boy.

They all looked at him. They didn't know who he was or how he had landed with them. There was a certain amount of begrudging him even the small space he took up. And he rarely moved, so it was usually the same small space, about the size of a smock.

'To be honest Smock Boy we still don't even know who you are. No one has heard of you. You've not even heard of you. I've been haunting the library for a couple of days and...'

'Technically Sir Guy, you weren't haunting, you were just there looking at books,' said Sir Everard.

'... and none of them mention you.'

Smock Boy coughed. Not in the way that Elizabeth coughed which was always a full stomach emptying bile piler, but just a gentle release.

'And if I wasn't haunting the library then what was I doing? I don't have a library card and I did enter by the eastern wall.'

'Don't you mean the eastern windows?'

'What's the difference?'

'I think we all know the answer to that one. Glass, brick. Brick, glass.' There was a group nodding and no one's head fell off. Smock Boy just shuffled a bit.

'Anyway,' spoke Thomas. 'Shouldn't we visit, have a look around, and put in an offer?'

'We could do a bit of spooking at the same time,' suggested Sir Everard. 'Seems such a long time since we got out.'

'Good idea,' offered Sir Guy, seemingly coming round to the idea, and that the place might have carpets, although mostly because he never liked to miss an opportunity to try and appease Sir Everard. 'You said it had carpets?' He thought he ought to check.

'Only one way to find out,' said Thomas.

Thomas Footitt had hung himself in 1831. It seemed to have done him the world of good. Since then, he had been quite the upbeat character and now lived death to the full. He was the most likely amongst them all to get things done. And once every hundred years or so there came upon them things that might well benefit from getting done.

The way of things seemed to be that if you wanted to view a place you just turned up. Ghosts didn't have estate agents. Well, they did, but they were the sort of people who were kept apart from everyone else on account of trying to sell them things they couldn't have. Twice The Lady In Green had been caught out in pursuit of a rather fine, white dress and then, on another occasion, a nice lace number in black. She soon discovered that all they could sell her was an idea and that was no name changer.

Sir Everard Bevercotes, Sir Guy Saucimere, Elizabeth Palmer, The Lady In Green, Thomas Footitt and Smock Boy took the long walk to the Corn Exchange.

'I still don't understand why we can't catch a bus,' said The Lady In Green.

'Because we're ghosts,' answered Sir Guy.

'And you know what happened last time one of us tried to catch a bus,' said Thomas. He looked at Elizabeth. She didn't need to reply. They all remembered the embarrassment of seeing one of their kind throw herself at the moving object, fly through, and land in the hedge on the other side. That's the thing with ghosts and moving objects. And bus stops are just too complicated to even start thinking about.

'I just think a lady of my status shouldn't have to walk everywhere.'

'We're ghosts. It takes no effort,' said Sir Guy.

'I just expect better.'

They let the silence speak for itself.

On arrival in Newark and standing outside the Corn Exchange they found a suitable wall and walked into the building.

'Carpets,' announced Sir Guy.

'Curtains,' added Thomas.

'A bit colourful,' commented Elizabeth.

'Potted trees, a bit common,' said The Lady In Green.

'You might clash,' said Sir Everard. He got stared back at in return.

What greeted them was an abandoned nightclub. There was still a dance floor. There was a bar. There was beer. There was a dead mouse. There was the ghost of a dead mouse, but no one noticed. The actual dead mouse was more likely to get the greater attention. The ghost mouse looked at Smock Boy and decided that things could be worse.

'All it needs is a woman's touch,' suggested Sir Guy. Elizabeth rebuked him by moving too close and pretending to cough. Even a pretend cough would have seen most people reaching for half a dozen boxes of giant size tissues. Sir Guy checked himself for unnecessary phlegm, or at least phlegm that had not already been there. The moment of dying invariably does not find anyone at their cleanest.

'Have you seen this?' said Thomas. 'We can have a disco.'

'Or a rave,' said Sir Everard. Six hundred years dead but he was down with the kids, or something like that.

'That's where they dance. Where they did dance. Where we could dance.' Sir Everard looked around for someone to dance with and then halted his plans.

'I wouldn't go in there,' said Sir Guy to The Lady In Green.

'Eeeuuggh!' she said coming back out and wishing she had heeded the warning. She nearly collided with Elizabeth which might even have presented a better option than the ditched and forsaken gents' toilets that she had made the error of inspecting.

'And this could be yours,' said Sir Everard, pointing at and inside a cupboard.

'This?' muttered Smock Boy, peering in and looking quite pleased.

'Sorry. No.' Sir Everard laughed. 'I didn't mean all of it. That bit over there.' He pointed into one of the recesses. 'Such a delightful little spot. And with shared shelving.'

Smock Boy felt obliged to move into the space and to stand there and see how it felt.

Some stairs took them up to another floor and a central bar with spaces and seats and rooms.

'It is rather big,' said Sir Guy.

'And a bit, you know, cheap.' The Lady In Green had hoped for something more regal as she considered befitted her status. Although it was fair to say that no one knew what her status was beyond the ownership of a green dress and access to a lake. She usually kept quiet on the subject. Claiming high status rarely works if there is too much detail.

'I like it,' offered Sir Everard. 'We could really death it up here.'

The Lady In Green coughed. It was a release of her anxieties about what Sir Everard was contemplating.

'Could do worse,' offered Thomas.

'We are doing worse,' replied Sir Everard.

'And when the new owners eventually move in?' said Sir Guy. 'What will it be?'

'They need to clear it out completely and return it to its former glory if you're going to get me to move here,' said The Lady In Green. 'I will not be doing with plastic trees.'

'I hope they keep it as a nightclub,' said Sir Everard.

'Looks good to me,' announced Thomas Footitt.

These seemed to be the firmer opinions. Sir Guy felt obliged to support Sir Everard. Elizabeth Palmer knew that wherever they ended up she would be kept at arm's length. Her arms were different lengths so the longer one. And Smock Boy was still in his cupboard, not all of it, just that bit that might one day be his.

And so, via various walls, they left The Corn Exchange, each of them with different thoughts about the place and all of them soon realising where they were returning to. They would await news. That was how it seemed to be with ghosts and properties. It had worked for the past eight hundred years so why change it now? Of course, they had forgotten about Smock Boy who was still in his cupboard, not all of it but he had shuffled a little and found a new bit of shelving. Thomas returned for him.

***

Several days went by. The barracks were feeling less and less like home. They had been thinking about carpets, curtains, rooms, lots of them, walls, lots of them to walk through, lights and music instead of damp bricks and empty aerosols.

Then one day (a day that had seemed no different to any other and of which, if you are a ghost, there are plenty rolling along one after the other until the weeks add up and then time can be measured in months and before you know it, they've invented a new way of cleaning your teeth) Thomas came crashing through the wall. A couple of bricks vibrated and corrected themselves. 'The Corn Exchange has gone,' he announced.

'How?'

'What?'

'It's gone to Lady Ossington.'

'Lady Ossington,' said more than one of them and possibly all of them.

'She's already got Ossington Hall,' added Sir Everard.

They all looked at Thomas. They all looked around at the derelict officer's mess. They looked back at Thomas. He was their point of outrage. He was the messenger. 'Apparently, she's going to be allowed to use it as a holiday let.' Their outrage doubled.

'What?' Again, probably said by all of them.

'Travelling ghosts!' exclaimed The Lady In Green. It didn't bear thinking about.

'NOOOOOOOO!!!' they all screamed. Definitely all of them. Well, except Smock Boy. He quite liked the idea of keeping his few inches where he didn't have to share with a shelf. Not even enough room to swing a smock.

Never Forget

by Samantha Hook

I ZZY SQUINTED ANGRILY at the words on her phone screen.

"You have arrived," they declared.

"No I bloody haven't," she thought.

"Help us improve Google Maps. How was the navigation on this trip?"

Izzy jabbed at the sad face in the gallery of emojis on offer, looked up and was met by the equally displeased face of Mr Prager, the overall manager of Peterborough and her line manager.

"OK," she smiled, unconvincingly. "There seems to have been some mistake with the postcode, or something..." She trailed off as she saw more suited figures approaching from the direction of the station, each following their own misguided digital assistants.

"Just give me a second," she said, raising her voice above the traffic. "I'll bring up the website. It can't be far".

Izzy thumbed a website address from memory.

"Hmm. We're Having Trouble Finding that Site," the screen read.

Izzy looked up at the small, expectant group that had now gathered. She daren't look back at Mr Prager but could feel the heat of his anger from where she stood.

Trying to quell a growing sense of panic, Izzy opened her inbox and began to search for one of the many emails received from the hotel she'd booked. Finding no sign of any, she thumbed in the website address once more in the hope that she had mis-typed the first time. The same cheery error message appeared, infuriating Izzy with its assumed palliness.

The crowd around her was slowly but steadily increasing in size, as Izzy tried to put thoughts of the 106 expected delegates far from her mind. A hundred and six delegates in search of a conference.

There was probably about a third of that number here now, standing in a confused and agitated group in the middle of a busy crossroads in a small market town. Most of the women had walked the fifteen minutes from the train station in high-heeled shoes, more suitable for sitting behind a desk than walking. The men were no more comfortable in their office attire of hot and itchy business suits. All had negotiated suitcases of varying sizes to this spot and most had some sort of laptop or briefcase also. None were smiling.

Actually, that wasn't entirely true. Izzy noted one grinning face. Clearly amused by her discomfort, Michael looked her directly in the eye with a wide, pearly white, shit-eating grin; the one that made her palm tingle with the urge to slap it off his face. Hate was a strong word, thought Izzy, but not where that twat was concerned.

Izzy was snapped back to reality by an amused voice.

"Hey me duck, you lot look lost." A small famed, ruddy-faced gentleman and a small, white dog looked at Izzy inquisitively.

Izzy took the man's arm and gently turned him so they both had their back to the increasing crowd of delegates, thankful for a potential ally.

In hushed tones she said: "Yes, I think we are. I'm looking for the Robin Hood Hotel."

Izzy frowned at the laughter this prompted.

"Is it very far away?" she asked.

"Ooh, about 23 years away I'd say!" The man chuckled at his own sparkling wit. He must remember to tell Nora that one when he got home.

"What?"

"It were knocked down, me duck. Then they built this Travelodge." He nodded to the building behind the really rather sizeable crowd now blocking the entire pavement.

Izzy looked up at the clear, white lettering above the crowds' heads. It did indeed read "Travelodge". How had she not noticed that before? No matter, she had booked this conference with the Robin Hood Hotel and had the emails to prove it. Emails she couldn't find right now but I.T would no doubt help with that. Unless she'd received ghost emails from a hotel that had ceased when she was three years old, this poor old boy was clearly mistaken.

The little white dog took a few steps, seemingly bored and eager to be on his way. The man's eyes twinkled as he looked from Izzy to the irritated faces of the office workers behind her. He didn't know what was going on here but guessed at some sort of wheeze at this young girl's expense.

"Good luck!" He nodded and followed in the direction the small dog was pulling.

Izzy turned to see a pleasant looking, middle-aged couple crossing the road towards her.

"Excuse me..." she smiled.

Once more she was told that this Travelodge stood where the Robin Hood Hotel used to be. She asked if there could be another Robin Hood Hotel but was told, no, there had only ever been one in the whole of Newark. As Izzy thanked the couple for their help, wondering if this was some sort of weird local joke, she heard Mr Prager ostentatiously clear his throat.

Izzy pushed her way through the crowd of chattering delegates to reach him.

"This will make you laugh," she began, doing her best to sound breezy as she explained the situation to her manager. She was in no way surprised when he did not, in fact, laugh.

"It's not that bad," she said but before she could continue, Mr Prager interrupted.

"I can assure you Miss Antill," he spat. "It is indeed that bad."

***

Izzy could see her whole career, past and present, whizz before her mind's eye. She needed some space to think and take stock of the situation. Scanning the area, she became aware once more that they were all stood outside a Travelodge. Staring once more at the big white letters, Izzy felt dread realisation drag its ice-cold fingers down her back. The postcode she had fed into her phone's Sat Nav had brought her here, to a Travelodge. Which was a hotel. Not the hotel she thought she'd booked but undeniably a hotel. And didn't that guy say it was built on the site of the old Robin Hood hotel? The hotel she thought she'd booked? None of this made any sense, but she had to investigate nonetheless.

Pushing her way through the sea of middle-management, she was strangely comforted when the glass doors of the Travelodge opened to welcome her in and closed behind her. Inside the lobby the chatter and the traffic noise were replaced with the muffled voices of radio ads playing quietly through a PA system. The room was warm with low lighting and she could immediately feel the tension start to leave her.

There was no-one behind the reception desk but there was a bell, which she rang, then she stood nervously tapping her fingers on the desk. When, after about thirty seconds, no-one appeared, Izzy rang the bell two more times, a little impatiently and shouted to the door behind the desk:

"Hello? Hello? Is anyone there?"

Izzy looked around the lobby, not allowing her gaze to stray toward the glass doors and the impatient crowd beyond. To the left of the welcome desk was a blue wall with the words "QUICK AND EASY CHECK IN" in bold, friendly white letters. Underneath was a plinth on which sat a screen showing a photograph Izzy recognised as the castle they'd seen from the train window upon arriving in Newark. Over the image were simply the words "Check In. Touch to Start".

Izzy heard the glass doors shoosh open and turned to see the most unwelcome sight she could have imagined. Michael's tall and well-tailored form was approaching, his perfect smile even broader than before.

"Hey. Having a spot of trouble?" he asked, tilting his head and wrinkling his nose in an exaggerated show of concern. "Mr Prager asked me to come and see if I could sort out your mess because people are getting a bit impatient and..."

"Everything is in hand!" interrupted Izzy with a little more irritation than she had intended.

She turned her attention back to the screen and was surprised that the greeting message had changed. It now read:

"I think, therefore I am."

Izzy frowned, she recognised the quote and was trying to place it. Then it struck her and she asked "Why is the check-in machine quoting Descartes at me?"

Michael peered over her shoulder at the screen. As before, it clearly displayed the words: "Check In. Touch to Start".

"I don't think Descartes ever said that," he said, dismissively.

Izzy frowned.

Her options looked pretty limited at this point, so she followed the instructions. The next screen prompted her to enter a booking number, which she didn't have, not having made a Travelodge booking. Before she had much time to consider her next move, figures started to appear, one at a time, in the prompt box. "1... 2... 3..." all the way to 9, then an 0 completed the sequence. At this point Izzy had no clue what was going on but duly pressed the "Find My Booking" prompt next to the number.

Next she was presented with some additional options: "Late Checkout" and "Breakfast to Go" but almost as quickly as these appeared, they were ticked and the screen changed again.

"Welcome Miss Isobel Antill" it said, as it started dispensing key cards for rooms.

For a moment Izzy stood in dumb shock. Had she somehow booked the entire conference into a Travelodge and then blacked out or something? The cards kept coming. At least the delegates would have rooms, or at least some of them would have rooms. How many rooms did the hotel have? More importantly, where on earth were they going to hold the conference itself?

Izzy's racing thoughts drifted as the DJ announced the next song as "You're Beautiful" by James Blunt.

"Oh, I love this song!" said Izzy

"Urgh!" spat Michael "That's it, you're on your own!" and he began moving towards the door.

At that moment, the radio's volume suddenly increased, stopping Michael in his tracks. Izzy grabbed his arm, a little harder than necessary.

"You're going nowhere. Help me count these."

She scooped up a hand full of cards from the small pile that had formed under the machine and thrust them towards Michael. He made a groan of protest, but Izzy couldn't hear him over the sound of James Blunt, now paying uncomfortably loudly.

They both heard the peal of thunder, however, and were aware that the lobby was suddenly darker. They turned towards the doors to see a rain-soaked horde fight their way through.

Mr Prager pushed his large frame to the front; his round, sodden face a shade of red that Izzy imagined described as "Cardiac Arrest" on a Dulux chart.

"Izzy!" he shouted. "What the hell is going on?"

The James Blunt song was now so loud that Izzy was reduced to reading Mr Prager's spittle flecked lips. Michael was shaking his head and biting his bottom lip, expressing mock sympathy and barely disguised glee.

Izzy looked back to the terminal.

"Hell is other people," it now read. Either Izzy was losing her mind, which seemed possible, or the hotel was a philosopher. And a bloody good judge of character.

Izzy walked purposefully back to reception. Placing both hands firmly on the desk, she lifted herself, one knee at a time, flashing her spanx to all. Then she stood up, a 5' 2" Boudica rallying her troops into glorious battle.

She took a deep breath, ready to make herself heard over the deafening sound of music. At the very moment she opened her mouth, however, the music was abruptly cut. She screamed at the top of lungs across a silent room:

"WELCOME TO NEWARK!"

The silence was broken only by a snort and a snigger that Izzy recognised immediately.

"So," Izzy continued at a more acceptable volume. "You're probably wondering why we've brought you to a Travelodge, and where the conference itself is going to take place!"

A sea of blank expressions met these words.

"Well, you know we like to do things differently in Peterborough and this year's conference is no different! So, welcome to our Magical Midlands Mystery Tour!" Izzy lifted her hands and clapped, nodding to encourage the assembled attendees to join in. A few even did. Most stared back in confusion.

"First things first. We're going to get you checked into your rooms, then we'll meet back here in... erm... an hour, when we'll head out to our mystery location!"

Izzy gestured to Michael to start handing out key cards. Michael opened his mouth to protest, then closed it again without speaking. If Izzy was hell bent on making a complete fool of herself, he wasn't about to stop her. Instead, he did as she asked, handing cards to his confused colleagues.

A tall girl in a royal blue trouser suit walked towards Izzy. She had matched her suit with a white blouse and bow tied at the side of the neck and her hair was tied in an aggressively tight chignon. Izzy expected her to ask, "Beef or fish?" and offer her a hot towel. Instead, she demanded,

"And how are we supposed to know what number room we're in?"

"I'm glad you asked!" replied Izzy. She was not glad she had asked. "That's all part of the fun! Your first challenge is to find your room!"

A low grumble could be heard across the lobby. It did not seem as though many of the delegates shared Izzy's sense of adventure, although some had dutifully filed through the door marked "Rooms" and had begun trying their cards against each door in turn.

Izzy smiled at Mr Prager once more and once more Mr Prager did not smile back

"Is this some kind of joke, Miss Antill?" he asked.

Izzy gestured for him to follow her to a corner of the room occupied by two large vending machines.

"Something very weird has happened," began Izzy. "I booked a hotel. A different hotel. A big hotel with a ballroom for the main speakers and smaller rooms for break-out sessions. There were emails about the number of rooms we needed, catering, room lay out, bottles of water and those little pads of paper and rubbish pens."

"So why are we in a Travelodge, with none of those things?" asked Mr Prager.

"That's the weird thing," continued Izzy in hushed tones. "It turns out the hotel doesn't exist. That is to say, it did exist, but it doesn't anymore and, somehow, I seem to have booked all the bedrooms here."

Izzy was reminded of one of her mother's many platitudes: "Magical things happen in hotels!" She considered sharing this with Mr Prager, looked at his darkening expression and thought better of it. Besides, Izzy suspected the "magic" her mother was talking about had more to do with the first night she met Izzy's father than anything David Blaine would recognise. The mere thought made her shudder.

Mr Prager rubbed his eyes, he could feel the start of a headache.

"Let's just assume for a moment that this is an insultingly stupid lie, but that I don't have time to deal with that right now," he continued, matching Izzy's hushed tone. "You've told everyone that we're going to register them and take them to another location. Do you have another location arranged?"

"Well, no, not yet," admitted Izzy.

Mr Prager could no longer keep his voice down. "So what the hell do you suggest we do about that?"

A few of the delegates who were still in the lobby looked over, raising eyebrows and murmuring amongst themselves. Izzy could have sworn she heard the word "Slough."

"It's OK," said Izzy, in what she hoped was a re-assuring tone, "I'm sure there are some pubs with function rooms or church halls or... I saw online that there's a museum and a theatre here. I'm sure I can get us in somewhere. We can say it's a chance to shake things up. Give us a new perspective and to see the real Newark. It'll show how creative the Peterborough team are, how we think outside the box."

Mr Prager sighed in defeat. "You've got..." he glanced at his watch. "55 minutes. Don't let me down. This was supposed to be a chance to rebuild our reputation. This must not become another Slough!"

Izzy shivered at the mere mention of Slough and the memory of the last time Peterborough had been given the responsibility of organising the annual conference. That was five years ago and she was surprised they'd been entrusted with it again so soon.

"Guys!" Michael had now joined them and was waving his phone at them. "I don't mean to make a bad situation worse..."

Izzy narrowed her eyes. She was almost certain that was exactly what he meant to do.

"It's just... there are 106 delegates, yeah? Well, it looks like there's only 66 rooms here. And they're nearly all double beds."

Michael bit his bottom lip, Izzy was sure he was stifling a grin.

"OK," she said. "That isn't perfect BUT we can say it's all part of the unique charm of the event! You know, a way to really get to know your colleagues."

"By sleeping with them?" asked Michael.

Mr Prager had heard enough. He left them and walked through the door to the rooms, knocking on the first door he came to and insisting that the occupant swap key cards with him.

***

Forty-five minutes later the lobby was full of the sounds of infuriated delegates but, through some miracle, everyone seemed to have found a room and a room-mate and whilst most were unhappy, none were currently complaining to Izzy.

A further miraculous result came from her panicked phone call to the town's museum and theatre. The theatre was dark for the weekend and, after some hard negotiation, Izzy had secured the whole building, its staff and café, albeit at an eye-watering last minute rate that she was not looking forward to justifying to Accounts. But that was a problem for Future-Izzy; Current-Izzy was high on adrenaline and ready to march her troops through the streets of Newark.

Even Mr Prager's ire seemed somewhat cooled and the mood in the lobby was considerably lighter once Izzy announced the location for the conference. Even the weather worked to enhance the atmosphere; the rain having passed on, leaving warm sunshine, drying puddles and the prospect of a pleasant walk through Newark town centre.

Izzy felt triumphant. And Michael could suck it.

All eyes were on Izzy as she made her way to the glass doors. Turning her head to the delegates with a confident hair-flick and her first genuine smile she said, "Follow me!"

She was starting to enjoy the attention as it turned from livid to miserable to intrigued. She could feel the crowd relaxing and opening up to the potential that this could be fun.

Her confident stride was broken once she reached the door and was brought to an embarrassing halt as it failed to open. Izzy searched the walls for a sign of a button or any other kind of opening mechanism but found nothing. The delegates started to take turns in approaching the door and performing increasingly bizarre and extravagant gestures in hopes of alerting some hidden sensor to their presence.

Disappointingly, no amount of advanced Tai Chi had convinced the door to open. Some delegates were gathered around the reception desk, ringing the bell to no response; a young executive had removed his jacket, vaulted over the desk and was loudly knocking on the door to the office beyond.

There was a definite sense of mounting panic as Mr Prager shouldered his way to the glass doors and began pulling at the edges with all his strength, his face returning to a worryingly puce tone.

It was at this moment the volume on the radio suddenly returned to its deafening level as, for the second time that morning, Radio Newark delighted its audience with James Blunt's Magnum Opus.

The radio was too loud for Izzy to hear the word screamed by Mr Prager, but she could clearly read his lips and it wouldn't have been hard to guess.

***

As soon as the song finished the radio returned to a quiet murmur.

Michael, who had thankfully left the lobby for a few blessed minutes, was now back at the "Rooms" door. Hand in the air he said, loudly,

"Excuse me everyone, I've found a fire escape. The door seems jammed though, so it might take a few of us to get it open."

"Or you're too weedy to get it open," thought Izzy.

"Good work, Michael!" said Mr Prager, following him back through the door to the rooms. Izzy closed her eyes and imagined Michael as a weak and terrified Roman Senator, cowering beneath her, the murderous Boudica, resplendent in vengeful beauty. The thought made her smile for a second before she opened her eyes and returned to the world of the Travelodge.

Pulling her phone from her back pocket Izzy typed "Travelodge Newark" into a search engine. There must be a Manager or something who could sort this out. Her screen filled with search results, all identical and none for the Travelodge.

They all read "The Robin Hood Hotel, Newark".

"Mr Prager!" shouted Izzy, waving her phone in the air as she fought through her colleagues to follow Mr Prager and Michael. Something weird was definitely going on and, more importantly, it seemed like this wasn't her fault.

Izzy pushed open the heavy door under the "Rooms" sign and made her way into a brightly lit, blue corridor. She saw no sign of Mr Prager, Michael or the fire escape but she soon came to Room 17, outside of which sat her suitcase.

Izzy heard a click and the door opened without any assistance from her. This was definitely odd but she was becoming accustomed to things being out of the ordinary today and simply shrugged, then entered the room.

Once inside she threw herself back onto the double bed, staring at the ceiling for a few moments, trying to gather her thoughts. Then, propping herself up on her elbow, she turned to the telephone on the bedside table. On it was a sticker suggesting she should "dial o for reception." She picked up the receiver and pressed the "o" button, then sat for a few seconds listening to the line ring without an answer. This was as she expected; after all there had been no sign of human life on reception or anywhere else for that matter. Just as she was about to replace the handset there was a click, as if the line had been answered and she smiled with relief, welcoming the chance to speak to someone who might be able to help. But instead of the voice of a saviour there came a static crackle followed by the sound of tinny recorded music. The song was "You're Beautiful" by James Blunt.

Izzy slammed down the receiver and screamed into a pillow.

She was interrupted by a loud banging on her door. Upon opening it she was met by a despondent looking Mr Prager.

"Did you get the fire door open?" asked Izzy.

"Yes," said Mr Prager. "We got it open and I'm currently in the Theatre about to start my key note speech!"

"OK," said Izzy, trying to sound unflustered. "I'm guessing that's a no. So..." her attention was broken by the sight of Michael, standing behind Mr Prager, his head lifted to the ceiling, holding what looked like a clump of wet papier mâché against his nose.

Izzy frowned a silent question to Mr Prager.

"Oh, him," he said, his voice heavy with disappointment. "The silly boy did get the door open, but not for long enough to actually pass through it!"

Michael removed what turned out to be an improvised cold compress made of loo roll and ice from a dispenser next to the fire door, revealing an alarmingly red swelling on the bridge of his nose.

"The door wouldn't budge for either of us," he explained. "We both pushed on the bar at the same time, nothing. Then, I gave it one last really hard push and it just sort of gave, with no resistance. The door opened, I lurched forward with all that momentum and then it slammed shut. Hard. In my face."

Mr Prager closed his eyes and inhaled deeply.

"And now," continued Michael, "it's shut tight again. And my nose really hurts."

Izzy bit the inside of her mouth. Whilst she wasn't petty enough to find pleasure in Michael's physical pain, she wasn't above enjoying Mr Prager describing him as "silly boy," or the sight of a flaw on that perfect face he was so proud of.

Mr Prager turned back to Izzy. "Please tell me there's a Manager, caretaker, cleaner or someone coming to let us out."

"Funny thing," said Izzy. "Well, not funny ha-ha, more..." she was starting to ramble. "Anyway, it's weird, there doesn't seem to be any people in the hotel. I've tried calling reception and..."

Izzy paused for a second, not wanting to appear totally out of her mind. "There was no answer. I can't find any other telephone numbers and if I search for the Travelodge online I just get this."

Izzy hurried back into the room to retrieve her phone from the bed and the two men followed her. Looking at her screen, she felt a now familiar sense of disappointment as, instead of the strange search results, all that appeared were two words "No Internet".

"Damn," she said. "I've got no internet connection, in fact I've got no signal at all."

Her two companions pulled their phones from their pockets, only to find that they too were without any phone signal.

"Weird," said Michael. "You'd think there'd be some sort of WiFi, but I've looked and... nothing. Ooh," he said, hoping for redemption. "Have you tried the television?"

"Are we boring you, Michael?" asked Mr Prager.

"No, I was thinking, there might be some sort of info channel, or at least a screen with a contact number or something."

"That's actually a good thought," admitted Mr Prager.

"Bugger," thought Izzy.

Michael pushed past her to pick up the remote control from the table opposite the bed and point it at the large screen on the wall. A soft focus, sepia toned close-up of a couple in fedoras appeared.

"Here's looking at you kid."

Izzy sighed, she loved old movies and Casablanca was a favourite.

Michael changed the channel and Rick and Ilsa were replaced by Jack and Rose at the helm of the Titanic, another click of the remote and Rhett Butler appeared, declaring to Scarlet O'Hara that she should be "kissed often, and by someone who knows how."

Click. Celia Johnson was leaning from a train window to gaze longingly at Trevor Howard. Click, Audrey Hepburn and Gregory Peck were tearing up the streets of Rome on a Vespa. Click, Mark stood in Juliet's doorway holding his "To me you are perfect" sign. Click, Jerry Maguire declared "You complete me."

"I love a good romantic movie," sighed Izzy.

Michael was squinting in confusion. "They're on every channel!" He was clicking furiously now as the screen showed a montage of lovers, most star-crossed and all declaring their devotion.

"Stop!" shouted Izzy. "Go back."

Michael duly reversed his search, slower this time, until Izzy said, "There!"

"I don't recognise this one," she said. "And it looks different, grainy and a bit... shaky, like old home video."

"Alright, Kermode and Mayo," said Mr Prager, raising his voice. "Excuse me interrupting the film reviews, but there is a slightly urgent situation at hand!"

"Yeah, of course," said Michael, before letting out a surprisingly high-pitched whelp and throwing the remote control into the air.

"What now?" asked Mr Prager. Izzy noticed that the colour of his face was once again entering the deep red end of the Dulux chart. Currently it was somewhere between "Gazpacho Death" and "Livid Port".

Michael was rubbing his hand. "It shocked me! The remote control, it gave me an electric shock."

Izzy's attention, however, had been drawn back to the screen.

"Oh my God, that's it! That's the hotel, the one I booked."

Although fuzzy and grainy and occasionally skipping forward in time a few seconds, the video was clear enough for them to make out a smart looking young woman in a tweed pencil skirt and short jacket holding the hands of two small boys, both around the age of 6 or 7, dressed in long shorts and incongruously smart jackets, like two very small chartered accountants making an impromptu trip to the seaside.

They were emerging from a dark doorway in a large black and white building with ornate leaded windows and bright, cheerful hanging baskets. Above their heads was a glass sign clearly reading "ROBIN HOOD HOTEL."

"Well, this is all most edifying," said Mr Prager. "But can we concentrate on GETTING THE HELL OUT OF HERE?"

"Yes, of course, Mr Prager," said Izzy, glancing at the remote control but deciding not to risk injury and instead allow the video to continue playing.

For a moment all three stood in silent thought. Finally Izzy spoke.

"I think we just need to alert someone from the outside and ask them for help. Has anyone got any phone service?"

The men looked at their phones and then back at Izzy, shaking their heads.

"Oh my God, we're so dumb!" said Izzy, causing Mr Prager to raise an eyebrow. "The windows!"

She ran over to the large window opposite the door and the daub of a painting gracing the wall next to it. She pulled at the handle but couldn't get it to budge. Mr Prager tried to the same effect whilst Michael kept his distance, not wishing to incur another injury.

"OK," said Izzy, trying to keep her voice measured and without any tell-tale sign of panic. "The door in the lobby is glass, so let's just get someone's attention through that."

Mr Prager nodded in agreement and Michael opened the bedroom door. The hallway outside was dark.

"The bloody lights have gone now!" said Michael.

Izzy joined him in the doorway and immediately the hallway was illuminated. "Oh," she said, "it seems to have sorted itself," and she started to walk back towards the lobby.

Michael stood in the doorway for a moment in confusion.

"Excuse me, Michael," said Mr Prager with more than a hint of irritation as he pushed past.

Izzy and Mr Prager were already a little way up the corridor when Michael stepped out of the room. Immediately the lights where he stood snapped off.

"For Chrissakes," he hissed. Looking ahead he could see the part of the corridor where Izzy and Mr Prager were walking was still illuminated, so, like all lost souls, he walked towards the light.

As Izzy and Mr Prager reached the door to the lobby they heard the sound of an Armani clad body hitting the floor, followed by a stream of industrial strength profanities.

With a quiet click the whole corridor was once more fully illuminated and they could see Michael gingerly rising from where he'd fallen, face-first and spread-eagled. Under him was what turned out to be the remains of a Roomba robot hoover.

"What happened?" asked Izzy.

"It came from nowhere!" said Michael, standing now and bending to examine his right knee, bloody and visible through the rip in his tailored woollen trousers. He administered a small kick to the broken machine in retribution then winced as this only made the pain in his leg worse.

Izzy thought it was odd that she had neither seen nor heard the machine before it met with its untimely end, but Mr Prager was already in the lobby. She smiled sympathetically towards Michael, then turned and followed her boss.

***

Four women were gathered around the reception desk, chatting. Each wore a slim fitting knee length dress in a vibrant, jewel colour: royal blue, jade green, peacock and shocking pink. All had abandoned their office shoes. Two were in socks, one wore a pair of poolside sliders and one was wearing a pair of well-worn grey slippers. They stopped talking as Izzy and Mr Prager entered the lobby, eager to eavesdrop.

Mr Prager nodded towards them then turned his back and leant in towards Izzy whispering, "try to get the attention of someone walking by outside but DO NOT make it obvious." Then he approached the women smiling broadly.

"OK," agreed Izzy, wondering how she was going to draw attention to herself, without drawing attention to herself. She needn't have worried, however, as the street in front of the hotel was strangely deserted.

Michael joined her and in the comparatively bright light of the lobby, Izzy could see that his nose was still alarmingly red and swollen and the skin around his eyes was darkening, suggesting a broken nose. He also seemed to be limping.

"You OK?" asked Izzy with genuine concern.

"No!" snapped Michael. "I am not OK!"

"Why don't you go back to your room for a lie down?" Izzy asked. Even an Iceni warrior queen could show mercy from time to time. "I don't think there's really much that can be done here and I'll get you if there are any developments".

"I don't need to lie down," said Michael and turning to the vending machines added, "I just need something to eat."

Izzy looked back out of the glass doors. The crossroads was still eerily quiet. She pulled her phone from her pocket, only to find she was still without any signal. As she began to consider how they were going to make contact with the outside world, her thoughts were interrupted by the sound of Michael furiously banging his fists against one of the vending machines.

She joined him at the machine as he started to shake it.

"It says there's no credit in there," she told him, helpfully.

"I know what it says," he bit back, "but I've put over five pounds in there now."

"I think you'll probably need to refund your cash and start over."

"Well, I would if it wasn't denying all knowledge of the money I paid," he said, as he continually punched the refund button with his left hand, his right hand still throbbing from the remote incident.

Finally he gave up and sat on the floor with his back to the machine. Izzy peered at the buttons over his head and pressed a couple at random. The machine started to vibrate gently as an item was released and fell into the dispensing bin.

Izzy reached in and retrieved a Snickers bar, handing it to Michael.

"There you go," she said.

He looked at it dismissively and said, "Peanuts".

"What?"

"It's got peanuts. I'm allergic to peanuts," he said despondently. "As tempting as it is right now to end it all through a severe allergic reaction I don't really fancy adding anaphylactic shock to my list of ailments."

"Oh," said Izzy, "I rather like peanuts."

Immediately, the machine began to vibrate so violently that Michael scrambled to his feet and both moved to a safe distance. One by one, a dozen items were dispatched into the tray. Izzy and Michael looked at each other wordlessly then Izzy reached into the bin, retrieving two bags of Peanut M&Ms, four bags of Reece's Peanut Butter Cups, two bags of KP Ready Salted Peanuts and three more Snickers bars.

"OK, this is weird," she admitted. "Let me try something."

"I'm thirsty," she said, raising her voice and attracting the attention of a couple of the technicolour women. Once more the machine shook itself into life as bottles and cans clattered into its tray.

Izzy reached in, grabbed a bottle of water and a can of Coke and handed them both to Michael. She then took a bottle of water for herself and one for Mr Prager.

"You want any crisps or anything?" Izzy asked. Before Michael could answer, Izzy's words had become the machine's command and two packets of salt and vinegar crisps dropped into the bin.

Michael narrowed his steel-blue eyes at his colleague, he didn't know what kind of trick she was pulling, but he was in no mood for it.

Before either of them could further contemplate this haunted vending machine and its selective view of its clientele, Mr Prager walked towards them with purpose.

"Well?" he asked impatiently.

"There's no one out there," said Izzy.

"Don't be ridiculous," said Mr Prager but as he looked through the door he couldn't deny that the previously bustling junction was now still and devoid of life.

Mr Prager's shoulders slumped, he looked defeated. Izzy had never seen any sign of weakness in the man before and this break with convention made her extremely uncomfortable.

"Mr Prager?" she asked, quietly. "Whilst we're stuck here, maybe we should just, you know, get on with it."

"Get on with what?" asked Mr Prager.

"The conference. I know it isn't exactly what we had planned, but everyone's here and, whilst someone is bound to walk past the door at some point and rescue us, right now we're stuck. So why not?"

Mr Prager would have written this off as yet another step down the rabbit hole to utter madness but the idea actually cheered him up a bit. He liked a conference. He liked giving key note speeches and God knows, he probably wasn't going to get much of a chance after this weekend.

"OK," he said with a resigned sigh. "Why not?"

Michael looked shocked. Had they both lost their minds?

"I want you and..." Mr Prager looked at a battered and bruised Michael then back to Izzy. "I want you to amend the schedule. I'll hold the keynote speech in the lobby, people will have to spill out into the corridor but it's the best we can do. The break-out sessions will have to happen in the bedrooms. You can figure out the details, I trust you."

"Alright," nodded Izzy slowly. "We can handwrite new schedules and put one under each bedroom door."

"You're going to write out 66 schedules by hand?" asked Michael.

"No," answered Izzy. "I'm going to write out 33 schedules."

"Oh?" he said, then realised who was going to write out the other 33 and his shoulders drooped. "Oh."

"Then there's lunch," said Mr Prager. "I, for one, am getting pretty hungry."

"Do you like peanuts?" asked Izzy.

***

Michael and Izzy returned to Izzy's room and she took a notepad and pen from her suitcase. Looking at Michael however, she could see he was in a bad way.

"Look, why don't you leave this to me, go lie down for a bit, you look like hell."

"Thank you," said Michael sarcastically, "but we have less than an hour. There is no way you can work out the schedule and copy it out 66 times on your own in that time."

"Don't tell me what I can and can't do!" said Izzy.

"Bloody hell, Izzy, that wasn't a personal jibe, it's just too big a task to do alone."

"OK, fine." He was probably right. "But why don't you a least have a shower, it might help a bit."

"Yeah, OK," said Michael, "I'll be as quick as I can."

***

Izzy pulled her suitcase onto the bed. She unzipped a compartment on the front and retrieved a couple of pads of paper she hoped held at least 66 pages then, after fishing around blindly for a moment, her fingers connected with one cheap biro and then another.

It was at this moment her attention was drawn back to the television in her room. The old documentary still appeared to be playing but an abrupt change in the sound-track had made her turn. Polite tea dance music from, she guessed, the 1940s gave way to a song she recognised but couldn't quite place.

It was a pop song, but one from before she was born. It sounded like one of the boy bands her Mum used to listen to, but she could name neither the song nor the band. They all sounded the same to Izzy but as the song continued, the words urging Izzy not to forget where she came from, it became more familiar, in fact she was sure it was one of her Mum's favourites. What was the band? Boyzone? No, Take That, she remembered.

The film seemed to be of the same hotel as before, but everything looked different. It was in colour for a start, sharper and less jerky. The paint looked a little chipped in places, the hanging baskets a bit threadbare. There was a young couple at the door this time, they appeared younger and were dressed far more casually in jeans and t-shirts. The girl's hair was spiky at the back with a long streaky blond fringe sweeping across her face. She wore a knee-length skirt over her jeans, which Izzy found odd, and had her head down, covering her eyes to protect them from the shock of bright sunlight, after the darkness of the hotel's interior. There was something familiar about the way she walked, however.

Before Izzy could give this much thought, Michael was back, knocking on her door. When she opened it, there he stood, looking slightly defeated.

"My card's stopped working, I can't get into my room," he said sulkily.

"Let me try," said Izzy, holding her hand open.

"Why?" he asked. "I know how to open a bloody Travelodge door! It's. Not. Working."

Izzy said nothing but gestured to her hand.

"Fine!" said Michael, slapping the card onto her palm.

Izzy couldn't explain why but she was unsurprised when the door clicked open as soon as she held the card to the reader. Michael couldn't bring himself to look at her as he pushed open the door but when she advised, "I'd prop the door open if I were you, just in case," a black Gucci brogue appeared in the doorframe, followed by Michael's good hand, its middle finger jamming skywards.

**

Izzy sat on the bed, surrounded by conference notes, wondering how to begin creating a new schedule to suit their new surroundings. She looked back at the television, still showing the old hotel documentary, and then at the remote control, considering turning the set off to help her concentrate. Remembering how much pain the attempt had caused Michael, she thought better of it.

She allowed herself to be distracted once more. The Robin Hood Hotel was once again shown in its heyday, its dark wooden panelling and wide sweeping staircases pristine. Izzy smiled as women in beautiful full skirts and taffeta petticoats were waltzed around the grand ballroom by tall men in tailcoats.

Next, she was watching a scene in one of the hotel's bars. She smiled at the extravagant sideburns, the tall, permed hairdos, the flares and the blue eyeshadow, as a happy crowd of revellers laughed and drank and smoked.

The next scene returned to the ballroom, but time had moved on, as evidenced by the casual attire and dance style and by the slightly tired décor. Wallpaper looked faded and the furniture she could see was mismatched. Izzy did recognise the music this time: "I Wanna be the Only One" by Eternal, a timeless classic in her opinion, and she didn't have to guess at the time period for long, as a crude banner declared "NEW YEAR 1996".

Izzy smiled as she thoughtlessly swayed to the music, enjoying this glimpse into the world before her. The camera moved through the crowd as revellers, drinks in hand, sang and danced. Then the film seemed to stop, caught in a freeze frame, although the music continued. Izzy stopped moving also and stared at the faces on the screen, the smile and the colour draining from her face.

It was the couple from the doorway earlier, spiky hair and her beau, both faces now fully visible as they smiled directly out of the frame at Izzy. They looked young, younger than she was. The man flashed bright green eyes; the same eyes that made boys in bars ask Izzy if she were Irish, in a pitiful attempt to start a conversation. The woman's broad smile revealed a slightly wonky right incisor, causing Izzy to subconsciously run her tongue over her own teeth, stopping at the one that had never quite succumbed to her teenage braces, remaining slightly out of place.

Whilst they were much younger than Izzy could ever imagine them, these were, undeniably, her parents.

"Well, well, well," she said aloud. "I guess this is where the magic happened."

***

Izzy's reverie was broken by a sudden blood curdling scream, so loud she could hear it through the wall. She leapt to her feet and rushed through her door and across into Michael's room. The room was full of steam and in the door to the shower room she could just about make out the shape of Michael, wearing a bath towel. The humidity was stifling and even after a few seconds Izzy was becoming more than a little sweaty.

As Michael moved towards her she could see that he looked painfully red.

"That bloody shower!" he shouted.

"Why is it so hot?" Izzy asked. "You always talk about the importance of cool showers?"

"I was having a cool shower, and all of a sudden, this..." He gestured to the steam filling the room.

Izzy went to investigate the shower room and the steam started to abate. There was no way to reach the tap without putting her hand through the stream, but she couldn't leave it running, so she scrunched her eyes tight and jabbed her hand towards the tap, aiming to turn it off as fast as she could. It took a second to register that, to her surprise, the water was pleasantly tepid. In fact she would have described it as the perfect temperature. She turned the tap off, dried her hand and returned to Michael.

The room was still uncomfortably humid and Izzy wished she could open the window. Michael however was slowly returning to his usual olive skinned self and, thankfully, didn't enquire as to how Izzy had coped with the heat of the water.

A little while later they were both sat on the floor in the relative cool of Izzy's room, hurriedly making copies of the schedule. Michael was still dressed only in a towel, his skin still being far too sensitive for clothes. Izzy had never seen Michael in anything but bespoke tailoring and was irritated to note the perfection of his torso, sculpted, no doubt from hours spent in the gym. God he was vain. He was also relaxing back into that sense of smug self-satisfaction she found so infuriating.

She stopped writing for a second and looked at him. "You're enjoying this, aren't you?"

"Enjoying what?" he asked.

"Watching my conference go spectacularly to shit."

"No, I'm not."

Izzy raised her eyebrows in an extravagant show of disbelief.

Michael lowered his head, focusing on the itinerary he was purposefully writing. Izzy stared at him, willing him to lift his head, before returning to her work, carving the words into her sheet of paper like they were a declaration of war.

After a few seconds Michael stopped writing, dropping the pen and paper by his side.

"OK, yeah, maybe a bit," he admitted. "But can you blame me? It's not like you've been my biggest fan lately."

"Ha!" shouted Izzy. "I'm so sorry I haven't joined the Michael Bloody Pritchard Fan Club!"

In her anger she made a mistake on the itinerary she was working on, angrily scrunching the paper into a ball and throwing it across the room, staring at Michael the whole time daring him to comment.

Michael simply tutted and returned his attention to his own writing.

The music from the television had returned to a faint background murmur, the loudest sounds in the room the scratching of ball-point on cheap note-pad paper and the ripping of pages from the pads.

A couple of minutes passed.

Michael stopped writing again.

"You're so full of shit," he mumbled.

Izzy slapped her pen down onto her pad. "What the fu..?"

Michael turned to face her and clearly this time said,

"You're full of shit! That's not what I meant and you know it."

"Oh really?" Izzy replied. "So you don't have your little office harem?"

"What are you talking about?" asked Michael, trying to appear calm.

"You!" Izzy pointed a chewed biro at him. "You expect every bloody woman in the office to fall at your feet!"

"No, I don't!" Michael was starting to lose his composure.

"Yes, you do! You try in on with every woman that walks into that office."

"No, I do not!"

"Yes, you bloody do."

"No, I don't!" Michael was starting to raise his voice in anger. "I never tried it on with you for a start."

"I KNOW!" Izzy shouted, immediately regretting the outburst.

Michael snorted in derision. "Oh my God! Is that why you've been such a stone-cold bitch? Because you're jealous?"

"Jealous?" snapped Izzy. "Fuck you, Michael!"

For a moment there was near silence, the only sounds coming from the television and the heavy, slow breathing of the two combatants.

Michael picked up his pad and slowly began writing once more. Without looking in his direction, Izzy returned to the job in hand also. The scratching of pens was slower and more deliberate this time, occasionally interrupted by a sharp exhalation of breath and frantic scribbling as one or the other let their concentration slip.

After an uncomfortably long time, Michael sighed. "OK, so I shouldn't have called you a bitch."

Izzy continued to write, staring at the paper.

"This is where you apologise for what you said," he added.

After a further uncomfortable pause Izzy said, "OK fine, I'm sorry. But really, jealous? I'm not jealous."

"I know."

"But I'm sorry I told you to... you know," she said smiling weakly at her indiscretion. "You just waltz around the office, flashing your smile and everything just kind of falls at your feet. Everything comes so easy to you."

"It really doesn't," said Michael, "I like to pretend it does, but I work really freakin' hard. And then Mr Prager still entrusts all the important jobs to you. Like this conference."

"Yeah, and look how well that turned out!" laughed Izzy ironically.

"It could be worse!" said Michael.

"Oh yeah?"

"Yeah, I'm pretty sure my nose is broken."

***

After an hour, a new schedule had been pushed under every door, delegates had gathered in the lobby and the corridor and Mr Prager was standing atop the reception desk, as Izzy had been earlier. The vending machines were empty, having provided the conference attendees with the closest proximity to lunch they were going to find, and the mood was better than Izzy had feared it might be.

The delegates had enjoyed some unexpected down-time, taking the opportunity to indulge in a long shower, to play a card game or just chat with work friends, old and new. Most had dispensed with the formality of ties or jackets, and a few were even in their pyjamas. Some delegates had evidently enjoyed more than a drink or two from bottles of contraband booze, smuggled in for the expected after-parties.

"So," began Mr Prager. "This is one for the history books!" The crowd murmured in agreement. "It could be worse; we could be in Slough!"

Izzy gasped at the word, but the crowd appreciated this self-depreciating, tension-breaking humour. They laughed.

"Slough!" he repeated, making Izzy wince. "We don't like to talk about that conference in the Peterborough office. I understand some of you have swear jars in your office?"

A few delegates nodded.

"Well, we have a Slough jar. This speech has cost me over a fiver already!"

Laughter rippled through the crowd and echoed down the corridor as his words were relayed to those too far to hear clearly.

He continued, following loosely the speech he had written and rehearsed to perfection, but also ad-libbing and riffing off the crowd. And the crowd loved him. Izzy looked around at her colleagues, a sea of smiles and laughter. She was laughing too, even Michael looked less miserable. Mr Prager was funny. Actually, genuinely funny. Who knew?

After 90 minutes, Mr Prager was drawing to a close. "Right, well you've all listened to me for quite long enough."

A few shouts of "no!" and "encore" came from the crowd in a kind of reverse heckle.

"No, no, there are far more people to hear from than me! We hope you all enjoyed your slap-up Mars bars and packets of crisps and we're really glad you're embracing this somewhat unorthodox conference." He looked at Izzy and, much to her surprise, he smiled.

"Now, I'd like you all to thank young Izzy there," said Mr Prager clapping his hands. The delegates all dutifully did likewise. "She really had something very special planned for us all this weekend, but events, some really weird events, put paid to that."

"However, she's done an amazing job of bringing us all together and allowing you all to hear some truly inspiring people. Like me!"

More laughter.

"Now, please don't anyone worry, I know it has been a strange day but it won't be long before we're all out of here. After all, I have my very best minds on the case!" He smiled again at Izzy and Michael. "Isn't that right?"

Michael and Izzy looked at each other nervously. "Ah-ha. Absolutely!" they nodded, their smiles a little too broad to be altogether convincing.

"Great!" Mr Prager concluded. "Fifteen minutes then everyone off to their break-out sessions."

***

Break-out sessions continued to take place in the bedrooms throughout the afternoon. Some rooms, with charismatic speakers and intriguing titles, were standing room only. Chris

Mitchum (Norwich) ran a session on Communicating to Generation Z and Beyond that proved so popular that the room was full, and some attendees were forced to watch from the corridor and the shower-room. Angela Pickles (High Wycombe) foolishly attempted to stand on the toilet and the ensuing damage caused the room to flood and the session was brought to a premature close.

This was good news for Gerald Newbold (Glasgow) as some delegates joined his workshop A is for Accounts Receivable! Doubling his audience from three to six.

Izzy and Michael did not attend any sessions, instead they were back in Izzy's room trying to devise an escape plan.

In the background the television was still playing quietly as Michael asked, "Have we tried all the windows?"

"Well, no," answered Izzy. "I suppose there are some bedroom windows we haven't tried but honestly, I feel like we've tried enough to know they won't open."

"Air vents!" said Michael. "We're all still able to breathe so there must be air vents somewhere."

"I guess..."

"No, I've got it!" Michael sat up and smiled at Izzy triumphantly. "The vending machine. A few of us could probably lift it between us. I'm sure I'm not the only one who lifts weights."

Izzy rolled her eyes, but Michael didn't seem to notice.

"If enough of us could get behind it, I reckon we could break the glass doors."

"That seems pretty extreme," said Izzy.

"This seems like a pretty extreme situation."

"Perhaps we should look to see if there's anyone outside yet?" said Izzy, raising her voice as the sound of the television was slowly getting louder.

"There hasn't been anyone out there for hours."

"What?" shouted Izzy.

"There's no-one there," shouted Michael. "WHAT THE HELL IS GOING ON WITH THE TV?"

At that moment something truly spine chilling happened. For a second, the video's soundtrack fell into silence, then a voice started singing. The song was, by now, horribly familiar.

Michael jammed his hands over his ears but Izzy stood up and approached the television, mesmerised by the opulence and elegance of the hotel that once stood where she was now. Two familiar figures slow danced into the frame, the young woman's head resting on the man's chest as they moved together.

Izzy turned to Michael and said, "I know what I need to do," and the music suddenly stopped.

***

The break-out sessions were due to finish at 5.30 pm and at 6 pm Mr Prager was scheduled to deliver his final remarks, after which delegates would normally return to their rooms to freshen up for the gala dinner.

It was ten to six and Izzy was nervously looking out of the glass doors onto the deserted street when Mr Prager approached her.

"Hello, Mr Prager," she smiled.

He smiled back, looking tired but less stressed than he'd been for most of the day.

"I'd rather hoped we would have some good news to deliver in the final address," said Mr Prager.

"I rather hope we might, but I need you to trust me."

"OK," Mr Prager said slowly, fearing what might come next.

"At the end of your address, I need you to tell everyone to go back to their rooms and watch the documentary on channel 96."

Mr Prager looked perplexed.

"I know this sounds weird, but I think it's what the hotel wants us to do," said Izzy

"What the hotel wants..." started Mr Prager.

"Yeah, I know, crazy," admitted Izzy, "in fact that's not half of it. I think the hotel brought us here. Brought me here."

Mr Prager closed his eyes, he could feel another one of his headaches coming on.

"Think about it," insisted Izzy. "The emails I couldn't find, from a hotel that doesn't exist. The fact that the hotel has locked us inside and that there doesn't seem to be any actual people working here! Not to mention all the other weird stuff that's happened, like the music. Also..." Izzy checked that Michael hadn't entered the lobby and said quietly, "I think the hotel is trying to kill Michael."

"OK, that's enough," said Mr Prager, starting to lose his temper. "I know this has been stressful for all of us Miss Antill, but I really need you to pull yourself together."

All across the hotel lights flickered.

"Mr Prager, please I know I sound crazy..."

Air vents that had gone unnoticed most of the day started to blow icy cold air throughout the building.

"Izzy, no, this is quite enough..."

There was a banging on the door marked "Rooms".

"What the hell is that?" asked Mr Prager.

Izzy ran to the door and opened it. A dozen Roomba vacuum robots swarmed into the lobby, forcing Mr Prager and Izzy to climb onto the reception desk. They clung to each other as icy wind blew hard in their faces.

Distant screams and shrieks suggested that similar scenes of domestic appliance based terror were taking place throughout the hotel.

Izzy now had to shout over the noise: "How do you explain all this?"

"I have no idea, but assuming any of this makes any sense – which it doesn't, no offence Miss Anthill – but why would the hotel specifically be targeting you and Michael?"

Izzy thought for a second. The whole thing was already sounding so crazy, she may as well just say what she was thinking. "I think... I think it considers itself... like... my Godfather. Or something."

The Roombas banged themselves against the desk, some of them cracking their plastic shells with the force of their bombardment. The cold wind was biting Izzy and Mr Prager's faces, forcing their eyes shut.

"And Michael?"

"Well, he was pissing me off..." shrugged Izzy.

Then the music started.

"FIIIIIIIIIIIIIIIIIIIIIIIIIIIINE!" shouted Mr Prager and all at once there was stillness and silence.

***

A quiet, nervous crowd was gathered in the lobby at 6pm.

"Well," said Mr Prager, trying to sound avuncular and jolly. "I'm sure you'd agree, that was quite the haunted house, er... hotel, experience Izzy created for us all!"

Delegates looked at each other and there was the sound of dozens of muffled conversations, "Could it be?", "Was it really all a trick?", "Wow, that must have taken quite some planning!", "I've never experienced anything like it!"

From the hallway behind the door came the sound of clapping. Just one person to begin with, then it started to spread. More and more delegates were joining in and the clapping got louder and louder until the sound echoed throughout the hotel. The clapping was soon joined by cheering and whooping, the euphoria heightened by a palpable sense of relief.

Mr Prager smiled a broad, genuine smile, then put his fingers to his lips, silencing his audience.

"There is just one more task for you all before you can leave our haunted hotel." The delegates looked up in hushed expectation. "Everyone, and I mean everyone, must now go back to their rooms and watch the documentary on channel..." he looked at Izzy.

"Channel 96."

"Channel 96," repeated Mr Prager.

"It's really important that everyone does this!" Izzy couldn't help but interrupt. "If you don't watch the film all the way through, the hotel will know."

"Oh yes!" laughed Mr Prager. "You don't want to upset the wrath of the hotel now!" He looked at Izzy and for a second the smile left his face as the importance of this instruction dawned on him. Then he turned back to the crowd.

"So it is REALLY important that you do watch the film. Can't emphasise that enough. Do watch the film. After that you are free to freshen yourselves up and we'll all meet back here at 7.30pm to leave for the gala dinner. Now, off you go."

Slowly the lobby emptied until only Izzy, Michael and Mr Prager were left.

"Well, what now?" asked Mr Prager.

"Now I guess we go get ready for the dinner and meet here at 7.30."

"Oh," said Mr Prager. "Good, good." And he left to return to his room.

Michael smiled in relief as he asked, "How did you know that will work?"

"Oh I don't," said Izzy, "I just have a hunch."

"A hunch?" asked Michael, eyes widening. "And what about the gala dinner?"

"Well, I had booked that with the Theatre so I'm hoping that they've been preparing it, even though they haven't been able to get hold of any of us."

"And if they haven't?" asked Michael, panic clearly rising in his voice.

"Oh, then we're screwed," answered Izzy, sounding strangely calm. "But I wouldn't worry, if we can't get out of this hotel we'll probably starve to death anyway."

"So what do you suggest we do now?"

"Dress for dinner?" suggested Izzy. "Although I'd give the shower a miss if I were you."

***

The hotel lobby sat empty and quiet save for the soft murmuring of radio adverts.

Throughout the hotel, delegates sat on their beds, drinking cups of instant coffee with UHT milk; they dressed, put on make-up and styled their hair. They finished off the last of the alcohol they'd smuggled into the conference. Whatever they were doing, none spoke, all were watching their televisions, tuned to Channel 96, learning of the splendour and the history of the Robin Hood Hotel.

***

An excited group had now gathered in the lobby, awaiting the grand finale to the day's events. Some had clearly been enjoying their contraband refreshments and clung to each other, swaying and giggling.

Mr Prager stood at the door with Izzy, who was wearing a long, forest green velvet gown and had piled her hair into what she hoped was an elegant, loose bun. Michael approached her in a dark grey, double-breasted, perfectly fitted suit. He would have looked immaculate had it not been for the limp, the matching black eyes and the slippers that didn't quite complete the ensemble.

"Oh, these," Michael said as he caught Izzy's glance at his slippers. "My left toe has swollen quite badly. I think it happened when I kicked the Roomba."

Izzy shook her head in disbelief and Michael laughed. "I think maybe this hotel is trying to kill me."

"I think when, or if, this door opens," said Izzy. "We need to take you straight to the nearest Urgent Treatment Centre."

"Are you kidding?" asked Michael. "No, I'm going to dinner with my friend."

Izzy smiled, then, much to Michael's surprise, threw her arms around him and hugged him tight.

"But then, yeah," he said. "I think I need to find a hospital."

Mr Prager looked at his watch. "It's 7.30," he said to Izzy. "Everyone should have watched the film and everyone should be here."

"Only one way to find out," she said and nodded to the door.

Mr Prager put his hands out and stepped forward into the door. It opened. Fresh air had never tasted so good as Izzy and Michael stepped into the Newark dusk, followed by their laughing, cheering colleagues.

Izzy felt a vibration from her handbag. Opening it, she saw her phone was ringing. Tentatively, she answered.

"Yes, yes, it is... Oh yes, yes, oh that's brilliant... Oh yes, I was worried that when you hadn't spoken to me that... what? Oh, oh yes of course... Oh, I see... I have no idea how I could have forgotten, sorry! No, that's obviously not a problem... No of course that's understood... Yes, thank you, we're looking forward to it... We'll see you really shortly."

Izzy looked at Mr Prager and Michael.

"Everything is ready for us at the Theatre. And it's just as we requested earlier today, except that they can't allow smoking at the bar. It's illegal to smoke indoors."

"Of course, it is. Who asked if we could smoke at the bar?" asked Mr Prager.

"I don't know," said Izzy quizzically. "But at this point I'm not going to question anything, and I for one am ready for a drink!"

"Quite right!" said Mr Prager. "OK, I'll lead this lot on foot. Do you and Michael want to take a taxi, on account of..." he waved in the direction of Michael's lower half.

As the crowd dispersed, Izzy indicated to Michael to follow her back into the hotel. He did so reluctantly, gingerly crossing the threshold.

Izzy looked back to the automatic check-in point. The screen flashed blue, then the following text appeared.

"Never Forget..." That was it, Izzy remembered. That was the Take That song her Mum loved.

Izzy smiled. "We need a taxi to the theatre," she said to her surroundings.

"Erm, you might want to actually use your phone for that," said Michael. By way of response, Izzy simply gestured to the road outside the hotel, where a taxicab was already drawing up to the kerb.

Michael looked at Izzy, a little scared. "I'm going to be OK staying here tonight, aren't I?"

Izzy looked around the lobby again. The radio increased in volume once more, but this time it was just enough to draw attention to itself.

"Thank God, it's not James Blunt again," laughed Michael.

"No," said Izzy "It isn't, is it? For a while I couldn't quite remember who it was though."

Michael shook his head in mock disapproval. "You couldn't remember Never Forget by Take That? How ironic. And furthermore it's a classic, you heathen!"

With that the music's volume increased, just a little, but enough for Izzy to notice.

She smiled at Michael. "I think you might just survive the night," she assured him.

With that she linked arms with her hobbling friend, the door opened and they walked, arm in arm, to the waiting taxi.

St Catherines Well

by Lynn Roulstone

N OW, WHEN I hear that the floods along the Trent have
receded and I smell spring on the air, I think again
about slipping my bounds and going to visit him. I know the
way, though I have not walked it these last twenty years. Along
the Trent past the wharfs where the men load the barges, to the
banks beyond the town walls, past the women washing their
clothes and young boys fishing. There, where the Trent meets
the Devon I will find him, at the place that was our undoing all
those years ago.

I hear what people say when they think I am not listening.
How he supports the maimed and feeble minded, cures the sick,
helps young orphans find their place in the world. They think it
wise that I not be reminded of the time when he was Sir Guy and
I was the Lady Isabel. Now they call him Saint Guthred, and I
have been Sister Mary Magdalene, the penitent, under the rule
of Our Blessed Lady and Saint Catherine these long years since.

I lived in the castle. My father was warden and I had
chambers above the hall with the other maidens. From our
rooms we could look across the castle grounds, over the roofs
of the houses to the church beyond. I rarely went out, my father
liked to keep me close. So instead, I would look from my

windows and make up stories about what I saw passing before my eyes.

The tilt yard where the knights practiced was one of my favourite places. From the battlements I could see all that happened clearly. There was one knight that I called Sir Peaceful. He seemed to have no desire to engage in the games and tricks I saw the others play, and was always the first to come between those whose play seemed in danger of turning to real harm. Others were not so gentle. There was one I often saw putting burrs under the saddles of his rival's horses, and making rude gestures behind Sir Peaceful's head, to the amusement of the other young men. I called him Sir Sly.

I dreamed that Sir Peaceful might be chosen as my husband. I knew I had been betrothed twice since my birth. The first time my prospective groom had died. The second time allegiances had changed and the gentleman had married elsewhere. I was nearly fourteen and I knew from the gossip that reached me that plans were underway for a third match. My father had independent wealth and connections with the king that would make ours a useful family with which to be aligned.

On Twelfth Night I, along with everyone else in the castle from the pot boy up to my revered father, was at a feast to celebrate the season. The food was good and there had been music, dancing and games. Then my father's page called for silence and my father stood to give the last toast. I was standing near him, happy and slightly tipsy. I wasn't really listening until he said,

'And now some good cheer. My daughter is to be wed. Isabel my child, come here.'

A hand pushed me in the back and slightly staggering I walked towards him, I could hear the laughter, good natured in the most part. He signalled for me to stand at his right hand.

'Sir Everard, come forth and give your pledge.' I peered in the crowd wondering which of the knights was to be my husband. A man walked towards me. In the flickering light I could not see clearly who it was until he was almost at my side. It was Sir Sly.

'Hold hands now,' commanded my father. 'In front of this company I give my pledge that my daughter the Lady Isabel will be wed this coming May Day to Sir Everard Bevercotes.' I held his hand, damp, thick and rather hairy. My small pale one was swallowed up by it.

The next few months were in many ways joyous ones for me. I came down to dine with my father most nights now. Sir Everard would hand me to my seat, on the top table with my father's chief knights and their wives. He rarely stayed beyond the first course, preferring the company of his fellow soldiers to that of the ladies of the castle. The young wives enjoyed the status they had, and liked to compare husbands. One noticed the way I was always looking to where Sir Peaceful was sitting.

'His name is Sir Guy Saucemere. My husband says he is more suited to the cloister than the battleground. You are lucky that Sir Everard was chosen for you instead.' I did not agree, but knew I could not say so.

My father began to give me more license, little freedoms. I could, with a suitable escort, visit the town with my ladies to hear Mass in St Mary Magdalene on feast days, or visit the market to buy ribbons and sweetmeats. What I liked to do best though was to go riding in the countryside outside the town walls. I thought Sir Everard would accompany my ladies and I, but he rarely did so, and when he did he was scarcely civil. Instead the job usually went to one of the squires, boys little older than me. Then one day Sir Guy was in the courtyard, his hands holding the reins of my palfrey. He smiled when he saw me, and held out his hand to help me onto the horse.

'It is a fine day, and I find these walls gloomy when the sun is shining. Sir Everard has a mind to teach the young men some sword craft, which is not my fancy when the weather makes me think of spring. So, I will accompany you, if that is your pleasure.' I did not reply, but the look on my face was all the answer he needed as to my glad acceptance of his plan.

We rode down the Trent and then out by the Devon. As we went he pointed out the new lambs, and stopped to talk to the villeins sowing this year's wheat. He seemed to know much of farming, and knew most of the men by name. By Hawton church we stopped at a cottage where an Alewife gave us pots of her beer, and he talked to her of the craft of brewing. I enjoyed watching him, seeing the way he held his head as he listened carefully to all she had to say. He then turned his horse towards home, and I reluctantly followed. Each pace the horses took towards my home made me regret even more that this kind man had not been chosen as my husband. That was the only time Sir Guy accompanied me, and even now I think it was the happiest day of my life.

During our ride I'd mentioned my love of the battlements, so I wasn't surprised when, as if by chance, we met there a few days later. It was an hour before sunset and the whole of the world seemed bathed in a gold light. Rather than look at the town, he took my hand and pointed across to the low hills by Kelham. He told me of his own house on the other side of the hill, and the beauty of it.

'I have a garden of healing herbs. If I was not called by God to be a knight, I should like to have been a monk, to train in some great priory as to the right use of them. As it is my path is otherwise. And you, Lady Isabel, what would you wish for?'

I wanted to say to be your wife, to share your life beyond those hills. Instead I said something about being content to do my duty. I wish I had been brave enough to speak the truth, though I hope he knew what was in my heart. That is my one regret. If I had spoken out maybe things could have been different for us. Maybe not the way we wanted them to be, but not the disaster that was to engulf us.

The day of my wedding drew closer. The knights practised for long hours for the tournament my father was holding as part of the wedding celebrations. I liked to sit in our pavilion in the castle grounds to watch them. Sir Guy and I exchanged glances every time he passed where I was sitting. Sir Everard, on the other hand, did not seem to notice me. His interest was just in being the victor in any combat, and he used what ever means necessary to get that victory.

The tournament took place two days before the wedding. The marshal and the seneschal had worked closely to make sure that the event was worthy of the warden of Newark Castle. Sir Everard and I entered together, and sat in the place of honour. Behind me was my father and his specially invited guests.

The day started with a pageant on the theme of the holy bond of matrimony. I watched in envy as the scenes unfolded. I could not imagine the man sat beside me and I having a such tender moments as the actors portrayed. Then the games began. The jousts were designed to show the knights' skills, not to cause injury. The swords were blunted and the lances were of wood. Sir Everard watched it all keenly, but rarely spoke to me. Between the bouts there were other entertainments, dancers and jugglers. Despite everything I was enjoying myself. Then Sir Everard turned to me.

'The last joust is between me and Sir Guy. I think you would like him to be the victor. Maybe you would prefer him as your husband?'

'I am betrothed to you sir and will be to you a faithful wife.'

He squeezed my hand tight. 'I will make sure you are.'

He stepped down from the pavilion and waved at the crowds. He was popular and he did look the perfect pattern of a knight from one of the romances I had heard my father's minstrel's tell. He then turned so that he could receive a favour from me. This had all been planned beforehand, and I slipped the veil from my head and handed it to him as we had practiced. He bowed towards the crowd and went to prepare.

Known only to us, Sir Guy carried a kerchief I had embroidered with our names entwined close to his heart. I had managed to slip it to him the previous day.

As soon as they entered the lists I saw that Sir Everard had exchanged his wooden lance for a battle one, the cruel point glinting in the clear April sunlight. Sir Guy halted his horse, and I thought for one moment he would turn away. Then he gave the signal and charged forward. I wanted to close my eyes against what I thought would happen next, but I needed to see. Sir Everard's lance struck a glancing blow on Sir Guy's shield but he recovered and managed to unbalance his opponent by using the weight of his lance against him. Sir Guy jumped from his horse and drew his sword. Sir Everard was already on his feet, his sword in hand. He struck the first blow and I realised that he was not fighting with a blunted sword.

At that point the marshal who was overseeing the jousts raised his hand to stop the bout and stepped down to talk to them. I was too far away to hear what was said, but I could see the marshal trying to keep them apart. While this was going on my father had risen to his feet, pulling me to mine. The other spectators rose too.

'Now let the feasting begin,' he said, waving his hand towards the castle, as he led me away towards the great hall. At the door he stopped and signalled to two of the guards.

'Take Lady Isabel to her rooms and keep watch until I come.' I called out to him as he walked away but he did not turn his head.

It was only much later I heard that Sir Everard and my own Guy slipped away from the castle to those fields where we had spent those brief happy hours. Those meadows down where the Devon meets the Trent. There, they fought for the right to claim my hand. Even now I do not know why my love accepted such a challenge. We knew our love could not be, so why fight for it? He must have held his honour higher than I knew.

What really happened there only the nesting larks and the ravens flying high above saw, but shortly one lay dead and the other had fled. The dead man was my betrothed, his head sliced from his body by a single unhappy blow from my beloved.

The body of Sir Everard was found early the next morning. That night my father had me moved to this house just outside the town walls. He told me as he left me at the gate he would tell all that asked that I had died of grief, and that from that moment I was dead to him.

Here I have remained ever since, hearing the news of the town as though through a veil. I heard how a spring of water had burst forth where Sir Everard's head was found. I also heard that Sir Guy had vanished, though there were rumours he had gone to the Holy Land as a penance for his grave sin. These stories did not touch me, they happened to Lady Isabel not Sister Mary Magdalene.

Ten years ago I first heard rumours of a leper that had been cured by the spring where Sir Everard's head was found. I heard the story from many different sources, but minus the embellishments they all said the same thing. A knight stricken by the plague had seen a vision of Saint Catherine, who told him to bathe in the spring near the Devon. He did so, was cured and in thanks built himself a hermitage there. I was told much of the man's piety and good works, but it wasn't until he came to our door asking advice of our Abbess on herbs that I realised who he was.

I was not on duty in the herb garden that day, but from the orchard where I was picking the early apples I saw him. Still tall and thin, his hair now grey. I could see how he listened, his head on one side in a gesture I thought I had forgotten but which now bought back many tender memories. I stood in the shade of the trees, ready to gather up my skirts and fly to him, but something held me back. I trust it was Saint Catherine, that wise woman who knows so much. She must know what is best for us all, and that this life is the best for me, as his is the best for him.

Iris of Time

by Luke Settle

QUEEN'S HEAD COURT carries the last few remnants of Moira's perfume above cobbled flooring before dispersing into the late afternoon air. The journey back home to Lincoln is relatively short; likewise for her friend travelling back home in the opposite direction. Traffic is light which allows Moira to make driving a subconscious activity, enabling her to plan the evening ahead. Specks of rain begin to flick onto the windscreen of her car enticing her to click the stick of the wipers, initiating combat. Within seconds the clouds send in more troops, confirming that she is indeed heading into the eye of a December storm.

"Typical," she mutters. The night is drawing in with every junction passed, the road signs blur behind heavy rainfall as Moira Huddlestone drops her heterochromatic eyes to the fuel gauge. It's looking rather low and the BP garage up ahead begins to look necessary.

"Shit." Being broke not long after payday is painful and one-eighty a litre is pure daylight robbery. She pulls into the station and switches off the engine. It's silent, not a car in sight. Moira cannot fathom the station's ghostliness given that it is five-thirty on a Saturday. With extreme reluctance she gets out of her car to begin pumping away her pennies. She puts in a fiver more than she wants to and even goes two pence over that. It won't last long but it'll certainly get her home.

Not so many miles away, Olivia Bateman is running from the storm. The heavy clouds behind her are making their way down from Lincoln, over Newark and into Grantham. Olivia's SEAT León is heading back home, carrying a carefree twenty-eight year old. Her mousey blonde bob is bouncing around the frame of her face as she sings along to her car stereo which is playing a compilation of music from the noughties. With Moira on the forty-six and Olivia on the A1, two long-time friends create distance that'll be bridged by calls and texts until they meet again at the weekend — same place, same time.

Back in winter-dark Newark, Analetta, witch-chanteuse of The Tribe, drifts through Paxtons Court underneath black painted beams. She's almost skiing on tiptoes across the floor in ghost-like fashion. Her eons-long companion, Uriah Vanlow skips jubilantly down the same pedestrian passageway, thick dark strands of hair floating behind him as streetlights flicker under his presence. It's just a glimpse of their supernatural abilities as they appear far younger than they really are. The fact that they are able to transcend in this way means that she – 'the girl' – has been close. It isn't the first time they've felt it, it seems to now be a weekly occurrence. Next weekend can't come soon enough.

***

Saturday is already nine and a half hours old by the time Moira and Olivia meet again. The streets of Newark are frosty with last night's downpour turned to icicles and frozen sheets that resemble glass. The shine from polished cobbles is quite mesmerising. Each stone, eroded under decades of footsteps, seems to bend light in a way that reflects much more than its immediate environment. The market square is already bustling with market traders and Christmas shoppers. A young couple are debating whether or not one of the greasy-spoons-on-wheels is worth the risk and after further deliberation the two opt for something a little more commercial, just round the corner on Stodman Street.

Moira and Olivia walk past the town's Christmas tree towards Queen's Head Court and step into The Old Bakery Tea Rooms. They laugh at the fact they have somehow put on the same coat to meet today, an embarrassing indicator of how in-tune they are. They catch the waiter's attention; he's cute, young and very well groomed but hasn't a second more to chat past taking down their order. He's also new which means he doesn't know their order. They slowly recoup from the best kind of laughter, the sort that does in fact bring tears.

"Drinks, ladies?" Two small handbags are occupying the space the waiter requires to place their drinks down. The question was a nudge, a subtle technique used to influence change. It's failed on this occasion and the ladies stare blankly at the young lad whose brushed chrome name badge shines three bold letters into their reflective starry eyes — BEN. Without hesitation, Ben lifts one of the drinks from the tray he is holding and raises his brows in hope one of the ladies takes the hint. Moira makes room and the second her bag is off the table, her drink comes in to land. Olivia, observing the process, does the same.

"Thank youuuu," Ben says with an elongated 'Ooo' at the end of his sentence — a 'must-have' for any Gen-Z as part of their toolkit in customer service.

The morning moves closer to the afternoon with two women staying for a second drink, the same again but this time they add a mixed fruit and a cheese scone to their order before settling (and wrapping back) up. Olivia heads out first, warm walking boots providing comfort and insulation, a seasonal change from her preferred black knee-highs. Moira walks behind, looking back over her shoulder at Ben who's too busy to notice, which gives her a dull ache of disappointment, even though he's really too young for her. The door to the bakery shuts, closing off the thought along with the possibility.

Olivia has disappeared into The Secret Wardrobe — a unique ladies fashion boutique. The stock is relatively bespoke and significantly limited in comparison to most modern retailers. Moira stands for a second outside the door, reacclimatising to the English winter after the toastiness of The Old Bakery Tea Rooms. Olivia glides past hangers of clothing, evidently excited from the spring in her step. She gets a little giddy when surrounded by comforts, something Moira has come to know and love about her best friend.

"Livvy..." Moira catches her breath inside the boutique. Spinning round as delicately as she seemed to glide into the shop, Olivia turns to look square at Moira whose entrance is slightly dramatic given the silence within. Over her left shoulder, looking in through the window, is a beautiful looking young man. He may have caught Olivia's attention but he only has eyes for Moira. Hypnotised by the handsome Jack Sparrow wannabe, she walks closer to the door, dropping the cardigan she had selected from the rail. He truly is mesmerising — exceptionally striking in fact. Just stood there in a casual manner leant up against the wall, he seems to be enjoying the sport that is 'people watching.'

"LIVVY!" Moira shouts in her face, attracting the attention of an unhappy looking shopkeeper. Olivia blinks, turns her attention to her friend before looking back over her shoulder. What she sees is impossible. She blinks quickly in an attempt to stabilise what she is seeing but the vision remains. The gorgeous dark-haired man stood outside is now a frail old man with a grey, wiry beard that covers most of his face. She forces herself to blink hard, at least three times which now causes Moira to spin round, facing the old man that Olivia is trying so desperately to replace. He smiles, cracking the corner of his mouth in a way intended to haunt the recipient because right now, that's all he can do. Olivia's eyes are now rolling around in her head in search of an explanation. Moira stands still, too afraid to move. A handful of seconds pass where they watch the little old man shuffle away, leaving the girls with nothing but their own thoughts. Olivia pushes past Moira, out the door and up Queens Head Court, through the archway onto Kirk Gate. She turns left, takes a few more steps and then stops. Trailing behind once again, Moira eventually catches up.

"Oi, what's was all that about? Did grandad freak you out too?"

"I think I'm going crazy Moira. I felt like... I dunno, a... presence. Then when I looked up, I saw this gorgeous man. He looked all bohemian with colourful clothing and jewellery."

"I must have missed that one because all I saw was some old git with a beard in very colourful clothing. Unless you are saying *he* is 'gorgeous' of course?"

"Shut up, Moira!"

"I'm joking," says Moira, hooking her arm around her friend's. "Tell me what happened."

They stand still for a second, a sober tone replacing their normal levity.

"There's just no way a man can change before my very eyes. It was like he aged in an instant and the man you saw was the older version."

"Story of my life."

"I'm being serious." She looked it too. "He was like two people. I thought maybe he went this way but how could a little old man get away so quickly, where could he have gone?"

"His smile did freak me out, I'll give you that." A feeling of dread washes over them. The pair make steps down Kirk Gate to the Middle Gate turning on their left.

Out of sight, a woman dressed in a red and gold patterned shirt with baggy sleeves stands in Paxton Court, a little further down Kirk Gate. Her lower body is covered by a bright blue dress with pink and orange flowers. Her hair is beautifully long, jet-black with natural feral curls. Costume jewellery consisting of long necklaces full of red and white coloured balls and gold coins hang round her neck whilst bright purple and gold dream-catching earrings dangle against her jawline either side of her throat. She turns her face towards Middle Gate and sniffs the air.

The two girls carry on walking under frosted breath with no more clarity as to what one of them supposedly saw outside The Secret Wardrobe. The first few steps onto Middle Gate force Moira and Olivia onto the road. A group of youths occupy the width of the slippery path without any consideration for those approaching. Passing Boar Lane on their right, they revert back to a stereotypically British topic when no-one can think of what to say.

"Bloody cold isn't it, Livvy?"

"Sure is."

"You'd have thought by now us Brits would be used to it..."

"Yet we still moan. I know." Moira interjects. The two look at each other and smirk, aware that years of friendship are the reason they can finish each other's sentences so effortlessly.

The old man is still nowhere to be seen.

Conversation turns from weather to the approaching Christmas holidays. They hook left at the end of the road, almost completing a circuit and as they step back onto the Market Place, a cold wind sweeps in across the busy square, rustling the covered stalls. Threading their way past fruit and veg crates, bratwurst vendors and patterned rugs, Moira and Olivia come within aroma-reach of a locally-cherished delicatessen in a building with painted white lettering demanding people to 'try our smoked bacon.' They walk along the south side of St Mary Magdalene's Parish Church and are leered at by gargoyles perched high above their heads.

As the pathway of Church Walk gets nearer to Appleton Gate, it narrows to barely five feet across, penned in by wrought iron fencing and eighteenth century buildings. Set within the ancient red brick is a door to a watchmaker which opens thirty yards ahead of the two friends. Stepping out onto the pathway is the old man who was outside the clothing boutique only ten minutes ago. He had taken a right where Olivia thought he took a left. His head is down, bowler hat tight to his head and flamboyant clothing ready to meet the weather head-on. Moira and Olivia are just metres away from him but miles away in conversation. Uriah has just had his pocket watch refurbished to rid itself of all impurities. Except, it's not actually a watch, far from it. It's an heirloom of time waiting for the right moment to activate.

The man's face peers down at his artefact. Creased eye sockets have drawn in skin to form caves that shadow the eyes within. Thick dark brows hang just above, sharp to touch. Uriah's tinted beard is the product of two halves. One that has an absence of melanin and another that probably has too much of it. It hangs as low as his chest, over the top of his floral white shirt. His second layer of clothing is a black and tan coloured furry waistcoat with a variant of the floral design from his shirt.

The bottom half of Uriah is just as colourful, just as patterned. Reds and greens cover his trousers, all of which stand vibrant, like flecks of colour bringing new life to any black and white photo set in the streets of Newark. The bronze pocket watch in Uriah's right hand is detailed with black roman numerals around its edge with some peculiar detailing in the centre. He grumbles to himself in an obscure language and pulls the watchmaker's door closed. As he turns to the left he brings his eyes up, diverting his attention from the pocket watch to the girls up ahead. He stares with intent, confirming what he saw less than an hour ago, a beautiful anomaly. Heterochromia, signifying that two halves do indeed make a whole.

Each member of The Tribe has it and so too does the young girl up ahead. Moira's right eye is blue, her left, green. The Tribe all have the same left green eye but their right is brown. When Uriah Vanlow locked eyes with Moira Huddlestone for the first time, the dream of immortality evolved from centuries of hope into something actually possible. Grinning, he looks back down at his watch as he begins to pick up pace. If you were an onlooker, you may assume that Uriah was fleeing from someone or something behind him and technically that is true. He, like the rest of The Tribe, have been running from the hands of time and its outstretched grasp.

Behind Moira and Olivia, at the top of Kirk Gate, a slow, plaintive melody sung by a young, beautiful woman washes over the noise of traders from the nearby market. Analetta, dressed in contrast to the majority of those around her, uses her voice to cut through the wet air. It hangs solemnly, each note carrying pain from a different decade. In a flash, she morphs into an elderly woman of similar age to Uriah. After a few forced steps that signify a hip replacement is necessary, she reverses her appearance and is youthful once more. Those around her are oblivious, heads down on phones, focusing on the lives of others.

Analetta steps with pointed feet onto Church Walk. Uriah Vanlow has circulated the Newark area for decades. Analetta, not quite so long. The threat that time possesses against her natural beauty is real and each day she grows closer to wilting like the flowers on her dress.

As two young women approach the black bollard at the end of Church Walk, the old man bumps into Moira, causing her to become almost entangled within his unkempt beard. Olivia avoids the collision, instead, playing witness to the clash. The bronze pocket watch in Uriah's hand springs up, somersaulting before crashing down to the ground. It sits there, fully open to display the numerals around its edge and an hourglass of the same colour in the centre within the outline of a green eye. Olivia's attention is diverted from her friend to the shiny items that flew past her. She looks down but cannot make out the tiny detail in the centre of the timepiece. Moira is immediately apologetic and without thought, plants her hands on the old man's shoulders to steady him.

Olivia, feeling less apologetic, looks back up to yell, "MORON! Don't you look where you're going?" Moira is shocked at her friend's outburst from what appeared to be a genuine accident. For all she knows, this poor old man could be deaf, even partially sighted and therefore restricted to what or who was up-ahead.

"OI! OLD MAN! I'm talking to you!"

"Livvy! Cut it out, he's clearly shaken." Although he has kept his face averted, his colourful clothing allows Olivia to realise that he is the same old man that was stood smiling at them earlier. The hands of his pocket watch have stopped dead — twelve forty-nine to be exact.

"Sir... are you okay?" Moria's hesitant voice begins. Then, with a touch more uncertainty following every word she carries forward, "I'm ever so sorry. I was away with the fairies and my friend also didn't see you..."

"Yes I did."

"Shut it, Livvy!" she hisses over her shoulder with something of a serpent's tongue. "Anyway... I think you have dropped your watch over there... sir?"

"You think?" Olivia mumbles under her breath, the same way a child would bite back when being put in their place.

"Do you want me to pick it up for you?" Moira offers, realising that since the collision not a single word has been spoken by the old man. There's a shriek from the top of Church Walk behind them that carries on the winter wind, reflecting off surfaces of glass, brick and concrete. It's haunting. What comes soon after is a melody of folk music. It's an alteration to the one sung moments ago in Kirk Gate. It's slower, more pronounced. The ladies divert their attention from the man to the woman walking towards them. As beautiful as she is, there's something unsettling about her and both women feel intuition kick in. Olivia's face is crinkled with concern as they step away from Analetta onto Appleton Gate. She scans the street, becoming aware they are bizarrely the only people around at this hour of the day. Warm breath begins to escape past her lips forming small clouds of condensation, indicating an increase of tempo from her heart. Adrenaline pounds through her veins.

"Moira, I don't like this."

"Me neither. I think they're..." Moira's last word is jinxed as Olivia simultaneously jumps in.

"Together!"

And indeed they are. Dressed in similar colourful patterns, they've been waiting for this day — for this very moment. The woman at the top of the pathway is dancing theatrically behind Uriah. She wants to be noticed and take centre stage. As she joins him just in front of the black bollard, Uriah Vanlow finally takes his eyes off the pocket watch and turns his attention towards the two young women. His nails are in the same grotesque state as his beard and he gestures with them to the dark-haired young beauty beside him.

"Analetta." The whole thing is downright peculiar and the friends genuinely do not know what to say.

Being the cockier of the two, Olivia responds by mimicking the man in front, arrowing a much more feminine nail at her friend.

"Moira." The two different coloured eyes of Moira Huddlestone immediately roll in embarrassment. She doesn't want to antagonise the situation. Before she can do anything else, the singing comes to an abrupt end as the air seems to thicken. The eyes of the floral woman fixate on Olivia Bateman with an incandescent stare. Olivia scowls back at her despite her bones having just jumped in her skin.

"The hands of time, my dears... will be yours to keep." Moira and Olivia are piecing together the two characters before them. They're dressed rather bohemian and sound like they are still in the Middle Ages. But the biggest piece to this puzzle is how Miss Colourful is now floating! Uriah bends down to scoop up the pocket watch and present its face to them. It's stopped working – as a timepiece. But it has begun its other function.

"Ten-to one. Look... technology!" Olivia flashes her phone at Uriah. Judging from his appearance she wouldn't be surprised if he remembered the invention of the first telephone. Despite Olivia's proven ability to round up, Uriah makes no reference to it. Instead, shaking his head, he looks back down at the timepiece that still reads twelve forty-nine. As their eyes turn from watch to man they gasp. He's now standing as the handsome young gentleman that Olivia first saw outside the shop.

He stares at Moira.

"The key is not in spending time but in investing it." Uriah's words are met with blank stares before Analetta takes the watch from him to regard the static hands on the beautifully crafted face. Lowering her feet to the ground she takes the form of an elderly woman once more, hunchbacked and furrowed with fleshy lines deprived of hydration. The uncontrollable shapeshifting between the ages is a sign that their inner selves are able to at least taste the power of immortality that can be unlocked by Moira Huddlestone. The singular brown eye that The Tribe all have will turn green upon the acquisition of her soul.

Analetta morphs back into the younger of her two forms. Placing her hands on Olivia's cheeks, she makes an O with her lips and blows hard. A warm air that cools down to below freezing in milliseconds flies in through her mouth, tickling the inside of her throat on the way down to stabbing at her lungs. Olivia is pushed away so that the same can be done to Moira, followed by whispered incantations. She skips back, holding the beads of custom jewellery around her neck in a seductive display of celebration. Her singing changes to a more joyful tone, emphasised by a higher key as she rises back off the ground in small springy skips. Throwing the odd twirl in to lift her colourful dress she catches the eye of Uriah who simply stands there observing the ritual. They stare at each other for a moment before the pocket watch is handed back. He snaps it shut as they disappear into the distance until all that can be made out from afar are the bright colours of patterned fabric along with the tall silhouette of a bowler hat worn by a handsome young man.

Grey figures coalesce from the shadows shortly afterwards to regard the two young women standing in the street, tranced by Analetta's breath circulating within them. If Moira Huddlestone succumbs to her curse neither she nor Olivia will see another day.

Many *TICKS* are eventually followed by a single *TOCK*.

***

It's nine-thirty on Saturday, again. Moira and Olivia sit in The Old Bakery Tea Rooms. Has it been a week already? Neither can remember what they did throughout it but at the same time, daren't inform the other for fear of appearing a bit mad. Instead, they tell white lies and make something up just to move the conversation along. Ben comes back over having taken their order.

"Drinks, ladies?" They move their handbags, not learning from the first hiccup last week.

"Thank you," Ben says with that same elongated 'Ooo' at the end. The girls are surprised there appears to be no change in his rigidness from last week, maybe he just doesn't recognise them?

"Shit!" Olivia proclaims, "We have the same coats again!" Moira looks behind her then over Olivia, she's right. What are the odds?

"Why did you wear that again?"

"I could ask you the same," Moira bites back. "Seriously though, what are the chances?"

"Pretty slim. I'm going to sell mine," she jokes, softening her previous remark's tone.

"Same. Then we can go out and buy new coats, hopefully matching again." Olivia chuckles but something feels off today and they both sense it. They don't stay for a second drink this time, nor do they visit the clothing boutique just up the street because deep down, they're both quite afraid of something they do recall last weekend — the man they saw standing outside. They have trouble locating his appearance in their mind's eyes, nor can they recall anything that happened just afterwards, but they do remember him.

"Livvy..." Moira begins.

"Yeah?"

"Do you think you can get Alzheimer's at our age?"

"No idea. You suffering from amnesia?" She doesn't really want the answer, it may be too close for comfort if she says 'yes,' and besides, wouldn't that just raise more questions?

"It's nothing, don't worry." Olivia doesn't, she's good like that. After all, ignorance is bliss. The clock crawls closer to half-past eleven when clouds of thick charcoal begin to hang heavy in the sky like balls of smog — blocking out the light of day, spreading an eerie darkness all over town. Silently, between themselves, the girls fail to remember a downpour last weekend and almost simultaneously they feel better about things, discarding the thought of sinister hands at play in the background.

By twelve thirty-two the girls find themselves back near the church underneath clouds that have begun to leak droplets of water. With every minute that passes thereafter, the volume of water seems to double until an eventual downpour breaks at twelve thirty-seven. It's not until they see the vibrant colours worn by a beautiful looking man up ahead, that they realise those sinister hands scratching the back of their minds are in fact very real. Just before time can completely fall away from them again, a very youthful Analetta steps out of G.H. Porter Provisions, where the smell of smoked bacon escapes out into the street. She begins singing, causing the girls to turn in her direction. Distracted, Moira is touched by Uriah's pocket watch and the day resets slightly earlier than before but too slight for the girls to notice.

Many *TICKS* ...

A single *TOCK*.

***

Ben has just taken their order. A coffee and a tea.

 "Woah!" Olivia bellows. "How the... ?"

"Woah!" Her friend echoes. "Weren't we here just a—"

"Little while ago" Olivia interrupts. "Are we stuck in a loop?"

"That's ridiculous!"

"Is it?" The two sit in silence, frowning at the possibility whilst waiting for their drinks. Of course, they have the same coat as the week before and the week before that except it's the same day. There have been no weeks pass them by since their first encounter with Uriah and Analetta. In fact, they haven't experienced a minute past the incident involving the pocket watch.

"Are we in hell?" Olivia asks.

"Thanks a lot," mutters Ben walking past with a plate of cakes.

"Feels like it." Moira says, ignoring Ben. Then, "Excuse me..." she begins, "Do you remember us?"

There's a brief rush of embarrassment from Ben who is wondering what joke they are about to come out with. In an attempt to expand a little further and clarify her question Moira adds, "as in customers... do you remember us ever coming in here on a Saturday to order these drinks over the past fortnight?"

The blotchy redness that filled Ben's face only seconds ago sinks until it has completely disappeared. His face is now beaming with relief. Clearing his throat he answers, "I am afraid I do not recognise either of you beautiful ladies and trust me, I would remember." Despite the current situation they find themselves in, the compliment feels good.

 "Now if you don't mind, I must carry on serving? It's got so busy in the last quarter of an hour." Moira's smile is taken as permission to the rhetorical question he just landed her with. Unsurprisingly, they don't stay for a second drink, they don't joke about their coats and they still don't have a clue as to what is going on. Making her way out, Moira turns back to look at Ben. This time he looks up from the table he is serving, smiling back. It would appear that the hands of time are now playing by different rules and with this supernatural spike in life, so too are the hands of fate.

It's a little after ten so they have less than three hours before time jags back again. They both feel a need to keep walking, to distance themselves from the the bakery as well as the town centre in general. Heading down Balderton Gate they pass the statue of Irena Sendler and the memorial to Ethel Harrison. Something pulls them further down London Road to the tree-lined tranquillity of Newark cemetery.

Rows of white headstones extend into the distance to form perfect lines of symmetry. The graves of Second World War squadrons from the Polish Air Force stand immaculate with only cold wet footsteps being heard around the near four hundred graves. Amongst them are the graves of nearly fifty World War I casualties that are scattered around the cemetery, as well as the graves of former Polish and British soldiers who died after the end of World War II, requesting this cemetery as their final resting place. As saddening as it is to know how they came to be buried here, the memorial carved from Portland stone that stands tall in the middle of the path, reminds us all of their sacrifice. As the women walk further through the cemetery, standing tall in front of them is a four-point elongated cross embedded with a downward-pointing bronze broadsword. The base of the cross, covered in algae reads: THEIR NAME LIVETH FOR EVERMORE. The friends read the words and wonder exactly what their own 'evermore' is going to consist of.

Moira feels the hairs on the back of her neck prickle and looks up. Cloaked figures, standing in a circle around the memorial come in to focus. The friends regard the faceless group with extreme anxiety. They're motionless and the absence of vapour from warm breath indicates that they may be as otherworldly as the two individuals plaguing their existence. Olivia turns to Moira, "What now?"

"You tell me."

"HEY! Are you with them?" Olivia asks. The group before them immediately raise their right arms in synchrony, mimicking something of a pop-star's dance routine. They each arrow their index finger, one half of them at Moira with the others at Olivia. A strange, overwhelming sensation comes over them, absorbing what feels like all their energy, replacing it with a powerful, restrictive force hindering their movement. Their right arms raise to mirror the shadowy figures and their eyes roll back in their heads. They don't realise it but they're hovering about half a metre off the ground in the empty graveyard. Ancient knowledge is funnelled into their minds from the pointing strangers.

> The pocket watch is the key to breaking the Tribe's spell. Once you make contact with it, a Gateway will appear. The timepiece must then be thrown into the Gateway but be warned, it will only appear for a limited period of time. Failure to do so will lead to it closing for good.

Without warning, the girls are released from the forces controlling them, the figures around them vanish. They hold onto each other, dizzy from the experience.

"What," says Moira, "was that?"

Olivia shakes her head. "I don't know. Any clue on how to get out of this?"

"We need to get that watch."

"How? And then what do we do with it?"

"First thing we need to do is get back into town." They set off back towards London Road. As they approach Charles Street, specks of rain begin to fall.

"Urgh!" Olivia moans. "So is this the weather dynamic in this hellhole?"

"It's still England, isn't it?" A slight chuckle of sarcasm escapes them. Sixty seconds pass and the rain gets heavier. Another minute and it gets heavier still. This continues for five minutes. Dashing up Balderton Gate, a colourful figure appears from a sheltered shop doorway and taps them with the cursed watch. Before they have a chance to scream, they're back inside the Tudor building for the third time, waiting for Ben to approach.

***

"So hold on Moira... what you are saying is, the rain acts as some kind of, what, countdown timer?"

"Exactly!"

"Well that's just stupid!"

"Is it? Look, we..." Moira looks around, embarrassed.

She leans in to Olivia and lowers her voice. "We've *reset* with the memory of all that happened previously. I remember rain."

"So do I."

"Yes... and it's no coincidence that those two colourful weirdos seem to come out so soon after."

"True."

"What I also remember, is that we were thrown back here well earlier than before, Livvy."

"Over an hour earlier, I think."

"So with that, do we *use* the rain?" Olivia grins at Moira's suggestion and just then, as she is feeling a little smug, Ben appears.

"No thank you," she calls out, standing up as her friend mirrors the same movement. They haven't the time to waste. Ben looks flabbergasted as they rush out.

"So what now?" Olivia asks, expecting Moira to have the answers.

"I dunno, let's wait, wait for the weather to change and then be on our guard to not get tapped back to the tea room."

"But, hang on. If we have to avoid being touched by the timepiece, then doesn't taking it from them have the same effect?"

She has a point.

"Maybe we're meant to take it from them when they aren't touching it."

"That means we're going to have to get physical, doesn't it?" They both fall silent, waiting for the rain to fall, watching out for Uriah and Analetta. At eleven twenty, it begins. In the cold streets of Newark near the Palace Theatre, they look psychotic covering each other's tail, spinning around until dizzy. Onlookers regarding the pantomime wonder what the latest hit is on the streets these days and come to the conclusion that 'spice' is probably quite fitting.

"Junkies!" one bloke shouts, disgusted with their public display.

"Just ignore him Livvy, we know what we're doing."

"Do we?"

"I hope so." They continue spinning round, waiting for the two 'sorcerers' to appear. The rain gets heavier and heavier, as always. They must have less than a minute to go when out of their peripheral vision they see a familiar figure skipping down the street towards them.

"Get ready Moira!" Olivia calls out, thinking how Analetta's high skips remind her of the county high jump athletics championship she won not too many years ago at the South Kesteven Sports Stadium.

"I see her."

"Where's the other one?" The rain is hammering down now. If there were any time left at all it could only be seconds. They can't make out if Analetta has the pocket watch and they have no idea where Uriah even is.

"What if they... you know... don't get us?" Olivia asks, referring to the fact that there is a possibility one of the two may not make contact before the five minutes are up.

"Well... we must be close to finding out. Maybe we'll b—" Moira's word's disappear into a vacuum. It turns out that you can't have eyes in all places at once, even with a friend. With one eye fixed on Analetta and the other rolling around in their minds for the answer to Olivia's question, Uriah springs out of nowhere, from within the blindspot created by the girl's rotations. A delicate brush on the hip of Moira is all that is needed to send them back to The Old Bakery Tea Rooms.

***

They don't even wait for Ben, they just leave. Straight to St Mark's Place multi-storey where both their cars are parked. They set off in different directions to see if it's the *town* that is cursed. They have each other on call through their car's infotainment system. They're not ten minutes outside of Newark when the rain begins, becoming almost impossible to drive through after four minutes — it's not even ten o'clock. With rain coming down in sheets thick as lead, they begin to wonder how much further they can go.

At exactly the same time, each driver glances in her rear-view mirror to see an unexpected splash of colour sitting on the back seat. As the cars swerve violently on the rain-soaked roads, a bronze watch taps Moira on the shoulder causing the landscape to slip away so that the two girls reappear in familiar surroundings.

***

"So running away speeds things up and I'm guessing that if we were to kill ourselves..." Olivia looks unsettled by this comment "then we'd probably face some other effect. Anyway, I'm not even sure I *could* do that." A couple sat in the bakery look at Moira with concern, overhearing her suicidal thoughts.

"What about just sitting here, waiting for the day to reset? Would they definitely find us?"

"Only one way to find out." Moira stretches her arms and massages her neck. "How long have we even been awake now?" Olivia counts on her fingers. "Well, I think that this is the sixth time we have done this circus and I'll be honest ... I'm not tired in the generic sense of the word but my mind is feeling it. I don't think our bodies continue on the standard timeline. I mean, look..." she breathes out hard, "my breath would smell like crap by now and so too would yours, I'd smell it from here!" Moira takes a furtive sniff of her armpits to check. "Besides," continues Olivia, "our hair would be wet; makeup running and not to mention we'd be famished wouldn't we?"

"That's true. So you think we actually bodily reset along with the day?"

"Kind of... except for our memories. Whatever this curse is, it wants us to recall the same routines because it wants us to go crazy. Doing the same thing over and over, expecting different results... isn't that the definition of madness?"

"Don't forget those freaks in the cemetery. I remember their words."

"Yeah, they're crystal clear in my mind too. Maybe we should try and figure out what this 'Gateway' is," Moira says, raising a questioning eyebrow at her friend.

Olivia stares back. "Moira! Your eye!" Putting one hand up to her cheek, she assumes it's bleeding or leaking tears she cannot feel.

"WHAT? What is it?"

"It's..." Olivia hesitates, confused by what she can see, "changing!" The green iris in one eye now has a portion of blue that matches Moira's other eye.

"How can that actually be possible?" Moira opens her phone and flips the camera to the one used for taking selfies. She pulls down her bottom eyelid in disbelief. Olivia's right.

"So not a complete bodily reset, then." Olivia doesn't mention it but when they were spinning round covering each other's six near the theatre, she caught a glimpse of blue in Moira's green eye. That was two resets ago and she begins to wonder if something is taking over with the diluted iris being proof of it.

"Drinks, ladies?" They look up to see Ben standing with their order. There's no need to move their bags because they've already done it, sick to death of hearing that elongated 'Ooo' now, they've removed the opportunity for him to do so. He places the drinks down in front of them where they stay for more.

Remaining in one location seems to have the opposite effect as running away, the rain starts exactly five minutes before twelve forty-nine, so as the first droplets fall out of the dark sky and against the bakery's windows, Moira and Olivia begin to feel as though they are a step closer to escaping this nightmare — despite being told what they must do by figures in the graveyard.

It's twelve forty-four and the sky is thick with clouds, grey with depression and wet from the downpour. Less than forty seconds to go and Ben reappears. This is a new scene, one the girls have never created before. He's bringing their latest selection of drinks.

"And whose is this one?" he asks. Moira's hands move with her head to the direction of the lemon-smelling tea where she grasps a solid metallic object from Uriah's cold hands. Before she can comprehend his trickery, the world is undone and they start again.

**

Moria's left eye is now at a state of sectoral heterochromia. It's half blue and half green, the change increasing Moira's anxiety.

"How? How was that even possible Livvy?" This time it's Olivia that must be the more rational one, she's becoming increasingly aware of Moira's fragile state.

"We're in their world, right? Playing by *their* rules. Maybe it's time to take control and try to locate this Gateway."

They find themselves wandering the streets of Newark struggling for ideas. It's nine-fifty and one has a dripping fringe, the other, a soggy bob. They've tried to run, they've tried to hide, and now, (worryingly) Moira begins to chuckle in public as madness begins to take hold. Despite this new sensation of lost hope, deep down inside the genetic makeup of humans is an undeniable drive to survive and it's not until we are faced with such adversity that we truly shine. After the madness settles, her left eye loses the battle to blue just that little bit more. A moment to gather her thoughts outside Morrisons sparks a wave of inspiration within the sea of her mind.

"Come on!" she says, tugging at Olivia's arm, "let's go!" Olivia allows herself to be pulled down the pedestrianised street closer to the clocktower. They sprint across the main road and down The Wharf to the banks of the Trent.

"What now?" Olivia asks, panting with dewy skin. Moira doesn't answer but continues up a slight incline that, after walking and running, feels to Olivia like the world's most vicious gradient. Lactic acid takes piranha bites out of her leg muscles but soon they are standing on the bridge over the Trent. Moira scans the river, the banks and the nearby castle gatehouse while Olivia stretches her legs and wonders what happened to her schoolgirl athleticism.

"It's not here. The Gateway. I thought that an old crossing like this bridge might be it, but I can't sense anything. I think we're going the wrong way." Olivia says nothing, but puts her arm around her friend and they trudge back up past the Ossington and towards the civil war statue situated on the roundabout.

"What about that?" asks Olivia pointing at the defiant Cavalier and his drummer, just as the first of many droplets fall from the sky. Moira frowns, unsure, but maybe the rain indicates this is the place.

"Right, Livyy, eyes peeled!"

"Yeah, let's do this!" There's a touch of uncertainty in both their voices. They make it through the first three minutes before the rain begins to severely restrict their vision. They squint through the rain, straining their sight.

"This must be it, Livvy. This must be the place they were talking about."

"I hope so!" They're both shouting now, shouting to be heard over torrential rain as they enter the fourth minute.

"What do we do?"

"We wait! They'll be here!" Then just like that, at twelve forty-nine and forty-four seconds — shifting through the rain quicker than the human eye can see — is a beautiful young man wearing a bowler hat. His unpredictable movement gives way to the solemn tones of Analetta ringing from afar. The girls are torn who to look for. Twelve forty-nine and fifty-five seconds, the singing is within earshot with Uriah even closer, Moira brushes her hair back and in that second of lost concentration, contact is made. A bronze heirloom resets the world for a seventh time.

Moira's once-green eye, is now three-quarters blue.

***

"Where are we going now?" asks Moira as Olivia guides them away from Ben's Tudor tea room and across the Market Place.

"You said on the bridge that we were going the wrong way. So let's try a few different directions and see if you get a feeling that we're on the right track." Moira wrinkles her nose at the plan, worried that she might be imagining any additional senses, but she doesn't have any other ideas.

They've trekked around the castle ruins, hiked along the Navigation towpath, explored the area around the Police Station and Friary Park, poked around the College and are now staring at the Odinist Norse temple hidden away just off Barnby Gate. Olivia turns to her friend.

"Do you think that could be it?" Moira's silent, unsure whether to answer. Olivia's patience soon grows thin under the pressure of a looming reset, "Moira! Could this be it? YES or NO?" She's noticed the near full transformation of Moira's iris and believes it's all linked to an inevitable conclusion.

"I... I don't—"

"Spit it out!"

"I DON'T KNOW!" she screams with a tear falling from her eye. "I don't know Livvy and if I have to stare at one more building or statue then I think I *will* kill myself." Olivia reaches out and hugs her best friend.

"I'm sorry, I'm sorry, ignore me. I'm just getting stressed because, well, look, it's nearly twenty-past twelve so at best, we have thirty minutes. We've just got to keep trying."

The conversation is closed off and they begin walking back, downtrodden, towards Carter Gate where they turn left and trudge up to the traffic lights and cross over the road. Standing outside the Travelodge Olivia sneaks a glance at Moira's left eye. It's so odd to see eyes of almost unified colour after all these years spent with her. She'd got so used to the beautiful blue and green that she forgot it was a rarity. Right now, Moira is about to lose all of that as The Tribe close in on their prize.

Wondering where to go next, Olivia sees a grey cloaked individual on the opposite corner of the junction and another standing in the middle of Carter Gate.

"Look!" she says, pointing at the one in front of her by force of habit. The grey Observer points back immediately, initiating contact. Olivia rises from the ground, her eyes roll back white and that strange, overwhelming sensation takes hold once more as the download begins.

> She's close, almost complete. There isn't much time and at best you have one, maybe two resets. The rain will come soon and when it does, you need to be ready. It is you, Olivia, that needs to take charge, take the lead. You need to find the strength.

She's released from the forces like before, but unlike before, the hooded figures remain and they're all facing the same direction, staring down London Road. Moira, who stood silent for the interaction is now unfazed — a sure sign of her imminent surrender with every minute that passes. They loiter for a second as Olivia digests the words in her head. Moments of pondering allow her nasal and sinus cavities to sense a change in barometric pressure. They're a step ahead in comparison to the rest of her body leaving her face to be subsequently rain-kissed as specks fall out of the sky. The advanced warning from her heightened senses was subliminal and now the physical touch of rain on her face has occurred, she cannot help but grin.

Moira's face (although rain-kissed too) is expressionless. This time, it's Olivia who takes Moira by the hand to lead her across the junction. A minute later the gates of heaven open just that little bit more as they dart past the petrol station then the car park that leads to the Odeon and the glass-panelled library. They keep going, pulled towards a vertical beacon. Taking the path on their left through some bushes into the municipal gardens they stare at the sight before them. There stands the Beaumond Cross, clearly glowing to Moira's eyes.

"Is this it? This must be it, surely," Olivia mutters. Moira is breathing heavy but unresponsive to communication. They enter the third minute and the rain slams down hard. Olivia feels that the next one-hundred and-twenty seconds will be biblical and with that thought in the forefront of her mind, Uriah Vanlow and Analetta casually walk down the path into the gardens of Newark from the other end of London Road. There's an air of arrogance among them as they close in one last time with the hope of finally achieving immortality. Their eyes are almost perfectly green — the same green as the cross before them. Uriah is shaking the timepiece in his right hand just above head height, Analetta is skipping next to him — both appear vibrant and youthful. Her tone has risen to that of a cheery folk melody, discarding the eeriness, which in turn makes it all the more unsettling. Uriah tosses the watch into the air, once, twice, a sign of supreme confidence.

Olivia knows what she has to do and she's glad of her footwear choice that feels like a lifetime ago. Leaving Moira alone she runs towards the cross, skips up the steps at the base of the cross, walking boots giving sure grip on the wet stone, and launches herself into the air towards the two members of The Tribe. It's a risky manoeuvre, one which requires an impeccable degree of accuracy but recalling her athletic triumph, her muscle memory takes hold as she flies towards Uriah. He hasn't been watching her and the watch is in the air for a third time, out of his hands.

Olivia twists in the air and connects with the pocket watch as Uriah claws towards her in hope that he can snare the acrobat. He misses. Olivia Bateman's usual landing place for the high jump was a large blue crash mat but this time it's Analetta that breaks her fall. Uriah's timepiece has been knocked back down the path beyond the extension of his reach. It shines under clouds fit for an apocalypse, fully open and full of water. Without hesitation, Olivia lifts herself up and pushes with all her might towards it. She feels the rough jagged nails of a (now) old woman scratch her calf through skinny denim jeans, drawing blood. Uriah has also morphed, resembling the frail old man she first encountered near the church all those resets ago. Olivia kicks back and makes contact with Analetta's face, leaving a Doc Martens footprint across her mouth and cheek. Scooping up the watch, snapping it shut as she does, Olivia dodges Uriah and dives to her right, headfirst over the bushes onto the perfect grass of Newark bowling green.

From within the Beaumond Cross, a dark blue whirling mass is expelled, where it hovers gracefully under the sound of a faint hum. Moira, staring open-mouthed at what has just appeared, comes to with the realisation that they may actually pull this off. Those in pursuit of immortality have also had the same thought, which has caused them to shift back into their more youthful forms as they begin to ascend into the air and over the bushes in ghost-like fashion.

"MOIRA!" yells Olivia, running along the edge of the bowling green, as she launches the pocket watch into the direction of a determined-looking Moira Huddlestone. The bronze heirloom from an ancient world dances through the air, the rain doubles and they enter into the final minute before the reset.

Analetta and Uriah rotate their heads, following the motion of the watch as it flies towards the young woman. There's a gasp from Moira followed by a huge sigh of relief as it lands in her cupped hands. Without so much as a thought, she climbs the same four steps that Olivia catapulted herself from only moments ago to see at least a dozen grey Observers standing around the gardens of Newark. They point at the person now in possession of the watch, passing on one more piece of ancient knowledge. Realisation dawns on Olivia, they have to be together, on the cross before the gateway closes. Moira confirms her friend's understanding with the most desperate of pleas.

"LIVVY! This way!"

Olivia makes a run for it with both Uriah and Analetta smirking at the possibility of further failure from the girls. Moira stands like a general, almost completely blue-eyed on the top step of the Beaumond Cross, watching her friend dashing on the grass below. It's something of pure majestic delicacy the way she dances in between the young man and woman who are desperate to tackle her. Olivia's willowy frame allows her to contort in a way that in itself, seems inhuman. Moira smiles, for what feels like the first time in a long time.

"QUICKLY!" She cries out to her friend, who attempts to vault back over the bush of bare branches. But Olivia's legs are feeling heavy once more and she barely makes it, tumbling over onto the path below. Moira runs down to recover her friend and they both stagger to the steps of the cross. Uriah and Analetta are gliding towards them with venomous looks on their faces.

The rain is at its most intense, and there must be less than ten seconds before the day resets, or worse still, the whirling mass disappears.

As the two girls climb the fourth step, hand in hand, Olivia snatches the pocket watch from Moira's hand and hurls it into the colourful abyss. A loud crack of thunder pounds their ears leaving Uriah and Analetta with the confirmation that immortality has just died.

The cross seems to vibrate and the girls note that the dark blue, whirling mass looks thick to touch, almost gooey. Olivia sees that the Gateway's dark blue centre blends effortlessly with an outer shade of purple — *Like a tie-dye shirt,* she thinks. They only get a few more seconds to be absorbed by its beauty before it expands, shrinks — shrinks some more and then simply, disappears.

The seconds that follow seem to hold no actual time.

Uriah and Analetta are aged and earth-bound once more, the price to pay for manipulating time and yet they were so close to having eternal life. Now stripped of all power, they'll be lucky to make it through the week.

One of the two girls resists the urge from human emotion to call back after the elderly pair whilst the bolshier of the two resists the urge to deliver more Doc Martens sandwiches. The true cause for dispelling these desires is trepidation. The girls aren't certain of the 'rules' in play beneath the veil of life anymore, so whether they truly believe that the old folk before them have been stripped of their power is not something they wish to test. As the saying goes, let sleeping dogs lie. The Observers simply fade into the light of the day, as if signifying their purpose has been fulfilled.

Time ticks over to twelve-fifty, the sky brightens and all evidence of rain evaporates in an instant. The cross itself is no longer glowing. The time-worn shaft of quiet, grey stone has returned to being a monument, the way the town intended it to be.

The rest of the day is spent, somewhat ironically, in The Old Bakery Tea Rooms, at least until closing time. They regularly check the clock on their phones. They don't talk much but instead, enjoy the comfort of familiar surroundings. Moira breaks their peace with, "familiarity is a face that welcomes you home." Followed by a smile.

Olivia feels like she has heard that somewhere before, possibly even read it but is unsure where. She smiles back, understanding its meaning.

***

The following day an odd thing happens. Moira, who has been sat on the wooden bench just to the right of the Beaumond Cross looking out to the gardens is joined by Olivia. The two have not planned to meet, after all it is Sunday. Olivia sits down beside her best friend, closest to the cross. She notices that Moira's left eye is fully green again. She's always secretly loved the fact that the two of them have been referred to as 'oddities' by the majority, both in body and in mind. Being 'labelled' is often confirmation that you're a threat, which in itself is a form of power.

"Fancy seeing you here."

"Likewise."

They're both sure that it's over, despite the odd glance by Olivia at the cross next to her. The sudden departure from The Observers and apparent defeat of The Tribe leads them both to believe that all has been resolved. They find it strange that they've been burdened with the memories of it all. Having learnt a lot about themselves and finding strengths they did not know they had, the two girls now feel god-like.

It's around two-thirty and not another word is uttered from them in the hours that follow. Birds chirp as the sun shines a low winter's light on a monument once proven to hold infinite power. They both sit, waiting for that Gateway to reappear, in order to satisfy their own doubt. The time regained — time they have control of once more, is spent returning to this very spot 'just to make sure', leaving them to wonder if they ever really broke the curse of repeating the same day over and over again.

The Blue Bell

by Mark Smith

I AM INDEBTED IN the telling of this story to a gentleman I met in The Blue Bell public house in Farndon. I was also able to verify it from a copy of the *Nottingham and Newark Mercury* although the official record did seem to have less detail than that which I was told. Make of the elaboration what you will, but I am informed that this gentleman is a regular teller of the tale, as indeed he is a regular frequenter of the aforementioned establishment, and with each telling he seems to remember things that had previously been forgotten. That, I assume, is the power of good beer with which he keeps regular company and with which I, like those before me I am sure, ensure such company is not lacking. It is the unspoken price of this yarn.

There seems to have been some agreement that the character at the centre of the story should be called Jack Thomas. How this agreement and indeed this name has come about I do not know. Whether it is a matter of committee, individual or group discussion cannot be clear. I suspect it is a matter of knowledge that were it an apple, it would have been found to have fallen far from the tree from where it originally flowered and grew.

Where our story begins is somewhat clearer. Mr Daniel Jameson of Dry Bridge in Newark would be the person to see if you wished to buy a carpet. This is as reported in *The Mercury*. And that establishment is where we will start.

This event occurred last year in June, although one telling did place it on a hot summer's day in August of that same year. Time has not weathered the details.

The gentleman who has this story to tell, I should now name. He is known as Sam. He once was known as Mr Sam Miller, but with ill fortune he seems not only to have lost that fortune but also the greater part of who he is. For now, he is neither Sam Miller nor Mr Miller but merely Sam. For my witness to the telling of the story, he was also accompanied by a Mr Kirton and a Mr Farthingworth, who both seem to have retained their titles. These were gentlemen whom I would assume have never had much to lose but to their credit have not lost that little that has kept them in the lifestyle to which they are perhaps less accustomed and more resigned. They were also the voices of credibility, confirming the details as if they had been there themselves, which I am to understand, they were not. That said, the beer had the impact on Mr Farthingworth of allowing him to cast the occasional doubt on something which earlier he had sworn to the high heavens themselves to be the absolute truth and strike him dead if that was not the case. I believe he has survived these last few days and is still alive.

We can assume that it was a fine June afternoon in 1831 when Jack Thomas arrived at The Blue Bell with a thirst and a carpet to sell. Indeed the carpet must have played no insignificant part in his keenness to welcome such refreshment. Sam was at that same time the only person already acquainted with chair, long table and tankard of ale. The whereabouts of the landlord I am not told and feel no need to ask.

The carpet itself was twenty-five yards of the finest Wilton and you would not find anything better this side of the Trent for many a mile. There were no questions to be asked other than what the price might be. Sam then observed the events as I will now tell. The carpet had of course accompanied Jack Thomas into the beer house for fear that there might be people out there, not unlike himself, with a keen eye for the kind of bargain where no money has to be exchanged. Sam therefore had seen the evidence and such was the nodding and muttering of Mr Kirton and Mr Farthingworth that one might easily have supposed them to have been there too.

It turned out that in this part of Farndon there was no one in need of carpeting. Or, at least, no one who could afford it beyond wildest dreams. Those present could assuredly confirm this on the part of The Blue Bell itself and several wealthy neighbours. Even the church appeared to be represented in the form of a gentleman who had once been inside and knew there to be pews and a stone floor but no need for a carpet. Although he couldn't answer on behalf of the vicarage, but suspected they were not lacking for much. On this matter, he could have added much more and might be available to do so on a different occasion and for the right amount of attention to his thirst.

I should add at this point that my visit, or more accurately, the opportunity for yet another telling of the tale, has attracted further numbers. I am sitting at the long table. At the far end, on the corner, is the tapped cask from which we are drinking. At my end are Sam, Mr Farthingworth and Mr Kirton. We now have additional gentlemen, some seated due to gathered interest and others standing as if familiar with proceedings. Whether for these attendees it is the story that interests them or they are attracted by the reactions of a stranger I do not know, nor do I care. I just note their presence and that our numbers have been augmented. It is all good business. There is just one fellow who seems less engaged and more concerned about his pipe, both lit and unlit.

Jack Thomas was not in any haste to follow his arrival with departure. He seemed to have taken a liking to The Blue Bell and especially its beer. And the beer, whilst not having the memory-enhancing qualities it seemed to have given to our friend Sam, had loosened the tongue of Jack Thomas.

And so he told how he had had the good fortune to come about this carpet that very same morning. To start, he had informed Sam that the carpet had been a gift from God. He had been dozing on the banks of the Trent near some spot where it juts out a bit and he had found, for want of a better word, a small beach, with an equally small drop down from the field against which to rest his head. He had awoken to find the carpet placed next to him. This was not credited, even by the gentleman who had once been inside the church and who might have been a potential believer. It was a part of the account that made Sam laugh and then take a larger swig of his beer. Mr Kirton and Mr Farthingworth both nodded. It was not clear to me if this was as one in agreement with the tale so far, or in acknowledgement of Sam's merriment.

Jack Thomas's tongue then seemingly fully loosened, he told the tale as is now reported by Sam and made significant corrections to what had been said thus far. And so it was that that morning he had walked into the carpet shop on Dry Bridge in Newark and seen the carpet rolled and ready. With a confident air and strength of both mind and arms he had picked it up, put it over his shoulder, and walked out and away, unchallenged. The means by which he had acquired the carpet he told with the simplicity of how it had just been described. In reading a report from *The Mercury* of this incident it does state that the man we are calling Jack Thomas approached his crime in a "business-like way" and that he "excited no suspicion". I assume from this, a previous familiarity in such matters that might lead one to believe that carpets have gone missing before and there might be more than one establishment that has found itself better refurbished on account of one Jack Thomas.

Jack informed the group that he had walked along the side of the Trent and, only when he had got as far as the place where he had previously tried to put everything to a brief intervention by God, did he then have a look at his gains and knew enough to know it to be Wilton and around twenty-five yards. Jack Thomas did feel, at least, that God had blessed him, even if he had not directly contributed the contraband. No one seems to have challenged this judgement on the deity's choice of divine intervention. The preference seems to have been to keep the story going. I wonder if other such omnipotent activity of a dubious nature has also been disregarded for the sake of the continued telling of a good tale. Jack Thomas had then set off again and The Blue Bell had been the first place he had come to which he considered to be far enough to take a break. Far enough perhaps being safe enough. Here Jack Thomas had hoped to sell the carpet but then settled for selling his story instead. It was bought with several beers, just as I seem to be buying this account in similar fashion.

The Blue Bell is of course situated on the pedlar's way which accompanies the Trent as it meanders between Nottingham and Newark. A good spot for rest, food and drink. Despite the proximity, perhaps not a good place to take to the river. Mr Farthingworth did inform me of bodies found in the river. This being something in which he seemed to take unfortunate great pleasure. One person's misfortune is entertainment for another.

Sam and Jack had made very much an evening of it. And perhaps out of fear that, under the influence of such a good time, Jack Thomas might have not found a straight route along the river, and could have at any time wandered drunkenly into deeper waters, it was reassuring to hear that he was persuaded to sleep the night at The Blue Bell.

This in itself brought another smile onto the faces of our Mr Kirton and Mr Fathingworth as they anticipated what then was a tale of one man insisting that he could not be parted from his carpet, and the sight, as then told by Sam, of how Jack Thomas had not only got himself up the stairs but the carpet too. Apparently, it was hard to tell at times if Jack Thomas was taking the carpet up the stairs or the carpet was taking Jack Thomas. Sam had not offered to help as he had to admit that he too was very much in the drink and might only have added further chaos to what had already become a situation of farce. He had sat, indeed he had had to move to watch, but he had taken sighting of the ascent of man and carpet whilst drinking a final brandy. It was an image, he said, that had accompanied him on his short journey home.

The next morning both man and carpet were gone. They had gone so quietly and unnoticed that it was as if the whole afternoon and evening before had been no more than a dream, or perhaps the consequence of beer-infused imaginings. The sort of ghost that visits when it knows our senses to be very much off their guard. Jack Thomas, as named, had gone, and so the story ended.

Sam, Mr Kirton and Mr Farthingworth do seem to have found their place with the telling of this tale, bought for the price of several beers and now sold several times over for much more of that very same currency. It has given them a common identity that I have observed all too well as they encourage each other with smiles, taps on the table and the occasional pat on one another's backs.

I inquired of Sam as to whether or not the carpet did get sold. Not in The Blue Bell was the answer. And he was sure that it lay now nowhere in Farndon but further down the river and more likely nearer to Nottingham.

Sam's telling of this story rarely ended, as I am told, without consideration of the risk that had been taken, for had Jack Thomas been caught - and in which case we might have known his real name - then apparently and, according to Mr Farthingworth, who claims to have knowledge of such matters, he could have expected at least several months in the Southwell House of Correction and, more likely, transportation for numerous years.

It intrigues me that despite the offence, the severity of the sentence that could have been given out, and the loss for the poor carpet seller, Jack Thomas has gained some sort of hero status. Then again, it is not unmatched by the regard that also comes to the fore for the storyteller and embellisher of these events. It probably sells a little more beer too.

I leave The Blue Bell and walk alongside the river back to Newark. One thing strikes me, and that is the strength of the man to have made the reverse of this journey carrying twenty-five yards of Wilton carpet. And then to have gone further the next day. And I wonder where now lies that twenty-five yards of Wilton and whose feet are treading on it.

Pining for Fanny

by Abigail Ted

Part I

I N, WHAT WAS otherwise a very unremarkable year, the town of Newark, and its various genteel circles of company, found itself in want of men. 'Want' is perhaps too presumptuous of a word, but it may truthfully be said that the male inhabitants of this pretty town had, all at once, taken up the habit of disappearing. Almost every wife found her husband called away to some other part of the country for business, or recreation, or simply 'attending a matter of great importance'. The sons, the brothers and the lovers had all heard the calling of the Navy or the Army, or some field of study or employment that the town could not satisfy. Tradesmen were in such scarce supply that Mrs Barlow took it upon herself to learn joinery. And on the first Sunday in April, a butcher, a young man come home from the university and the reverend of St Mary's church were the only men to be seen walking out at all.

This lack of men in the town was particularly troublesome to Mrs Singer who kept The Clinton Arms, for she had never in this year many travellers take up lodgings in her establishment, the principal part of her usual customers being of the male variety. Mrs Singer was a virtuous woman of five-and-forty and was apt to be punctilious in matters of propriety. Had she, a year earlier, witnessed a young gentleman named Byron improperly admiring the comely person of her serving girl, she would have told him, in no uncertain terms, that he was not welcome to stay at her inn. But young Byron had not happened into the town a year earlier. The gentleman did not hesitate to show the colour of his money, and the accounts of her business being most fragile, Mrs Singer enrobed Miss Hetty's fine person in an unflattering smock and convinced herself to overlook the man's imprudence. So, in Newark did young Byron stay.

That the women of Newark were much left to the society of only their own sex was not a truth unknown to its newest visitor; rather, it was the very reason for his visit. A good-humoured young fellow, a friend of Byron, had, several weeks before, passed through the historical town briefly, and – finding its prettiest creature abandoned by her usual watchmen – had shortly left on a spontaneous journey to Gretna Green. The giddy prospect of a singularly beautiful and extremely unsuitable wife could not blind this young man to the duty owed to his dearest friend, and as such, he had scribbled a brief note informing Byron of the opportunities to be found in Newark.

For the viewing of the reader, an excerpt of a letter from the above-mentioned gentleman to his friend, Byron, forwarded to The Clinton Arms:

> 'If you have been a good lad and taken up my hint, I hope you will lodge at the establishment of a Mrs Singer (I forget the name of the inn, but it is in the far left corner of the square, depending, I suppose, on which way you stand). I recommend to you this place because I can vouchsafe that under that roof you shall meet with a temptation I was forced reluctantly to resist. There is only one servant

for the guests, but she is uncommonly charming, and whatever drab and ugly clothes the landlady will put upon her, there is no disguising how generously and pleasingly her person has developed. She is often blushing and seems little used to conversing with men. You will, I know, be very pleased with her, and may thank me for directing you thither.'

'Today is the first day since my meeting my little wife that I have not been deep in my cups from breakfast, and I begin to think the wine has convinced my heart into taking a step my mind could not tolerate when sober. I thank God my eyes have not been similarly deceived; she is, in *all* her parts, as perfect as I had first determined (I shall describe them to you when I have the leisure of more time to write a long letter). You know it has been my determination for this year to vex my mother by marrying our name and fortune to some very improper family. In that respect, I cannot be displeased with my choice. Still, I have reasons to be disappointed with my wife.'

'I cannot yet say whether I would advise you to be encouraged or discouraged in taking a wife so far flung below our station in life. I am mostly "*sir*" to her, and she cannot be happy unless she is performing some errand for me; this I like in her very much and not only because it is so improper for a woman of her new wealth. Though, I am becoming quite taxed by finding things for her to do. Last night, I would have put her upon stuffing my pipe, but she told me she did not know how to, and, begging my leave to speak frankly, the pretty little servile thing told me she hated the odour of smoke. I have not picked up my pipe since! But what is this? Have you ever known me to consider the likings or dislikings of any girl AFTER I have been abed with her? By God, Byron, I am sure I never intended to marry a girl whose opinions should be of any concern to me!'

'She has put the servant here entirely out of humour with her, for she is always interrupting even the most menial task to say, "No, indeed, *I* should like to do that for my husband." *My husband!* With what vivacity has she adopted the use of that appellation! You may say *she* is very pleased with the match! And I can see that I have become *too* pleased with her, because I begin to fear what cruel usage she will suffer from my family and all our friends. I wish I had married a girl not half so charming and sweet! I must rely upon it that the better acquainted I become with her person, the less I shall care for her. All women are fated to be unremarkable, given enough time. A few weeks north of the border with this darling girl, and I doubt not, I shall be quite ready to deposit her at home with my mother and no view of returning to either woman but once a year!

Your most etc., Jack B.'

For the viewing of the reader, an excerpt of a letter of reply from young Byron to his friend Jack:

'If you had consulted with me *before* running off, you would not now, Jack, find yourself in this unenviable position. I should have liked better for you than to be married, at the none age of two-and-twenty, to a girl who has mastered the art of simplicity, for you will inevitably fall in love with her, and remain in that awful condition so long as she keeps up the pleasing pretence. There will be, among our own ranks, no hope of being led astray. Even if you find a comparable beauty – and you have told me she is *singular* in the appearance of her person – you will never find a girl able to feign such pleasing manners in amongst our set. The young women of your equal birth are incapable of affecting such simple manners, for they are all brought up to think of nothing but themselves! For your sake, I shall hope your wife is acting a part and grows tired of the pretence quickly. If she is in earnest, and you have married a girl who is in possession of a singular beauty *and* uncommonly pleasing manners, then you have only yourself to blame. Though I shall be sorry to lose a dear friend at such a tender age.'

'Though I did not receive your recommendation till after I had chosen my lodgings here, Providence directed me to the very place in which this pretty Miss Hetty resides! As it is Sunday tomorrow, I had hoped that Miss Hetty would remain here while her gaoleress went to church. No such luck! The blushing beauty told me, in that charming awkward manner that makes her appear like some fairytale creature who has been locked away in a tower all her life, that they *all* go to church together. I told the dear thing that never in my many travels have I missed a Sunday service. Ha! It was quite a strain to prevent a smile from breaking out across my face. She seemed very pleased to hear it, Jack. How might anyone say a lie is a bad thing when it can make a pretty girl so happy? Besides that, it found me an invitation to join the house on their visit to St Mary's in the morning.'

–

'I am returned from church, Jack. I found the experience unbelievably stirring, not least because I had the honour of sitting beside Miss Hetty dressed in her Sunday gown, which afforded me the most spectacular view. That was, till my eyes happened upon another young lady. If you believe you have taken the prettiest girl from this town, let me tell you now, you have been deceived. "Who is that woman in the brown pelisse?" said I to my charming serving wench. Hetty, leaning her parts towards me, whispered that the girl is called Miss Fanny Ridge, and she is running the print shop while her father is gone from town. Rum chance, indeed, Jack!'

***

Part II

Nothing could be more prudent in a respectable lady innkeeper than a hearty disbelief in the honesty of any man and a dominating watch over the virtue of her female servant. Weighed against such qualities, Mrs Singer was the very best of her kind. That her rooms were all pleasant and clean, her meals always hearty and her hearthside forever warm was by the bye when compared with her exemplary record for preventing unChristian happenings occurring under her roof. Indeed, once she had been much pleased with herself for turning a young couple, who purported to have been married five years, away from her inn and into the arms of a cold, winter storm after uncovering their deceitful act by detecting that the two seemed too much pleased with one another to be *really* married. Though she later discovered the couple had been forced to take unhappy shelter in a far bawdier – and therefore unmentionable – inn and that they were known by other persons to be truly married, she could not be displeased with herself. It was better to turn away an honest couple than admit the doers of the devil in her house.

Of course, life in Newark had much changed for Mrs Singer since that happenstance. And what a handsome young devil she housed now! Pecuniary misfortune might have forced her to accept young Byron's custom, but she need not lessen her moral resolve. This matter only increased her niceness in watching over the most important of social punctilios. The weather at that time was not very hot, though neither was it very cold, and pretty Hetty the maid, whose exertions in her toil were productive of much warmth, found her labours and their warming effects ever increased by the growing number of clothes she was forced to wear by her mistress. A line in a letter of Byron's in which he licentiously described the '*frontal development*' of the poor young dear had fallen accidentally across the path of Mrs Singer's eye while she had been in the course of snooping through his writing box during one of the gentleman's many outings to the printing shop. For this young man's crime, the punishment was all Hetty's and she shortly found herself in possession of a large knitted vest that had belonged to the late Mr Singer and which she was required to wear about her person at *all* times.

For the viewing of the reader, an excerpt of a letter from young Byron to his friend Jack:

'Oh, Jack, that you could see a glimpse of my pretty Fanny, you would care nothing for your new, stupid wife. How she works in beauty! Who could have guessed that the most beautiful creature to inhabit this Earth should work in a printing shop? I have passed my whole day staring keenly at this Fanny Ridge. Even now that the dusky hours produce their wicked obstacle in the course of my pursuit, even now that my perfect prospect of her has been stolen by the dark, my heart beats only for the thought of Fanny! Cannot you see by the vigour in my hand how much this angel excites every part of my person, my mind and my soul?! I think I must needs write a poem before my heart collapses under the weight of my affections. Adieu, my friend!'

–

'What have I to tell you, Jack? The pretty bird wants not to be captured. Do not I always say that poetry penned by the hand of a handsome man is to young women as cake is to dogs? They are compelled by their nature to devour it and care never to estimate its quality.

Who is this girl to defy my maxims on women? You will gather that she cared not for my poems. I wrote a dozen, Jack. Last night, my mind had been the most virile tiger, swiping with sharpened claws at the verses of love; each poem more brilliant than the last, and each one for *her*. Tired-eyed, I ventured to her shop this morning with the greatest haste. I had barely slept, for when I eventually took to my bed, my thoughts boiled over with images of Fanny.'

'I entered her shop under the pretension of having come to Newark especially for the purpose of printing my poems. She would have taken my money and the poems to be printed with little more than a glance at them, "I am undecided, madam," said I, throwing a pitiable look across her countertop. "I am not convinced the poems are worthy of printing." The pragmatic little creature told me, as I was burdening the expense of the printing myself, that the only measure of their worthiness must be in my own reckoning of them. I tore at my hair handsomely and affected a manly listlessness to reply, "These words are too much part of my soul, and the beloved object from which they sprang too precious to my heart for me to be any judge of their worthiness. Would not you, madam, read a little of them and give me your opinion? Your eye for good poetry must be, by your work here, rather sharper than most."'

'If I did not love Fanny so well, I would perhaps express some dissatisfaction with the perverseness of her spirit. At first, she would not consent to my plan, and seemed ready to turn me from her shop if I could not decide on printing my poems, for there was, by then, another customer arrived. But I have never been put off my point by the presence of an audience. I threw myself upon her benevolence – I have never, you know, Jack, been afraid of a little begging. "The lady, madam, whose beauty inspired these lines, you must comprehend my mortification if she should judge that their merit falls below the brilliance of my affections for her. Would not you take pity upon the frenzied mind of an ardent lover and give him the honest estimation of your thoughts on these poems?" The pretty thing can indeed be made to yield. I shall remember that, Jack! Miss Ridge took my collection of poems and said she would read over them that evening and that I might return to her the next day to hear her verdict.'

Several days passed before Byron's next lines to Jack. Within the passage of these few days, the gentleman's ideas of Miss Ridge had changed remarkably. No longer was she the delicate, ethereal queen presiding over the dominion of the print shop, but a sarcastic-tempered, tormenting wench who possessed an external beauty far surpassing the merits of her mind. Byron was more intent than ever to carry his point with her. Indeed, he now hoped to break her ill-humoured heart. Fanny was a very pretty young lady, and though her thirty years had not diminished the quality of her person, it had naturally increased her discernment for good poetry and her propensity for speaking honestly. Young Byron's poems were not very bad at all, and had his subject been something milder she might have, in good conscience, recommended he put them to print.

Verses to impress upon the heart of a young lady, though, was an entirely different matter, and she could not satisfy herself with approving any of the poems he had given over, for they all made him appear a little ridiculous. While all this was said with the greatest delicacy within Fanny's power, it did not prevent the young gentleman from becoming instantly and greatly incensed with what he called her 'rejection'. All his previous charms fell off with such a suddenness that it could not but shock dear Fanny. Her fear, though, was quickly abated by that part of her nature that was compelled to mock all rudeness. She withheld not one of the sharp witticisms upon his poems that formed shortly in her mind. What a sweet smile she proffered when she began to pity aloud the poor object of his clumsy lines. If she were ever to learn that her own existence had inspired such mortifying poetry she should heartily regret ever having been born!

In a rage, Byron flew from the shop and returned across the marketplace to Mrs Singer's inn. The devil would take him if he could not make this Fanny Ridge quiver at his poems! Indeed, who was *she* to criticise his verse thus? What could *her* thoughts be to anything, to anybody? He would make her see her error and ensnare her upon lines no lady could resist. Back and forth the gentleman went between the print shop and the inn, each time returning to Miss Ridge with a better, more potent poem. Still, she would not condescend to acknowledge their improvement. Indeed, so vexed was she by his previous rude treatment of her, that she had no intention of ever thinking his poetry good whatever the truth might be. After several, frenzied days of this behaviour, Byron ran, in the silence of the night, across the cobbles to Miss Ridge, knocking upon all her doors and windows till she deigned to stick her pretty head out the upstairs window.

She would not read his poem that moment, but shouted, that 'if the gentleman would kindly leave her to return to her sleep, and push the paper beneath the shop door, she would read it over breakfast and tell him her thoughts to-morrow.'

***

Part III

For the viewing of the reader, an excerpt of a letter from Jack to Byron, forwarded to The Clinton Arms:

'Did you ever venture to Newark? I have heard nothing from you, nor any congratulations upon my marriage to the most amiable girl in the world. I suppose you are piling high your daily scribbles to send me in a thick packet. You ought to have a very diverting tale to share should you expect forgiveness for your incivility. Let this, if nothing else, excite your writing hand: if you do not rescue me soon, Byron, I fear I shall be at risk of becoming happily married, irrevocably.'

For the viewing of the reader, an excerpt of a letter from young Byron to his friend Jack that was added to his already heaped stack of letters to be sent and which would not be sent for several days hence:

'Jack, you may tell the world that I am cured of my obsession with Fanny! After she had so cruelly bid me turn back into that cold air of the night and I had left my poem under her door, I began to feel, on my journey of several dozen yards between the printing shop and the inn, that I was unhooked from her. And, by the time I saw old Singer's face greet me, I was convinced I had not a single passionate thought for Miss Ridge remaining in my entire body. There was something like genius in those last lines I penned. I believe now my poem is too good for her! This night, as I heard the thud of her window closing, the notion began to dawn upon me that she is nothing but a very ordinary sort of girl. By the time I came to my bed, I was quite convinced she was perhaps rather plain. Then became my mind alive to the jewel who had resided under that very roof with me. Dear Hetty, how I had forgotten her! I was determined to make amends for my ignorance.'

'Fixed that I would leave this strange, female town the following day, I could not lose a moment in finding her out, and shortly discovered that the girl had not long gone to her bed. Thither my heart led me, taking steps by their two. There was not a thought of Fanny in my mind, my heart was all for Hetty! I blew out my candle and my hand quaked as it touched the door. What pretty parts must lie behind it, thought I! What parts indeed! And what words can I find to describe what I did find within, for it defied all my excited expectations? I heard the girl, as I thought, breathing quickly and furiously. "It is me, Miss Hetty," said I, "you need not be afraid. I desire only to speak with you a brief moment." Before I could utter another charming word, my ears came under the most violent assault as Mrs Singer, who it seems has been, since my arrival, sleeping in this room with Miss Hetty, began to cry and shout for help.'

'I would fain have fled that instant, but the old wench is of sturdy build and charged at me, knocking me to the floor, all the while crying, "Speak? SPEAK? Fie, sir! I know what you are about in *this* room, and it is not to be speaking with this poor girl!" And so, Jack, my hopes with Miss Hetty were dashed. I remained in the house only till daybreak lest Mrs Singer began another jeremiad against me, and having taken breakfast at another inn, I had only one remaining act of business to perform in this awful town before I could, at last, take my leave of it and its haughty female inhabitants; that was, to retrieve my poem from Miss Ridge.'

'Shortly before eleven o'clock, I ventured towards her printing shop. The vixen had the nerve to smile at me as I entered through the door. "You have hit upon it," said she, pushing my poem across the counter. "Hit at what?" said I. She replied to say that she thought the latest poem, that which I had left under her door, to be *remarkably well formed.* "It is", said she, "really rather good." Well, Jack, I walked coldly towards her and said only, "Yes, I know it is." And then I quit the town forever. If this had all been a jilt for nothing I would think with rage whenever the name "Newark" was spoken within my hearing, but for all her vile coquetry, I can say for Fanny Ridge that she has produced from me a quite excellent poem and for that alone Newark shall possess my affection!'

The Tragic Events in Wilson Street

by Lynn Roulstone

I T WAS A report of the events over Christmas and New Year 1891/92 in an anthology of famous Nottinghamshire mysteries that intrigued me enough to investigate further into the tragedy that occurred in Wilson Street in Newark that festive season. It is not as well-known as other similar cases of poisoning in the 19th century, but you will still find it occasionally in books of famous Victorian crimes.

1891 had been a hard year for the Copley family. At the start of that year they had been living in a large house on London Road, and James, the head of the family, and a successful Newark businessman had still been alive. It was his death in January 1891 that had laid bare just how fragile the foundations of the family's fortunes were.

James had trained as a pharmacist under his uncle in Newark. On his uncle's death he had taken over and expanded the business, diversifying into other areas. He had married his cousin Sarah, who was some years older than him. Gossip in the town was that it was the price he had to pay for inheriting the business. The marriage was not a happy one, and after several years they separated. Sarah and their daughter, also called Sarah, went to live with relations in the Mill Gate area of town, while James remained living over the shop in Barnby Gate.

In 1863 Sarah died and shortly afterwards James remarried. Mary Ann Norwell was the daughter of one of his business partners, and at eighteen, nearly twenty years younger than him. Shortly after the marriage they moved to a house on Balderton Gate and his daughter came to live with them. She was only five years younger than her step-mother, but they seem to have got on well. Children came along: Anthony, Elizabeth, Richard, Catherine and Edward. Sarah also married, a tenant farmer in Sutton on Trent, and had two daughters. The families were close, and visited each other often.

As the years went by James' business interests prospered. He was involved with the Trent Navigation Company and on the board of directors of several prominent Newark firms. In 1880 the family moved to a much larger, new house on London Road. The 1881 census lists the Copleys and their five children, as residents along with a Mrs Margaret Pepper, who is described as a cook. Three maids and a boot boy were also lived in.

Anthony, the eldest, left Thomas Magnus Grammar School at seventeen to train in his father's original chemist shop. The school's records show that he left suddenly before the end of the spring term 1882, eve though he was being tutored for the Oxford Entrance exams. The school's punishment book describes a reprimand and a suspension from the school for a week in the previous term when he was found to have put an emetic obtained from his father's shop in the lunch time drink of one of the other pupils. The financial records for the same period show a substantial donation from his father, and this may have been the reason why he was not expelled at the time. The clue to his leaving the school so suddenly a few months later may lay in the staff records. There seems to have been quite a few members of staff taken ill shortly before Anthony left, including his house master, who had been responsible for investigating the incident the previous term. This is all conjecture, but certainly James made another donation to the school shortly after his son left.

By the time Anthony was in his early twenties James' health was very poor, and Anthony was taking care of much of the day to day managing of the family's business portfolio . It has been suggested by some sources that Anthony was secretly poisoning his father, but I have found no evidence to substantiate this. In fact Anthony seems on the whole to have been a reluctant business partner. There is some evidence of his applying for posts in London and even a suggestion that he considered emigrating to Canada.

What may have changed his mind was his marriage in 1888 to Thecla Jamison. Thecla's father had invested heavily in James's business dealings and this marriage was very much encouraged by both families. The young couple moved to a house on The Park, a few minutes' walk from his parents, who they visited often.

The 1891 census highlights how different things were for the family, and what an effect James' death had had on them. Mary Ann was now living in Wilson Street in a house that had until recently been rented out as part of James' business portfolio. Most of their furniture had been sold to pay their bills and the family was reduced to one servant, the same Margaret Pepper, now listed as a cook/general. Anthony along with his wife and infant daughter Florence, and Edward, a pupil at Thomas Magnus Grammar School, were living there. The house in Park Street had been sold to help pay off his father's debts.

Of the other three children, only Elizabeth who was married to Dr Frederick Marston, doctor to the Newark workhouse, lived in the town. Richard was a medical student in London and Catherine was a pupil/teacher in a school in Lincoln.

By Christmas things seem to have settled somewhat. All the creditors had been paid, and Anthony was making a go of running the pharmacy business. Mary Ann Copley, whose reduction in circumstances must have been a shock, was determined to celebrate Christmas in the way the family always did. Both her daughters and her daughter-in-law advised against it. However, Anthony seems to have been keen for the celebration to go ahead. This is something that would be held against him later.

Eleven people sat down for dinner on that fateful Christmas Day 1891. All the children and the spouses of the eldest two were there. The party was completed by Mary Ann's stepdaughter, now also widowed, and her two children.

The family enjoyed parsnip soup, followed by oysters. The main course was goose with all the trimmings, and the meal ended with plum pudding and custard. There were various drinks on the table, including beer from The Clinton Arms on the Market Square, several bottles of claret and a bottle of port. It was this bottle that was to feature in subsequent investigations. Later in the afternoon, cake and mince pies were on offer. Finally, before those not staying in the house went home there was bread, cheese and ham for those who were still hungry, along with a variety of home-made pickles. This was accompanied by more beer and wine. The food was cooked and served by Mrs Pepper along with a friend of hers, a Mrs Harding, who had agreed to help in return for a dinner.

The party broke up at about ten and the family at Wilson Street retired to bed shortly afterwards. In the early hours of December 26th both Thecla and Mary Ann woke in agony. Richard, helped by his sister Catherine and Mrs Pepper, tended to his mother and sister-in-law. Edward was sent out to knock up the doctor. Anthony had been sent to wake Mrs Pepper, who slept in a room off the kitchen and was somewhat deaf. After that no one was sure of his movements. In his statement Anthony said he did not want to be in the way, so he had stayed downstairs ready to meet the doctor when he arrived.

Edward had no luck raising the Copley's usual doctor, Dr Cardew, who lived at the far end of London Road. He then walked to the workhouse on Bowbridge Road in the hope his brother-in-law was available. By the time he reached there it was gone five in the morning. Marston was reluctant to turn out and it took some persuasion from his wife and brother-in-law to do so. When questioned on this later he said he was paid to care for the inmates of the workhouse and felt his duty lay with them.

Marston headed towards Wilson Street, arriving there shortly after 6am. Edward had been furnished with the names of other doctors and had gone off in the direction of Farndon to try and find one.

When he arrived at Wilson Street, Marston found both women semi-conscious. He assumed it was food poisoning and ordered emetics, though they had both already vomited a lot. At around eight Edward arrived not having been successful in his search for another doctor. Shortly after this the Copley's own doctor appeared. He had been treating Mary Ann for various complaints, and though somewhat bemused by her symptoms he was not altogether surprised by her being so ill. He did not examine Thecla Copley in detail. She was not on his books, and she did not appear to be as gravely ill. He was informed by Marston that she had miscarried, and he assumed her symptoms were due to that cause, rather than anything else.

By midday, both women had, with the aid of large doses of morphia, been made comfortable. Over the next few days Thecla slowly recovered, but Mary Ann did not, and in the early hours of January 1st 1892 she died. The funeral was held a few days later. The death certificate gave the cause of death as heart failure. When questioned at the trial Dr Cardew explained that he had been treating Mrs Copley for that condition, and though no doubt the severe symptoms of what appeared to have been food poisoning might have hastened her end, he saw nothing untoward or suspicious in her illness.

The family seemed to move on from the shock of Mary Ann's death relatively well. Her life had been insured, and the money from that enabled Anthony to make a few improvements to the house. Richard and Catherine returned to their studies. In February, the Marstons moved to Kingston-upon-Thames, London, where Frederick had obtained a post in the workhouse. Edward continued with his studies, and Florence learned to walk and say a few words.

The main change was in Thecla herself. Before the events of Christmas 1891 she had been a fit young woman who was a member of the local tennis club and worked with the Ladies Guild in St Mary Magdalene church. Now she rarely managed to get out of bed for more than a few hours. Anthony and the doctor felt she was depressed over the loss of her baby, and various tonics were prescribed. None appeared to do any good, though she seemed to improve a little when she went to visit her family in Collingham. She said she found the air better there.

Then in May 1892 she was taken ill again. The symptoms were much as before, acute vomiting, stomach pains and severe chills. This time she did not recover, dying two days later.

Unlike the death of her mother-in-law, this death being unexpected, meant an autopsy was ordered. The results were to cause a sensation when it was discovered that there were grains of arsenic in her stomach. What had seemed like a tragedy had suddenly turned into something much more sinister.

The inquest was held at the Clinton Arms. The members of the family in attendance must have been contrasting that occasion with that of a few months previously when beer had been brought there in expectation of a happy Christmas. The place was packed. Inquests were always something of a spectacle, and this an inquest on a young woman from a well-known family promised to be interesting at the very least, and maybe even sensational. It didn't disappoint those looking for drama.

The jury, made up of a selection of local men, heard evidence from several doctors, and members of Thecla's family. Dr Cardew, who had attended Thecla in her last illness was very circumspect in what he said. Reading between the lines he appeared to think that Thecla had committed suicide. A Dr Madeley of Collingham, who had seen her several times while staying with her parents, thought she was in low spirits, and had prescribed several tonics. Anthony said he too had been concerned about his wife. He talked of how she found living in the centre of town too noisy, and of her worries over their daughter. He too had suggested various tonics from his pharmacy. Thecla's parents said their daughter was always much better after she had stayed with them, and thought her 'quite well' when she had returned to Newark after her last stay just ten days before her death. They hinted rather heavily that they thought Anthony was in some way to blame for their daughter's death.

After a lot of deliberation, and direction from the coroner, the jury recorded an open verdict, though they added a caveat that the police should investigate.

The coroner appears to have reluctantly agreed to this and the local police were called in. The case was led by Thomas Treadwell who had recently arrived in Newark as a detective. Treadwell had trained in London, but was originally from Nottingham. At the time detectives were still a relative novelty and his employment was considered quite an innovation for the local force. In discussions with the doctors who had undertaken the autopsy on Thecla Copley it was decided to exhume the body of Mary Ann Copley too. There was an attempt to keep this secret, but it soon became common knowledge and was hinted at in an article in *The Newark Advertiser* in early June.

The results of this autopsy were inconclusive. Arsenic was found, but in small quantities consistent with that found in some of the patent medicines Mrs Copley had been taking for her various ailments.

Treadwell started his investigation by interviewing those who had been at the Christmas dinner. Obviously there were no remains of the meal, but everyone agreed there were no dishes that were only eaten by the two Mrs Copleys. It was a well-known fact in the family that neither woman liked oysters, and would have been unlikely to eat them. Richard did not care for parsnips, and remembered being puzzled that the rest of the party had enjoyed the soup. Mrs Pepper and Mrs Harding had tasted all the dishes that were sent up, and admitted to eating a good deal of the leftovers. Mrs Harding also took some goose and the remains of the vegetables home to her family. Neither woman or the Harding family suffered any ill effects.

The remains of the bottle of port, the only item left from the fateful meal, was taken away for analysis. This bottle was considered important as several people interviewed mentioned that Mary Ann and Thecla Copley were both partial to the drink and had had several glasses. The only other person to have some was Elizabeth, and she had left half her glass as she said she didn't like the taste. The police also took away a variety of medicine bottles, including some patent medicines that were a speciality of the Copley's chemist shop.

Treadwell called on several experts in poisoning to examine the findings of the two autopsies. The consensus appeared to be that foul play was possible but not necessarily likely. It was his interviews with Anthony which made him think there was a case to answer, as he seemed very vague as to what his movements were after his mother and wife became ill, and he of all the people present had the easiest access to arsenic in various forms. The fact that he had taken out life insurance for both women in November 1891 was also seen as suspicious.

On those grounds, with maybe some urging from the Jamiesons, who had influence with senior officers in the force, the case went to trial. From the outset it was obvious the prosecution case that the two women had been murdered was based on very little concrete evidence.

The prosecution based its case on three main pieces of evidence. The first being that Anthony had access to a range of poisons, admitting that he used arsenic in some of the patent medicines he sold in his shop. The second was Anthony's recent insuring of their lives. The third strand, that Thecla's health improved when she stayed with her parents was probably the weakest, and not much was made of it in court, though the Jamiesons often referred to it in their evidence. Finally, there was an overarching theme that Anthony had not acted on the night of the 25th to 26th of December in the way one might expect a concerned husband and son to do. The rumours that he still had money troubles, and the talk of other business men that he was considered reckless, although not admissible as evidence, added to the prosecution's conviction that he was guilty.

All this was circumstantial, and though Anthony could be said to have the means and motives, there was no hard evidence. At times the case appeared to descend into farce. For instance, the bottle of port which the police had hoped might have been laced with arsenic. On questioning the chemist who had undertaken the analysis, he agreed that it had been tampered with. However, it wasn't with arsenic but with water and treacle. There was much laughter in the court at this. When she took the witness stand Mrs Pepper was questioned about this, but strongly denied that she was responsible.

'I've signed the pledge, and don't touch a drop,' was her reply. In her opinion it was 'that Edward, sneaking in my kitchen when I'm busy upstairs, and playing tricks again.' She mentioned several pranks he had played in the past, including putting out a plaster biscuit on a plate being sent up when the vicar called to back up her claims.

The expert doctors called for the defence both thought it unlikely the arsenic found in the bodies of the two unfortunate women would have been enough to kill them. The defence managed to show that the doctor called for the prosecution had little experience and had made an error in his extrapolation of how much arsenic the women could have taken.

The trial lasted four days and the judge's summing up made much of the fact that Anthony, being able to have committed the heinous crime, did not mean that he had done so. The jury spent less than two hours on their deliberations before returning with a verdict of not guilty.

Although he was a free man, Anthony did not find Newark a welcoming place, and shortly afterwards he sold up and emigrated to Australia. His daughter, who had been staying with her grandparents during the trial remained there. Later they changed her name to Jamieson. The other members of the family went their separate ways. Richard had a successful career as a surgeon in London. Elizabeth was widowed shortly after the trial when Frederick was killed in a riding accident in Richmond Park. Later Elizabeth joined an Anglican sisterhood. Catherine became a teacher in a girls' school in Grantham. Edward was sent away to boarding school. On leaving, he joined the army and died of dysentery at the siege of Ladysmith during the Boer War. Sarah and her daughters continued to live in Sutton-on-Trent and both girls married locally. Their descendants still live there. Treadwell remained with the Newark force for several more years before transferring to the Nottingham City force.

Shortly before her death in 1917, Catherine wrote her account of the events. She ended by saying, 'We could no longer be sure of each other. We knew it was unlikely that one of us had killed my mother and sister-in-law deliberately, but the thought that one of us could have done so, even inadvertently, still remained. Our family was broken by what happened that Christmas.'

Was Catherine correct in her assumptions that the deaths were not deliberate, or did the doubts that lingered have any basis in fact? Over the years various suspects have been suggested. An article in *The News of the World* shortly before the First World War was of the opinion Edward was responsible. Although she is not mentioned by name, the information in the piece appears to have come from Mrs Pepper. There is much about his slovenly habits and his love of practical jokes that sound very like her testimony at the trial. In the 1930s some writers from the Detection Club wrote a story that pointed to Frederick Marston. Much of what they wrote was fiction. There are no reports that he returned to Newark after he moved away in February 1892 for instance. There is enough fact mixed in though for some later writers to take the whole story as true and claim he was responsible.

I researched both these claims and found no evidence that either man could have been responsible. Instead, it seemed clear this was probably a tragic accident. However, I decided to trace what happened to Anthony after he emigrated. Others had tried but failed, but I have been able to trace him. He shortened his surname to Cope, and started using his middle name of George. He settled in a suburb of Melbourne and opened a hardware store. He married a second time in 1895 and had two children. In 1920 his second wife died in suspicious circumstances. Police soon ascertained that her breakfast porridge had been laced with weedkiller from Anthony's store, and he was arrested and charged. He died before the case came to trial, and until now no connection has been made between the tragic case in Australia and that which had happened nearly thirty years earlier in Newark.

The Kinema

by Mark Smith

'Killer Ants From Mars'

I SIT HERE IN The Kinema wondering what I might expect to happen. Norman Williams has invited me. That is to say, he had a careful and what I would have to call secretive conversation with me. First, to satisfy himself that I was someone he could rely on to say nothing should such occasion occur where nothing was required to be said. I knew I was being tested. Second, to gauge my interest. There was enough detail for me to surmise this without him giving anything away. And I think there was a third purpose. I have known Norman for the best part of ten years, but I think he had wanted to find something different in me to completely satisfy himself that I should be his companion for this late evening. I have also been introduced to others. He must have had that in mind. I am sitting here with time to think about all this.

The Kinema on Balderton Gate has changed ownership. It is now being run by Newark Cinemas but was previously built by Mrs Emily Bragg. Quite a woman one might say as she has now had the Palace on Appleton Gate built. I saw King Solomon's Mines there. I have only been to The Kinema once before. I know plenty about films and photos and what they are trying to develop and do next. Enough to suggest that it is not too much of a stretch of the imagination to think that one day we might actually get sound with the film rather than through an organist. This place is plush, with tip-up seats and plenty of red. I am wondering why I have not returned. Until now that is. But now I am a guest and one of only seven people here in this room that must be able to seat possibly somewhere near to a thousand people. We are positioned together, a few seats apart, but gathered near the front and in the middle. They are the best seats in the house.

Other than Norman, I know the other five people by introduction only. Gilbert Doncaster seems to be in charge. He welcomed me and then gave a brief introductory speech, befitting someone with authority. His welcome was cautious. It suggested that there was time yet for them, him, to change his mind. There was Stanley Peet, Archie Phipps and Montgomery Dickson. Finally, there had been a scene whereby Mrs Hartlight, arriving after myself, had introduced herself.

The scene had been due to her not being expected. She was the wife of Gerald Hartlight who had, it would seem, recently died. Gerald Hartlight therefore had not been expected at all, but having shared this 'secret' with his wife, she had taken up the option of taking his place. An option she alone had decided existed. And she presented as the type of person who was not going to be told otherwise. It had also seemed to raise a question about my attendance. What we both now knew confirmed that no one was to leave. There were seven of us. I cannot think that six had been any magic number.

An eighth person has now walked in front of the curtains. He has our attention.

'Welcome gentlemen.'

There is a pronounced cough.

'And ladies. Lady, I mean lady.' The man is nervous. He may not have been, but he is now.

'Tonight, I have for you a film that is entitled "Killer Ants From Mars". It may prove a little unsettling.' He clearly has Mrs Hartlight in mind. 'It certainly seems real, and I am to wonder if it is a tale of what is to come or just mere fantasy. I hope we can all enjoy it.'

At which point he disappears. The curtains are drawn back and the film begins to play.

I am stunned by what I see. It is a film. It has sound. This I did not know to be possible. It is in colour. This too I did not believe to be achievable. And it has a quality beyond anything, way beyond anything, I have seen before. It might as well be real. Gilbert is two seats away from me on my right. He looks across at me and smiles. He must have been waiting for this moment. He looks relaxed and ready to settle down and watch. I am not.

I have never seen anything like this before. Of course, I haven't. I want to watch. I want to take it all in. But I am buzzing. The film is about a battle between ants and man. The sound and colour make it too lifelike. I am believing what I see. How else can it be explained? Part of me scans the film for every detail. Another part of me is in shock.

At the end of the showing, everyone gets up and leaves. Norman accompanies me outside.

'What did you think?'

He sees that I cannot find the words. He just smiles. We part without words. I do not have them. He knows this.

'Smiling Jim'

A month later Norman Williams invites me to join him again. We are the same group. They have not met since the last time. Norman has informed me that they meet every month.

I think I know what I am expecting this time, but I am not sure. The last occasion was so unexpected that I must consider all possibilities. And I have not stopped thinking about it. Films in colour, where you can hear everything. That does not leave your head.

Norman has said nothing to me since the last time. I have seen him on a couple of occasions. It is clear we must not discuss this. It did not seem right for me to bring it up. He was not going to mention anything. I respected that. He had already established an expectation that it was a secret matter. I would have thought that films in colour with sound would have been something to shout out to the world about. And here in ordinary old Newark. But it was a secret. That had been agreed. I knew to say nothing.

The same man came out front again and offered a brief introduction. This was a comedy apparently.

I found myself in awe, as before. Once again, the colour and the sound. This served to confirm that the first occasion had not been a dream. But this time I had some sense to follow the story. Smiling Jim lived in some sort of future world where he always seemed to be getting into trouble but then found a way out which was where his smile came in, it would seem. He was a man with his eye on the main chance. He certainly liked talking to women. He wore strange clothes. They all did. I'm not sure I liked him. The colour and sound made him so real. It probably added to my dislike of him.

I now find myself wondering about these worlds I was being shown. Are they films? Are they real? Charlie Chaplin is an actor. You watch him, cane in hand, and you accept that it is entertainment, fun, a false world created just to make us laugh. But what I am watching now, I cannot think to be the same as that. It is too real. I'm not sure I can leave it behind in The Kinema.

'The Babysitter Just Ate My Sister 3'

I have to confess that this was hard to follow. Archie Phipps walked out but then walked back in again. I can't work out how the babysitter would be allowed to keep doing this. And how many sisters are there? It didn't seem to matter. To be honest there were times when I felt ill. Mrs Hartlight, I have to say, seems to be made of stronger stuff. Stanley Peet has whispered to me some disapproval of her. Apparently, Gerald was a gentle soul and knew how to keep his counsel. Mrs Hartlight, according to Stanley, is known for her forthright views and he considers this not to be the sort of place for such countenance. But this has only been a whisper to me and feels like a message that will go no further.

I am not clear what the 3 signified. There weren't three sisters. There weren't three films unless this was just the third film. Not a pleasant thought. But however unpleasant it all was I stayed and watched throughout. There was in me no desire to leave. I had no wish to miss any part. Again, I was mesmerised.

I find it hard to believe that along with the sound and colour, they can be allowing a film like this to be made and shown. Any film like this. I have entered an oh-too-true world that is vivid and real. The world we live in is turning grey whilst this new world is where the colour is. And when the content is as odious as what we have watched this time, then I am fearful for all of us. Once again, I will not sleep and will probably be ill. And despite this, I await next month with barely held-back anticipation.

'There's A Cow At The Bottom Of My Garden'

This film starts by telling us it is starring The Amazing Arthur Ramsbottom. The film, like all the others, is amazing. Arthur Ramsbottom is not. He keeps falling over, in and out of things, through things and ends up running off the screen with his pants on fire. There is no story. I did not find it funny. I cannot recall any of the others laughing like you would if it was Charlie Chaplin. The man was a fool. But what I would give to meet him in that world where there is so much more than anything we have now. If this is the future or what the future might look like, then we need to hurry there. I want to add taste and smell to what I have seen and heard. And to touch a world like that. I find myself detached from this grey world, putting everything on hold, and waiting ever more impatiently for my next encounter.

I have noticed also how we do not communicate with each other. We are an assembled group but lost individually in this world inside The Kinema. Gilbert Doncaster still offers a brief introduction, but we do not listen. The announcer gets our ear as we take from him some sense of what might be about to come upon us. Mrs Hartlight still offers the occasional moment of blunt candour. But it is all lost and forgotten in the stream of colour and sound that penetrates our eyes and ears and reverberates inside our heads. My associates I speak for as I cannot consider that they too do not feel this, as I do.

Recently I have started to have nightmares. And they are in colour. They wake me up. Thankfully, I have no one to disturb. I get up and walk around the room. I don't find it easy to settle again, but eventually I do. Always, the next morning, the dream is still vivid. During the day it fades, but always I am left with a flash of colour. I think it is probably making me quite ill.

'Dans Le Grand Palais'

This film is in French with the words typed underneath which is very clever but equally confusing. You either watch the film or read the words. It seems impossible to be doing both, which you would need to do to follow what is happening. I started trying and failed. I then concentrated on the words, but they made no sense on their own. I finished off just watching and could follow most of what was happening, and what was not clear I soon found I was making up myself. I think Mrs Hartlight can speak French as she was the only person laughing. That said, the experience of watching another film in colour and with sound was no less exhilarating. Nothing quite so upsetting this time. I have to say that the fellow who comes out and introduces the films does not seem to offer anything by way of expectation. I call him fellow which might impart some suggestion of him not being too old but having seen him several times now, albeit briefly, I would have to say that he is probably an older man. Were someone to suggest that he was a few years past sixty years old, I would not disagree.

I now find myself lost in the days between. I cannot wait for the next showing. I would sleep the days away if it got me there quicker. I have no understanding of how these films have come about. I remain amazed that I hear nothing of similar films anywhere else. Anything shown anywhere is in black and white and silent. The Kinema only announces such films on its billing. There is no reference anywhere to what I have been watching. Of course, I keep the secret. I once passed Stanley Peet near the marketplace. He did not acknowledge me. I am sure he saw me. I am sure he knew who I was, but there was no greeting. He walked on, possibly faster than his approach had been. We passed as strangers. To be honest we are all strangers when we meet. Nothing is said each time other than a brief welcome from Gilbert Doncaster and the man whose name I do not know but who introduces each film and then disappears behind the scenes. Norman Williams and I live two lives. We were associates out and about with cheery smiles and conversation but now say little when we meet. Indeed, it would be fair to say we don't meet at all now. We have become distant. I make my own way to The Kinema. It seems to be the only acknowledgement that I am an established and trusted member of the group. Likewise, Mrs Hartlight, who has need to say less now as her presence is substantially unchallenged. It strikes me that I really do know nothing about the other members. And I am calling them members as if we are some sort of club and one that allows ladies to join. Well, one particular lady, at least.

'Space Mountain – The Prequel'

I discover, on this occasion, that the gentleman who brings us these films is called Arnold. Mrs Hartlight is the only one with the audacity to ask. He does not want to answer but this is put on him with great force. He concedes his name. I think Mrs Hartlight has done well to get this as he does not look likely to offer anything else.

Once again it is a film that takes some working out. This must be set in the future and seems to be about the founding of a space society. Beyond that, I am out of my depth. We are not on Earth and probably far away on some planet around a sun, somewhere we do not even know. They are a community and led by a woman. I glanced occasionally across at Mrs Hartlight to see how this went down with her. She gave nothing away. Both Montgomery Dickson and Archie Phipps gave much away when one of the main characters turned out to be coloured. I found this to be unusual. To see a black face giving out orders. Montgomery and Archie were visibly unsettled by this. The utterings of one of them were echoed by the other. It was one of those rare occasions when after the film they walked off together in conversation, and both of them loud enough in their retained protestations to hear their disapproval. Colour film, sound, a woman in a position of power (Mrs Hartlight has perhaps led the way on this) and space travel all seem to have been accepted by them, but not Captain Johnson as a coloured gentleman.

I will not sleep tonight, as usual, due to the wonder of it all. I am a bachelor and have always lived more within my own head than most people, for lack of someone to hold conversation with, but now what is in my head, what has been planted there, is so much more enticing than anything I come upon in the real world. And there it is. I am not sure now what is real and what is not. And in truth, I wish to be in the world I am seeing in these films and not this world. And there lies reason for my struggle to sleep and that work does not reward me anymore. I feel like I am departing, but unable to get to any destination.

'In The Arms Of Dracula'

I arrive now having slept less and feeling nauseous with the waiting. It cannot be said that I sleep much at all. Days of anticipation are the days I live. And I have lost any sense of when night comes and goes. The curtains stay closed. There is no bedtime routine. I do not seek sleep. I wish to sleep, to sleep through to the next time, but this I cannot achieve. And then sleep will catch me and take me wherever I am. But it is never restful. It is fitful. And so, the whole month is just an impatient build-up to the world where I long to be. Not a world I can admit to knowing. Not a world that seems safe. And a world where much is different. But it calls me with each film we see. And it calls me in the dull routine weeks in between.

I am familiar with the writing of Bram Stoker. I am not sure that this film bares any resemblance to the book. But it is as frightening as anything I have seen to date. It is in colour but plays on the darkness of night. There are moments of light, daytime, and the only occasions when I can feel less fearful. But most of the action takes place at night and inside, where nothing can be seen except the horrors of the film. The music too, which seems to be a full orchestra, is there to set you up for each shock. I am not sure how I will ever sleep again. The fear has truly been planted in my head. I cannot see this as any form of entertainment. But then it has never been entertainment for me. It has become so much more. It has changed my life. It brings me extremes. The highs of each world I see and can believe might be there for me. Then the lows of who I am and what I am in this dreary existence I have. I am living at two ends. Or perhaps I am living at one end and dying at the other.

[TYPE FILM TITLE HERE]

And then it all ends. There is no invite. They are not meeting without me. I have worked out when any showing would be, and they do not happen. It appears to have come to an end. I find this hard to accept. The hole it has left is impossible to fill. I have a craving for more of this world. Although it would be more honest to say that I lack the desire to be in the real world which is dull, dull, dull. My head has been filled with so much that is far more enticing. I am not sure I have the will to live if now I must be only a grey man in a grey world. Gilbert, Stanley, Archie, Montgomery and Mrs Hartlight too are not seen, although they were all strangers otherwise to me. But Norman now has become equally distant. I do not see him anymore. We have drifted to the point that I do not know where to find him or how to make contact. It was more an association than a friendship, but now he is a ghost. And so, I have decided to make the simplest of enquiries at The Kinema just to see what is known about these gatherings. It will be a gentle questioning, but it will hold all my hopes for any revivification.

I go to The Kinema. The place stands over me with all that I know it can offer inside. It is a place of miracles to me. It has become my God. In truth, I now pass this frontage many times just to take in its glory and magnificence. It is the route, along Balderton Gate, that I will take from any one place to another just to take in that splendour. I am aware that from the outside it might not seem too special, but I know now what it can hold inside. It is wonderment to me.

And so, I enquire. And nothing is known. No one has any awareness and indeed they state the impossibility of such gatherings taking place. I do not mention the nature of the films. I fear they regard me already with some derision. I am seen as odd and my haggard appearance, as it has now become, cannot lay any denial to this.

There is a young man, I am told, and he knows everything and is seen as some sort of authority on what comes and goes at The Kinema. He has some slight familiarity about him although I have not met him before. Films are a fascination with him. He confirms the lack of activity and is the final diminisher of hope. It is now I realise that he reminds me somewhat of the gentleman who introduces each film. When asked about his father or more likely his grandfather, the former works in a bakery and the latter died the same day he was himself born. Indeed, he was named after him... Arnold.

The Otter

by N.K. Rowe

Phase I – Origin Story

H IS EYES ARE closed, crimson sunlight diffusing through his eyelids while his ears pick up an approaching boat, putt-putting downstream towards Newark. The noise barely disturbs the peace and quiet he has found on the north bank of the Trent, just ten minutes' walk from his flat. Off to his right is Newark Marina, delivering the occasional clank and shout as well as ad hoc river traffic. The subdued white noise of the weir further off to his left masks any other noise from the town. His right arm is behind his head and is starting to get uncomfortable. The fingers of his left hand flex in the long dry grass and pluck at cool stems tethered into the earth. Alex Deering is, for the first time in weeks, totally chilled and relaxed so when he feels a sudden sharp pain in his left hand he is immediately shocked upright with surprise and indignation.

"OwyaBITCH!"

He shakes his hand to lessen the pain and notices a brown furry body accelerating into the water to escape. The side of his hand has a small trickle of blood. He wonders if he's been bitten by a rat. It was a bloody big one, if so. A head pops up from the river, looking back at him and he frowns at his assailant. Looks like an otter.

"You little shit," he tells it. He didn't think they were aggressive but he knows people are killed by cows so why not anything else? They are wild animals after all.

Alex wonders what to do about his hand as it slowly drips blood onto the grass. He should definitely clean the wound but doesn't have any tissue on him. If it was a cat bite or scratch he'd put it in his mouth but he really doesn't fancy the idea of tasting any potential otter spit.

He looks around for inspiration and across the water on the other bank, between the buildings nestling off Mill Gate, he sees a man watching him. The man gives him a cheery wave, slaps his thigh and shakes his head.

"Glad to have entertained you," mutters Alex.

Taking care not to drip blood on his shorts or trainers, he gets onto his feet and briefly considers rinsing his hand in the river. It's cleaner than it was at the height of the industrial revolution but he's heard the stories in the news about sewage being released into rivers and seas and he reckons that otter spit might be the better option.

He plucks a nearby dock leaf and presses it against the wound to stop the dripping and belatedly hopes that it hasn't had a dog piss on it recently.

With a sigh he trudges off towards Mill Lane bridge, back over the river, through the Navigation courtyard and up Pelham Street.

By the time he's on Portland Street his hand is starting to throb and the warmth of the day has made his mouth dry. He passes the Organ Grinder pub and decides that once he's cleaned up his hand and got changed he'll pop back for a couple of drinks.

He turns right as Portland Street forks with Albert Street and crosses over to the black iron gates of Castle Brewery. He rents a flat – probably better described as an apartment – in the old red-brick brewery building. He prefers its towering presence to the smaller grey-stone-faced structure that once housed the offices, although he does like its clock tower topped with a Pickelhaube spire, which is good because he gets such a great view of it from his windows.

He's sweating as he passes through the large red door at the base of the building and although he promised to always take the stairs, this time he relents and takes the lift. It doesn't go all the way to the top and he still has a couple of half-flights to climb before he's at his front door. He fumbles for his keys again and realises he lost his dock leaf at some point. The blood seems to have stopped flowing so that's encouraging.

Alex heads straight to the bathroom and turns on the cold tap, washing his hands and face, slurping at the water to quench his thirst. The warmth of the day is still present in the water, tasting unpleasantly tepid. His head feels out-of-sorts, a confused brain-fog that stops him from thinking straight.

He groans and heads into the open-plan living area, wishing the day was cooler. A cold bottle of Belgian beer from the fridge is welcome relief and after a long swig his shoulders relax. Outside a siren blares, a police car negotiating the Beaumond Cross traffic lights, and Alex flinches as the sound slices into his brain before dopplering away towards Farndon.

Sitting on the settee, facing away from the afternoon sun streaming in through the curtainless windows, he stares blankly at the framed poster he'd hung on the wall. It's the cover of Amazing Fantasy from 1962, introducing the world to Spider-Man. The bookcase next to the poster is crammed with comics and graphic novels – the full set of Neil Gaiman's Sandman and of course many of the American classics from the Seventies onwards. There's also a huge collection of work by Alan Moore, a local hero for Alex as they were both born in Northampton. Alex wonders if it would have been better if he'd stayed there instead of taking the Financial Analyst post with the consultancy in Newark. Maybe he would have got a great job in his home town but after his mum died and he split up with Becca he just needed to get away. It could have been anywhere but fate delivered him to Newark and for the past five years he's been diligently analysing spreadsheets, checking income and expenditure and watching life drift by. And now he's been bitten by a bloody animal with who-knows-what kind of diseases. Thanks, Newark.

He finishes the beer and wonders if a soft drink might have been a better option because his head is banging. He hauls himself up the metal spiral staircase to the mezzanine main bedroom and drops face first onto the bed. Maybe forty winks will help.

***

He's moving through thick fog, so dense he can't see much ahead of him at all. No, not fog, liquid – khaki-coloured water as opaque as soup. Something large and dark darts in front of him and is gone before he can react. His legs try to move him away but they feel stuck in the silt of the river bed. He realises he needs to breathe and thrashes upwards towards a rippling platinum moon...

He's standing in front of a huge monster, its dark brown head lunging forward to strike him, he flings himself aside but the flashing fangs rip into his arm...

He's Peter Parker, staring at a puncture wound in his skin...

He's Bruce Wayne, standing on the roof of Wayne Manor as bats circle in the night...

He's swinging down from the shadows to stop evil-doers from attacking a lone policeman...

***

He's got his head under the shower and he feels like shit, even after a long night's sleep. His left hand looks swollen and the wound has gone purple. He'll have to find a pharmacy open on a Sunday and get something to treat it properly. He gets dressed and after breakfast heads to Boots in the town centre.

"I can't dispense any antibiotics without a prescription," says the pharmacist. "You should get a doctor to look at that, really."

"Yeah, I s'pose."

Alex picks up his antiseptic cream and realises he's forgotten to bring a bag. Again. And he needs to get some provisions from Morrisons.

Ambling back from the supermarket with another Bag for Life full of shopping for one, he's just entered the Market Place when he becomes aware of movement and shouts from ahead. A young man weaves between some empty market stalls and sprints past Alex who turns and watches him run down Church Street before veering right into the churchyard and out of sight.

Another man, older, rounder and out of breath, jogs to a stop beside him.

"Why didn't you stop him?"

"What? Why would... what's he done?"

"Swiped some old dear's purse. If I was ten years younger, I'd've had him." The man sizes Alex up. "*You* could have stopped him."

Alex gestures lamely at his swollen left hand and then his shopping bag in his right.

The man gives a shake of the head and a dismissive tut for good measure as he walks back the way he came.

Alex looks down at his feet because they don't seem to want to move. His heart is now thumping away and a belated adrenaline surge is coursing around his system. He *could* have stopped him. He was *that* close. A step to the side and a simple trip would have been enough. And a full Bag for Life swung in a powerful arc into the thief's head would definitely have concluded matters.

He's breathing heavily through his nose and clenching his jaw. Did anyone else see how useless he'd been? He looks around and finds himself staring at a spray paint artwork on a boarded up former café. It's a stylised version of Newark's coat of arms: a shield supported either side by a couple of brown animals. On the right is a chunky beaver. But the creature on the left is the most bad-ass otter Alex has ever seen – powerful arms and chest narrowing to a slim waist supported by muscular legs. There are claws on its paws, a growl on its face and determination in its eye.

Alex swallows and trudges home. He's still not well; he feels spaced-out and his torso is covered in sweat.

He approaches the Travelodge junction and sees the Castle Brewery clock tower and spire poking above the adjacent Baptist church. As he gets closer his meandering thoughts make new connections and he realises that the neo-Gothic grey building resembles a mini version of Gotham City's Arkham Asylum. The hairs on the back of his neck rise. The massive red-brick Brewhouse building looms into view as he passes through the iron gates: all squares and arches and triangles. At night the whole area looks like it's a scene from Tim Burton's Batman.

All it needs is the caped crusader.

There's a weird fluttering sensation in Alex's stomach that he tries to ignore. He hopes he can get home before he throws up.

***

He's staring at his Spider-Man poster again. In that very first story Peter Parker allows a thief to escape, a thief who would murder his uncle. He wonders what the Newark thief might do next. Alex sips at a glass of water as he confronts what has been swimming around in his head. He could have stopped him. He would do it next time. He could make a difference.

"I just need to get myself back into shape," he mutters, rubbing the antiseptic into his wounded hand. "Get downstairs into the gym, polish up the old Judo moves and we're in business." He hasn't done Judo since he was fifteen but he thinks the muscle memory is still there.

***

Phase II – Apparel Assemble!

Four weeks later and his hand has healed. He's stronger and fitter than he's been in some years and he's joined the local Judo club and is starting to hold his own against some of the younger members who were previously throwing him to the mat with very little effort. Today is a special day because his costume has arrived.

He stands before the mirror in the thin black Lycra top and leggings and realises that Chinese sizes are going to be a problem. The cuffs of both refuse to meet hands and feet. He tries a few exercise moves and when he lifts his arms up he exposes his belly button. And he's going to need to dig out smoother fitting underwear too. His lumpy crotch is embarrassingly noticeable and some experiments with different layouts fail to provide an ideal solution. He wonders if Tom Holland had this issue when filming. But the worst thing is the mask. He plumped for a black Lycra ski mask with three holes for eyes and mouth. He looks like a sex offender on the prowl.

Five weeks and several iterations later, involving numerous internet searches of cosplay suits and Amazon orders, Alex has perfected the look. A correctly-sized Lycra outfit with silicone shoulder, knee, elbow and crotch protectors topped off with a re-worked Lycra and silicone Deadpool mask that now sports an enhanced brow and little round ears. On his feet are high-top Converse All Stars and a utility belt is secured around his waist because superheroes don't tend to do pockets. The belt is black but everything else has been sprayed a dark bronze. The paint has made his Converse laces all crusty so he's had to replace them with black laces from his Adidas trainers. (He will forget about this when he gets ready for a gym session and has to wear the bronzed Converse boots instead, which do not go well with his Royal Blue shorts and pale white legs).

He climbs the metal ladder from the bedroom into the glass cupola that sits atop the Brewhouse building, the pyramidal roof ascending even higher, from which hangs an ornate glass chandelier. The perfect spot for some Batman-esque brooding as the sun sets over the hills beyond Staythorpe Power Station. From here Alex can look down on the roofs of Newark and he has a great view of Beaumond Cross. He can see a couple of lads cat-calling after some girls as they head down Carter Gate for a night out. This is what he should be stopping, or at least monitoring from a closer position.

He's at his front door before he realises that he can't go out in his costume. He's sure Matt, his landlord, said something about 'protected by CCTV' but he wasn't really paying that much attention. There's nothing obvious on the landing outside his door but he can't take any risks bumping into his neighbours. He racks his brain to think what the characters in the comics do. Adam West's Batman had poles to slide down into the Bat Cave, Spider-Man just hops out the window. Alex throws open his wardrobe and examines his options. Ideally, he needs a trench coat that he can stash somewhere. Alex doesn't have a trench coat. He's got a winter parka that he tries on but the bulky coat above his skinny lycra-clad legs mean he looks like some kind of bizarre relation to Sesame Street's Big Bird. He chucks it aside and pulls out an old grey shell suit that he sometimes wears for jogging. The ankle-zips allow quick changes so he rapidly dons his mufti outfit over his costume and pops his mask into his latest Bag for Life.

"Finally," he mutters to himself as he checks he has his keys before locking the front door.

By the time he's on Carter Gate the lads he had spotted from his eyrie have long gone. The grey tones of dusk are now being punctured by streetlights and Alex begins searching for somewhere secluded to change and stash his civvies. He needs somewhere away from the night-time economy and he's just thought of the perfect place. Alex spins on his heel and heads down London Road to the Iceland car park, just behind Castle Brewery.

Checking that no-one is watching, he plunges into the shrubbery between the road and the car park, whips off the shell suit and stuffs it into the bag which he then tucks as far out of sight as possible. Then he remembers that his mask is still in the bag, so has to retrieve it before re-concealing his gear.

He's been waiting for this moment for weeks and had wondered whether he should deliver a corny, semi-ironic declaration, but now he's not so sure. Bugger it, why not, he thinks. He clears his throat.

"Tonight, the streets of Newark are protected by... The Otter!"

He listens to the traffic passing by. He feels a bit of a tit.

He takes a deep breath and crosses the road and heads towards Beaumond Gardens, planning to access the town centre by the stealthiest route, but the gate has been closed. Should he climb over it, thereby managing to step on the wrong side of the law within the first minute of his new life as protector of justice, or should he walk through the Odeon car park?

He walks through the car park.

He keeps as close to the hedge as possible, brushing the bonnets of parked cars. A group of teens are hanging around outside Costa and Domino's and he really, really hopes that they don't see him. He's in luck because they're too busy staring at their phones.

He ninjas along to the library, doing his best to slide into the shadows, until the tree-lined path ends and he is level with the Peugeot dealership. His objective lies down the side of the building: a cut-through to Carter Gate, where he can keep an eye on passing activity without being spotted.

He's only been lurking for a few minutes when he hears someone coming down the path behind him. Alex frantically looks around for somewhere else to hide but there's a gaggle of people in front of him on Carter Gate. He drops his head down to his knees and pushes his shoulder against the wall, pretending to be ill.

"You alright, bud?" asks a male voice.

"Yeah, yeah, just a bad pie, earlier," he replies.

"Bad pint, more like it." There's an accompanying snigger and the pair are past.

Alex glances up at them and sneaks back further down the cut-through and squats behind a parked car. In comics and films the heroes always watch from a higher vantage point. He notices a sturdy-looking drainpipe and reckons he could use it to clamber up to a thin ledge, away from ground-level perspectives. He scuttles over and gives the drainpipe a shake. Satisfied, he grasps it with both hands and places a foot against the wall. Just as he places his second foot on the brickwork the cast-iron pipe comes away from the wall. Alex jumps backwards in alarm, sprawling onto the floor in a heap. Thankfully the pipe is still attached in a few places so he's able to push the pipe back into its fixtures. He gives it a pat and it pops back out again. He sighs and heads back to his squat-station next to the car. Nothing much happens for the next hour and he nods off.

A shout startles him awake and he realises his legs have gone dead. He hauls himself up using the car and staggers about as pins and needles surge through his limbs. He mutters profanities as he gets his legs working again.

The sound of feet running down Carter Gate reminds him of why he's here and he hops gingerly through the arched passageway to peer around the corner and follow the noise up the street. Just lads larking about, from what he can see.

But then one figure, walking past the main group, is pointed at. Shouts and jeers follow and they're crowding their victim. He pushes past and tries to break away from his tormentors but there are too many of them. Alex counts five. He can't take on five of them. He doesn't have any special powers. He doesn't even have any weapons.

But this is what he's here for.

He steps into the centre of Carter Gate, assumes what he believes is a powerful pose (legs astride, shoulders back, chin up) and shouts, as deep as he can manage, "OI!!"

The hubbub twenty metres in front of him quietens.

"Who the f–" begins one of the group and their victim takes the opportunity to sprint away. He pounds past Alex without a glance or word of thanks.

Alex wonders what he should do next.

The youths start to walk towards him. Discretion, he thinks, would definitely be the better part of valour. He gives a cheery wave and then legs it back through the archway. He can hear feet thumping after him but his escape is blocked by a van that is driving slowly towards him, headlights blinding. He staggers against the wall and the drainpipe he semi-vandalised earlier rattles free and drops vertically to the floor beside him. His would-be attackers are now coming through the archway but Alex realises that they will also be blinded by the headlights – and nicely illuminated.

He hefts the iron drainpipe, which is as tall as him, levers it horizontal and rolls it towards the running lads. The first steps over it and closes on Alex, but the second trips and brings down two others following behind.

The first lad reaches for him, such an easy move to deal with. He pivots his hip into his assailant and flips him over and onto the ground; when the youth's back hits the deck there's an audible 'oooofff' and Alex knows he's winded and not an immediate threat. The other three are still scrabbling on all fours while the last has paused and is clearly thinking better of a single-handed glory mission.

Alex takes advantage of this moment of indecision and charges towards him, roaring as loud as he can. The last man standing turns and runs, allowing Alex to power through the three on their knees and turn right into Carter Gate with the intention of looping back around to the library.

Instead, he runs into a couple of yellow fluorescent jackets who have just jogged up to investigate the commotion.

"Woah, woah, there," says one of the police officers, hooking his arm around Alex and arresting his progress.

"What's occurring, then?" says the other, who turns out to be female.

The adrenaline is banging hard through Alex's system and he struggles to form a coherent sentence. "They... ran... chased... there was a lad who... stopped them but..."

"Right, right. And you're on your way to a party or something, are you?" asks the male cop.

"Erm..."

The female cop has checked out the cut-through and sees figures melting away past a van with its headlights on. "Is this your drain pipe, sir?"

"Erm. I... er... no."

The male cop loosens his grip on Alex's arm. "Would you mind taking your mask off, sir?"

"I'd rather not. It's a bit of a faff to get back on properly."

"Can I take your name, then?"

Alex cleared his throat. "It's The Otter."

"Lee Otter?"

"No, 'The' not Lee. I'm 'The Otter'."

The policeman stares at him. "Right you are, sir. Are you in the film industry? Or perhaps got lost on your way to a Comic-Con?"

Alex is a bit surprised that the cop knows about comic conventions.

The female cop walks back to them. "Not thinking about any dubious vigilante behaviour, are we?"

"No, no, just, you know, out for a walk."

"In a costume? At this time of night?"

Alex looks at his watch. It's just gone ten thirty. "God, is that the time?"

There's a shout from outside the pub on the corner with Balderton Gate and the cops turn to see some minor scuffle taking place. Alex takes a step backwards, turns and sprints as fast as he can up Carter Gate towards Beaumond Cross traffic lights.

Jogging round the corner towards Iceland and his stashed shell suit he decides that this is enough for one night, especially his first outing. He stopped one possible mugging, avoided getting the shit kicked out of him and didn't get arrested. Not tremendously heroic but he counts that as a win.

But after scrabbling around in the bushes for a few minutes he concludes that some bugger has stolen his Bag for Life and shell suit. He thanks his earlier decision to keep his keys in his utility belt and he's past caring about being caught on CCTV. He pulls off his mask and trudges over to Castle Brewery's back gate. He needs a few beers & a bit of telly to wind down.

**

Phase III - Endgame

Over the next three weeks Alex makes another seven excursions into Newark town centre and on top of his day job, plus his sessions with the Judo club, he's feeling knackered. Being a local crime-fighter does not come easy and after his initial excursion things had thankfully been pretty quiet: a couple of low-key interventions when some blokes were following a couple of women; a bit of general preventative mooching. Then there had been a nasty car crash near Morrisons; the police and paramedics were already there by the time he arrived but it did make him sign up for a first aid course.

He stares out of the window of his office, wondering if there's anything going on in town and whether The Otter needs to be out and about or have another night off. He definitely needs to wash his suit again because it's starting to whiff around the armpits. And maybe re-spray it because the bronze is coming off. He ponders creating a couple of back-up suits to cover for washes and repairs.

"Wishing it was five o'clock already?" says a voice behind him.

"Hmm? Oh, no, sorry, mate. I was miles away."

His colleague, Chris, perches on the corner of his desk. "Fancy a few beers tonight at the Organ Grinder?"

"Maybe. I dunno."

"You've been very quiet these past weeks. Everything okay?"

Alex shrugs and waves his hands in a vaguely dismissive manner. "Yeah, fine, just, you know, not been in the mood much."

"So you definitely need a quiet session tonight. Just a few, straight after work."

"Yeah, that'd probably be good, actually."

"Cool. I'll see you in a couple of hours."

"Yep. Nice one."

Alex turns his attention back to his spreadsheet and tries to remember what he was doing.

***

They're in a corner of the Organ Grinder, half-way through their second pint, and Alex is enjoying simply relaxing with one of his few mates. They chat about football, office goings-on and the latest Marvel release.

"Oh, yeah, that reminds me, have you heard about Newark's superhero?"

Alex pauses mid-sup. "What?"

"Let's see if I can get the Advertiser site up on my phone. There's an article in there about it." He fiddles with his phone for a minute while Alex wonders what on earth he's going to hear. He hasn't done any interviews with the press and he's generally kept a low profile. Chris smirks and presents his phone. "Yeah, here you go: Otter-Man."

"Otter-Man?" asks Alex, taking the phone and scanning through the article. There's one grainy photo that could be anyone in a dark jumpsuit and balaclava but he knows it's him.

"Yeah, stupid name, isn't it? Maybe he got bitten by a radioactive otter."

"How would an otter get irradiated around here? And besides, why are they calling him Otter-Man?"

"That's what the cops are calling him."

Alex groans but thankfully Chris doesn't notice, he's too busy outlining Otter-Man's special powers. "Probably able to swim really well and hold his breath for ages. What else do otters do?"

"They eat my uncle's bloody fish out his pond, the greedy little beggars," says one of the regulars standing at the bar.

"So they're good at breaking and entering, then?"

"Oh, aye. Can't keep them out once they know there's fish to be had."

Alex is trying to ignore the conversation and read the article. It has quotes from a couple of people who have seen 'Otter-Man' flitting between the shadows of Newark buildings at night. A woman called Chantelle says that she finds it 'a bit creepy' while her friend Dawn thinks it's nice having 'an extra person looking out for ordinary people'.

Chris is still talking to the bloke at the bar and a few others are joining in. "I saw a man get bitten by an otter a few months back," says one, staring at Alex. "He looked just like yer man, although there was a river between us, so I wouldn't like to commit to it in court."

"Sure you did, Galloway. Can't trust anything you say, can we?"

Alex is wondering whether to contact the press to at least make sure they get his name right. Maybe set the record straight that he is on the side of the law. Being a 'vigilante' wasn't technically illegal, but doing any action a vigilante might feasibly do could end up with him being arrested. He passes the phone back to Chris.

"Maybe he's got lots of henchmen," says one man at the bar, "a whole army. A man with that kind of resource."

"What resource?" asks Chris.

"Haven't you heard about the Otter-Man Empire?" There are cheers and groans from those listening. Alex drops his forehead onto the table and closes his eyes.

"I heard he was trying to find his side-kick," says another. "Always out, looking for Beaver." Uproarious laughter and cackles.

"Maybe he's putting together a team, like the Avengers." The man puts on a deep movie trailer voice, "Otter-Man, Badger, Ratty and Mole are... the Super Furry Animals."

Alex gently bangs his head up and down on the table.

"Do you think he has a secret lair underneath Otter Park?"

"I'm sure he means well, but we just can't help to Tarka the piss."

More laughter but also a small voice in the background saying, "I don't get it."

"You 'otter' read more books, then," comes a reply along with a few cheers.

Alex's torment is relieved by the arrival of Chris's sister who has the same tall, rangy profile and mousey-brown hair as her brother, although hers is cut in a neat shoulder-length bob. She's wearing just enough make-up to be noticeable and seems to have expected them to be here. After introducing Jess to Alex, Chris orders another round.

"We were just talking about that Otter-Man character," says Chris to Jess.

"Oh, yeah, I heard about him from dad. Funny, isn't it? He's probably got some kind of issue, a need for positive affirmation or something."

"Can we not," says Alex rubbing his forehead, "talk about The Otter."

"That's not his name," says Chris.

"I'm not talking about it anymore."

"I thought you liked superheroes."

Alex zips his lips.

"No, you're right. We're just here to chill out." He beams at Jess and Alex and takes a mouthful of beer.

"So," says Jess, "Chris says that you're single?"

Chris spurts his beer over his trousers and is reduced to a teary, red-faced coughing mess. Alex is quietly sniggering and trying not to look at either of them or he will be in danger of actually pissing himself.

Chris manages to pull himself together and heads off to the toilets.

Alex looks up at Jess. "Is Chris trying to set us up, then?"

She smiles. "Yeah, he seems to think that the pair of us are miserable and need to get into a steady relationship. I've just got divorced – what I saw in that two-timing knob-head is an absolute mystery to me now – and apparently I'm ready to get back into 'dating', whatever that means these days. I have no idea what you might be looking for..." Her eyes widen, "Oh, God, if you're gay I'm so sorry about my idiot brother."

Alex laughs. "I'm not gay. I'm flattered. And a bit irritated, but that's fine. I'll find a way of getting back at him."

"Good. Chris says you're not originally from around here?"

"No, I grew up in Northampton. Been in Newark about five years now."

"Do you like it?"

"It's all right, I suppose. I've definitely seen worse." He takes another swig of beer. "So what do you do for a living, then?"

Jess brushes her hair behind her ear. "Work in a call centre up on Brunel Drive. Might have to find something that pays better now I'm back to a single income. I'm at my mum and dad's for a bit but I'm nearly thirty; I don't want to feel like I'm seventeen again, needing permission to come and go. And they don't need me moping about the place." She pouts and looks up at Alex with a sudden, shocked expression. "Oh, God. I don't mean to sound like I'm desperate to move in with anyone. I shouldn't have had that double vodka before coming out."

He smiles. "No, you're fine. I know what it's like to feel uprooted."

Chris comes back, trousers soaked. "I'm going to have to head off, my trousers are sticking to my legs and it's gross."

"Take them off, then," says Jess, "no-one will mind."

"I am not taking my trousers off. You two have a lovely evening and I'll catch you later." He winks at them both. "Be good."

Jess rolls her eyes and Alex shakes his head with a grin.

After more drinks and conversation Alex feels his stomach growl. "Hey, I don't suppose you fancy getting a bite to eat?"

"I grabbed a sandwich before coming out so I don't need much, but happy to do whatever."

"There's a Thai place around the corner if that's okay?"

"Sounds lovely."

***

By the time they leave the restaurant they have polished off a bottle of wine and are feeling cosy towards each other. Jess is leaning on his shoulder and he has his arm around her waist.

"Can I get you a taxi?" asks Alex.

"Maybe. Or you could invite me over to yours for a brew first?"

"You're very forward, aren't you?"

"Don't ask, don't get, that's what I say."

He leads her back to Castle Brewery and enjoys her expression as she gawks up at the six-story building. "How did I not know this was here?" she asks.

After taking the lift they puff and haul up the final flight of stairs to his door and he lets her in to probably the most unique living space in the whole town. She gasps as she walks into the main room.

"Bloody hell, Alex! This is amazing! It's like a proper penthouse. The spiral staircase and the beams and railings and stuff!" She looks out of one of the west windows. "Look at the views!"

"Yeah, they're not bad, are they?"

"Is this yours then?"

"I wish. No, renting it from a friend of a friend while he spends a year travelling the world."

She spins around, taking it all in. "Dusting is probably a bit of a pain, though. Why is there an old bike up on that girder?"

"It's Matt's grandad's. It was too much faff to take it down and to be honest it would feel odd now without it. There was a sword thing too but that got put into storage."

Jess strokes the wall next to the window. "And no curtains. I don't think I could live anywhere without curtains."

"Well, we're so high, no-one can see in." He walks over to the kitchen area. "Coffee or tea?"

"Tea, please. Can I use your loo?"

"Of course, it's next to the front door, on the right." He fills the kettle and finds a couple of decent mugs while Jess makes more astonished noises from the bathroom. Alex smiles as he pictures her cooing over the copper bath in the middle of the room, the ornate antique radiator, the baroque mirrors.

He puts the mugs on the coffee table and sits on the settee looking out of the north window towards the red-amber-green glow of the traffic lights of Beaumond Cross. He hears the bathroom door open and Jess's shoes clacking down the wooden corridor.

"It's not a bad bathroom, is it?" he says, turning to look at her.

His face falls and the blood drains away. She's holding his Otter costume. He remembers now that he hung it up in the bathroom with the intention of giving it a quick rinse in the bath.

She takes a deep breath. "Are you Otter-Man?"

"No." He stands up. "I'm *The* Otter." He takes the hanger and slightly whiffy costume out of her hand.

"I think I should go." She looks upset.

"No, please, stay. Let me explain."

"I don't think I want to know." She looks at the poster of Spider-Man. "Why do I always fall for the wrong 'uns?"

He isn't sure whether to step closer to her or sit down. He's still holding his costume which isn't helping. He tosses it over the back of the settee. "Why do you think I'm a 'wrong 'un'?"

"Well it's not bloody normal, is it?"

"What? Trying to help people?"

"Help how? By prancing around like some kind of spandex prima donna?"

"It's not like that."

"Oh, here we go with the 'it's not like that' speech. At least I've only been with you an evening rather than seven bloody years."

"Look, Jess, honestly, I was just trying to stop bad things happening. There was this bloke who had stolen an old woman's purse... and I could have stopped him but I didn't. I wanted to make amends."

"Okay. That might sound reasonable... if you were off your head. You're not on drugs, are you? That'd explain everything."

Alex sighed and sat down. "No, I'm not on drugs. And until tonight I've been keeping the beer count down too."

Jess stands with an arm across her waist and a hand over her mouth while she thinks. "Alright," she says eventually, "tell me what possessed you to act like such a twat."

He smiles and pats the settee. "Sit down and drink your tea, then." He raises his left hand and shows her the faint mark. "It all started when I was bitten by an otter a few months ago."

She sits down and takes his hand. "Seriously? So you have, what, some kind of special otter power or something?"

"Don't be daft. No, I got a bit of an infection and had a temperature for a few days. That's when I failed to stop the thief in town. And there were all these, I don't know, signs that I should do something. So I got into shape, took up Judo again. Got the costume together. I wasn't really sure what I was doing. The first time I went out was pretty intense."

Jess is sipping on her tea, eyes wide. "Go on."

He tells her about stopping a group of lads picking on a lone walker, checking that no-one is being hassled, calling CrimeStoppers about a few drug-deals. "That first time, though, when those five lads ran after me I was absolutely shitting myself."

"It seems to me that there are easier ways of helping people."

"Maybe."

"Look, I get it. You've done what you thought would help and maybe it has. Maybe you *did* stop a mugging or an assault or something. But there are so many other things you could do to make a difference."

"Like what?"

"Well, come down and help me at the local foodbank for a start."

"I suppose."

"Even if it's just sorting out incoming donations, or doing some admin, or whatever. There are people really struggling out there and we all need to pull together."

"Yeah. You're right. And it sounds less exhausting than running around town at night."

Jess nods. A smile creeps across her face. "What if, say, we could get Otter-Man... I mean, The Otter, to do some promo stuff for the foodbank? Help get people to donate? You're a local celebrity now, mate."

Alex takes a deep breath. "Oh, I don't know. I wanted to keep it all, you know, low-key."

"Too late for that now." She places her hand on his thigh. "So, I don't suppose I could get a selfie with The Otter, could I?"

Alex looks at her. "How do you mean?"

She nods over to the costume. "Let's see you in your full regalia."

"What, now?"

"Yes, now."

"It needs a wash."

"I'm not asking you to go out to dinner in it."

He sighs. "Fine, I'll put the damn costume on." He picks it up and pauses. "You're not going to run off are you?"

"No! I really want to see you in it. I'm sorry I reacted the way I did, but it was all so weird and unexpected. I've got used to the idea now. Off you pop."

"Right. Okay then." He goes into the spare room and after a couple of minutes emerges, somewhat bashfully.

Jess stands and stares at him. "Jeez. You look amazing. And those ears are so *cute!*"

He reaches up and feels one of them. He hadn't really thought about it before, he just tried to imitate Batman or Black Panther, but less pointy.

She has her phone out and is walking towards him for a selfie.

"Uh, could we take it somewhere that doesn't show that it's my flat?"

"Where do you suggest?"

He points to the corridor back towards the front door. "That's about the plainest bit."

Jess pouts. "Hmm."

"Or there's the master bedroom. That's quite dark." He points up to the mezzanine.

"Master bedroom, eh? Saucy."

"No, I didn't mean that."

But she's already climbing the spiral staircase. He drops his shoulders and follows her.

"Oh, it's so amazing up here. I *love* the triangular windows."

Alex is busy straightening his duvet and kicking dirty socks under the bed.

Jess turns to stare up the ladder to the cupola. "What's up there?"

"Oh, only a chandelier and some of the best views in town."

"Excellent." She clambers up and as he's about to follow he realises he will be staring straight up her skirt. He coughs, looks away and waits for Jess to get to the top before climbing after her.

"It looks so beautiful from up here," she says as he sits beside her.

He picks up a lighter and ignites a couple of candles.

She stares at the candles, the view, the costumed crime-fighter sitting opposite. "This is so... weird. I feel like I'm in a movie or something."

He grins. "I know. A crazy superhero-rom-com mash-up."

"In Newark."

"Not New Jersey, though."

"No."

He moves over to sit beside her and put his arm around her. She nuzzles his neck.

After a few minutes they climb back down the ladder to the bedroom.

"You're right," she says, "that costume does need a wash."

"Yeah, I'll take it off and slip into something a bit more comfortable on the nose."

"No," says Jess, pulling him to her and throwing him onto the bed. "Leave it on."

What Happened at The Ossington Coffee Palace (in ten & three half chapters)

by Martin Costello

Author's Note & Disclaimer

T HE EDITORS OF this volume have insisted that this essay on the Ossington Coffee Palace comes with a full and frank disclaimer by the author that this is entirely a work of fiction.

"Don't say it is 'based on a true story,'" said one of The Editors, "it doesn't bear the slightest resemblance to any kind of truth."

(I'm not sure if this was a legal consideration, or simply feedback on the quality of the essay.) In any case:

The author certainly agrees that this essay, on what happened at The Ossington, is neither the truth, the whole truth nor nothing but the truth, and further consideration of accuracy is to be found on pages 275 (*Galloway's Temperance*), 284 (*The Way I Walk*) and 302 (*The Pizza Chef*). Since after so much scrupulous research I am reluctant to leave this not insubstantial essay unpublished and idle on my laptop with no other place to go - for where else would it go, but in a collection of stories on the historic buildings of Newark? - I will agree to all demands of The Editors to confirm that the following is merely so much stuff and nonsense; voluntarily, ingenuously and sincerely adding that any similarity to any person living or dead is, inevitably, entirely coincidental.

If there is a further caveat it would just be to note that shop hours in this story are based on a true frustration.

Introduction – *The Ossington Coffee Palace*

Standing on the corner of North Gate and Beastmarket Hill in Newark there surely could have been no finer dole office in all of England. Built by a Victorian aristocrat to counter the degeneracy of the demon drink amongst the poor people of the town and to give working men a more salubrious space for the pursuit of healthy leisure in their time off, when their tiny hovel houses so full of children and women and noise and cooking and laundry afforded no rest for the wicked, it was a striking visual statement at the gateway to the town. A bequest to the people of Newark that they might become more erudite and more at ease, and less drunk, this house of temperance was amply furnished with coffee rooms, billiard rooms, reading rooms, rest rooms, bedrooms and an American bowling alley. Becoming a job centre in later life seems perhaps a natural maturing, or diminishing, of intent to help the poor to help themselves.

So desirable and spacious was the accommodation that the government twice requisitioned it during war time, and twice tried to avoid giving it back. After the first World War it took several years for the trustees of the late Viscountess Ossington, Lady Charlotte Denison, to reacquire the building from the Ministry of Defence who resisted vigorously. Lady Ossington had built the magnificent mock-Tudor coffee palace at her own expense, a whopping £25,000, and made provisions for it to remain in the hands of the people of the town - and to remain free of liquor. After the second World War, the Ministry of Health were even more vigorous in their desire to retain the palatial facility they had used as a wartime telephony centre, and this time succeeded in wresting the building from the trustees. It became a job centre and then a tax office, and later, when they had better options - likely cheaper to maintain - it was sold on to become at various times a fish and chip shop, a cheap hotel, a fun pub and a pizza restaurant. Today, as of writing, it is vacant - not for the first time - though the upper floors are divided now into exclusive and desirable private apartments.

The building has never been a commercial success. This would have been of no surprise to the Viscountess Ossington, who in her original provision stated:

> *A large building, like our tavern and hostelry, cannot be kept without considerable expense, and it is idle to suppose it will be a paying concern in the pecuniary sense of the word.*

When the government - having forced the Ossington out of the hands of the trustees and out of the possession of the town of Newark - had no further use for the building they sold it on to private concerns in the 1980s rather than handing it back to the town. A chequered period of failed commercial ventures, insolvencies, planning disputes, travesties of liquor-fuelled ill-behaviour and intermittent periods of extended unoccupied vacancy have ensued. Lady Charlotte could have told them it wouldn't work - indeed, she fairly did tell them.

Galloway's Temperance –
A Conversation at the Bean & Vine

"Here he is," someone said appreciatively, coming through the shop door.

I was in a Newark café, taking my morning coffee and contemplating the architecture of the square. In particular I was once again considering the conservation of the original sign over the shopfront at 5, Market Place: since moving to the town four years ago, I'd come to very much appreciate the words Pharmaceutical Chemist, gold painted serif carved into a dark wood panel. I liked the font, reminiscent somehow of Stephenson, Blake & Company's *Algerian* typeface though less loathsome - more authentic perhaps - than the inappropriately overused modern Linotype version popularised by Microsoft; and how the current residents of the shop, unrelated to pharmaceuticals - although arguably, perhaps not - had preserved the signage and mounted their own, The Bean & Vine, clearly above it. I thought it indicative of a respect for, perhaps pride in, the typographical heritage of this place. (The Bean & Vine type itself is also nicely rendered in a decorative yet sensitive capitalised serif font, with a modest flourish to the ampersand, apparently cut from a dark steel or tin plate and welded with fair craft into a decorative supporting frame of black-painted rods curved and mounted by bracket to the Georgian building.)

Nursing a full-bodied caffè Americano[1] I was surprised by the appearance of an old acquaintance of many years, the inveterate storyteller and champion liar Galloway, come in to the Bean & Vine to see me. Surprised because, in my experience, he rarely ventured far these days from his stool at the bar of The Local Tap, some miles out of town. He ordered a double espresso and joined me for what turned out to be one of his contemplations on the art of digression.

"How's the writing going," he asked me, "keeping up appearances, I hope?"

"I've not known you to take coffee in the middle of the day," I said, ignoring the quip.

He explained that he was observing a period of temperance for the good of his health, though I rather suspected it was no coincidence him being here now and declaring restraint from the modest delights of the ale, given that I had recently told him I was working on a story about the town's spectacular Victorian coffee house, the Ossington. Of his many delights in passing on false wisdom to the unwary, the opportunity to muddy the waters of historical research was irresistible.

History may be written by the victors, he had once told me, but truth is a contagion spread by bold deceivers. At the time - some years ago - he was trying to convince me of the importance of persevering with his walking tours of old time Newark, when the local Historical Society was battling to have him drummed out of town. A man dressed as a Victorian cutpurse had then just recently attempted to assault him while he decried the famous Newark printer Mr. Ridge - a cutpurse himself of sorts,

---

[1] *Sourced from Nottingham roasters 200° Coffee: their signature espresso blend "Brazilian Love Affair", which the company describe as 'a balanced espresso with a broad appeal, roasted medium dark for a full-bodied flavour with notes of dark chocolate that is bold enough to stand up in milky drinks'. Not that I take milk with my coffee.*

who had villainously profiteered from the success of our local Lord Byron during his lifetime by selling under-the-counter pamphlets of the poet's early observations on the varying degrees of moral lassitude amongst the townswomen of Newark. Galloway was quite sure the contemporary mugger (disguised in vintage attire) was a man of Historical Society connections.

This was at a time when The Ossington Coffee Palace had recently closed as a national training centre for Mr. Haddock[2], the since liquidated chip shop chain. In between a lurid account of the trials and tribulations of riding the cuckstool under the walls of Newark Castle and the legend of Prince Rupert's lion-eating dog Fydoe, on his walking tours Galloway would tell bemused tourists that when the environment agency discovered Mr. Haddock himself was nothing but a bleached and reconstituted brown trout scooped out of the sticky shallows of the Trent, the writing was on the wall for the piscine enterprise which went into financial meltdown soon afterward. The Historical Society had occasionally sent a stooge to dispute Galloway's accounts, but soon took to a persistent letter-writing

---

[2] *When I started my research into the Coffee Palace I was reminded of my one direct experience of the restaurant chain. My former wife, a native of Birkenhead in The Wirral, had introduced me to many local delights of a north west high street during a home-coming visit in our early days together including Stolen From Ivor, pre-nationwide Gregg's Bakery, Sharples News and Mr. Haddock. I recall we had a near silent but vicious disagreement in the chip shop after I had taken offence to someone dribbling their half-masticated chips onto their plate at the next table. It was only a month after my mother had died of pneumonia, at the end of a long battle with Alzheimer's Disease, and I was sensitive to manifestations of the struggles she faced in her terminal decline. Today I have no problem with dribbling or most other symptoms of late-stage dementia, though people rummaging endlessly through handbags whilst hoping for a reminder of what they are actually looking for remains a potent trigger. My wife quickly forgave my temporary intolerance but I don't think we ever went back to Mr. Haddock and eventually we were divorced.*

campaign to the Newark Advertiser from a safe distance instead, when the storyteller began to get violently defensive of his position. 'This is just the way I walk!' would become his trademark retort to any disruptive element on his tours, a precursor to lashing out with his fist.

"So," said Galloway, bringing me back to the present, there in the Bean & Vine, "you are planning, I assume, to write about what happened at The Ossington?"

This was an obvious cue, and I briefly considered how I might skirt around it, preventing my companion from launching into whatever dubious lecture he had prepared for me. I drew a blank.

"Well," I said, "I suppose that depends on what you mean by 'what happened at The Ossington'. I've got to write something, anyway."

"I've a few things in mind," I added, as an afterthought. Of course, he easily ignored this limp defence and proceeded to assist in my research with his - probably - unique grasp of local folklore.

Fugitive Piece – Provisioning at Porter's

Lunchtime was giving way to mid-afternoon when Galloway finished his third short coffee and his long story about a message in a bottle. The staff were eager to clear the tables now, encouraging us to move on. Early-closing Wednesday afternoon, a determination of the Shop Hours Act of 1904 that was repealed everywhere else in 1994, is to this day voluntarily maintained by Newark cafés along with early-closing Mondays, early-closing Tuesdays, Thursdays, Fridays, most Saturdays and definitely Sundays which are late-opening and very-early-closing-indeed. It was time to move.

Even on market days one could at least see the shop sign above Porter's Provisions on the far side of the square from the window seats of The Bean & Vine and on quieter days the red-and-white painted butcher's shop looked a neat compliment to the stripes of the market stall canopies. I was reminded, while Galloway delivered his wild theory on the truth behind what happened at The Ossington, that I needed a resupply of orange tea. It makes a light change from all the heavy coffees I am inclined to consume. After saying my goodbyes to my volunteer research assistant, the brazen meddler, I headed across the square to join the queue at Porter's coffee counter - it's a small shop and there was clearly a bit of a rush on.

"Shouldn't you be at home writing?" someone said behind me. When I turned around there was my friend Linda from The Writers Group.

"Shouldn't you?" I joked, by way of greeting.

"I'm half way between the Green Dragon and the White Horse," she said. I wasn't sure at all if that was code for something.

"Research," she added by way of clarification. Ah yes, the drinking story.

"How many pubs are you writing about?" I asked. While we waited for provisions, we fell to discussing our stories and our progress and the challenges of researching the historic buildings of Newark. I told her that since the building I was writing about was closed to the public, I was having to drink coffee all over town in the name of my studies whilst I contemplated how to accurately represent what happened at The Ossington. Fortunately, as Linda explained to me, having a range of public houses to write about and most of them still in business, she was finding the research perfectly accessible. As I was ordering my orange redbush at the counter, Linda mentioned that it must be a popular day for research as she had not long passed our colleague Sam coming out of the Travelodge hotel and Nick, who was one of the Chief Writers of The Writers Group, on his way to a riverside warehouse to measure how far you would have to fall from the upper floor to the lock below.

"...and here now," she nodded, "is Abigail. Are you researching too?"

Abigail, a prolific member of the Writers Group, was just coming out of Porter's butcher shop next door to the coffee counter with a parcel of fine cuts and a stewing bone. She told us that, as it happened, she was also on the research trail; we took a moment to discuss our stories and our progress and the challenges of researching the historic buildings of Newark. The butcher shop, of course, used to be the premises of Mr. Ridge the Printer, and Abigail was planning to write a story about Fanny.

"Fanny?" I asked.

"Fanny and Bryon," Abigail explained.

"Bryon?" asked Linda.

"Byron," said Abigail, "did I say Bryon?"

"Ah, Byron," said Linda, "maybe I misheard, I thought you said Bryon."

I thought she said Bryon too.

Abigail went on to outline the premise of her story, and we all agreed it sounded quite perfect for The Writers Group next anthology. I briefly wondered how I was going to make my story as interesting as all these brilliant ideas that were floating about, each of which seemed to be better formed and more interesting than my own. Perhaps I needed to spend more time with Galloway, who never doubted himself or his stories.

Linda looked rather distant all of a sudden, and then said, "There's Clair."[3]

We all waved to Clair.

"Well," said Linda, "I better get on. I've got a lot of ground to cover today."

We three agreed that if we were to meet the deadline for this writing project, we should probably all get on, and arranged to meet later for a sharing at the LetsXcape Together Café. I glanced up at Clair and she was still waving. I wondered if she was planning on coming to the meeting too.

---

[3] It took a while for Abigail and I to locate Clair, who was one of the Chief Writers of The Writers Group.
"Where?" I said. Abigail cupped a hand over her eyes, scanning in the direction Linda was looking.
"Up there," said Linda, pointing - and there she was, on top of the church tower, at the base of the spire, a long way up indeed.
"What...?" I wondered.
"She's researching St. Mary Magdalene's for her story, I suppose," said Abigail.
"Up there?" I asked.
Clair began to wave.
"Is she waving?" said Linda.
"I think so," said Abigail.
"Waving, or panicking?" I wondered. She was definitely waving with both arms anyway.
"She told me she doesn't have a head for heights," Linda pointed out.
"Waving, I think," said Abigail, reassuringly, "yes, definitely waving not panicking."
I wasn't so sure. Waving not holding on, I thought.
"It looks like we're all going the extra mile today," said Linda.

Message in a Bottle –
Under the Foundations of the Ossington

When I first undertook to write about the Ossington Coffee Palace, perhaps two things immediately leapt out at me that, in the end, were not the things I have written about here. One, most obviously, was the ghost story. Before I knew anything, before I had read a single line of research, I was to expect the inevitable equation:

historic building + (fiction researcher / coffee) = haunted house

'You know there is a ghost in the cellars there, don't you?'

How do you tell a generous interviewee you don't believe all that mumbo-jumbo without offending them? I will come to that later, on page 293 (*Gin on the Balcony*), precisely three sections from now.

The second teaser that elicited more enthusiasm on my part was the message in a bottle buried by one of the architects of the building. Placed under the foundation stone laid at the commencement of construction of The Ossington, the bottle was reported to have contained a set of freshly minted coins of the realm and a hand-written copy of the speech by the temperance philanthropist Lady Charlotte Denison, commissioner and funder of the Coffee Palace, delivered from the first floor balcony upon the opening of the tavern on 23 November 1882.

Why, in the end, did I reject this potentially rich vein of story when finalising my plans for this essay? My source tells me the message in a bottle no longer exists, and neither does the cash.

"A scurrilous ragamuffin dug up the bottle three weeks later," Galloway had told me, "and spent the proceeds in The Ram."

What about the hand-written speech, I wondered.

"He couldn't read," said Galloway.

The Way I Walk – A Guided Tour of Old-Time Newark

1. INGLEDEW MILL, MILL GATE:

A mechanic of the name Beck was making repairs to Ingledew's windmill, which had been badly neglected for some years - Ingledew being a legendary skinflint and all - and was fixing one of the sails when the faulty brake failed. It being a particularly windy spring day, the sails started up at a fair pace and John Beck was caught by the ankle. Alerted by his yelling, a miller on the premises managed eventually to engage the brake, by which time Beck had performed more than a hundred revolutions of the windmill and complained of headaches and dizziness for the rest of his sorry life.

2. SPECSAVERS, MIDDLE GATE:

On this site once stood Newark's first theatre, operated by the famous Robertson Family who had a monopoly of 'the Lincoln Circuit' of theatres in the region. The Newark branch was not a great success, blighted by a lack of interest in the town, and was eventually lost in the development of the Buttermarket. By coincidence it was in Newark Theatre that the seeds of the demise of the most famous Lincoln - that would be Abraham - were planted, so to speak. Miss Booth of Covent Garden was booked for the theatrical season of 1828 and a few months later she and her husband Junius Brutus emigrated to the United States with their new-born son, John Wilkes Booth, conceived after a performance of The Busy Body in Newark. J. Wilkes Booth grew up and maintained an interest in the family business, creating a major drama when he shot and killed President Lincoln at Ford's Theatre in Washington, DC.

3. QUEENS COURT, off KIRK GATE:

The industrialisation of Newark was no small thing, though small things were often made of it. The watch and clockmaker John Priest made the world's smallest steam engine that weighed half an ounce and was housed inside a walnut shell. The flywheel was three quarters of an inch in diameter and the engine could be kept in motion for several minutes at a time.

4. GOVERNOR'S HOUSE, MARKET SQUARE:

In between being the most important house for the most important person in the town and a Gregg's Bakery, the Governor's House was also The Home of Football, though it gets little credit for being the place where the global sport was invented. This may be because even back then it was still operating as a bakery, producing a large portion of the flour and water footballs that were used for the first ever matches which took place in the Square. Every Hercules Clay Day (March 10th) the bakery helped produce the 3,654 loaves required for extended games between the town's Rowdies and Rogues, and the practice dates back at least fifty years prior to the start of The Football League.

5. No. 5, MOUNT LANE:

At six o'clock one stormy Sunday evening of August 1831 there was a terrible flash that permanently blinded the minister in the pulpit of St. Mary's, accompanied at the instant by a tremendous peal of thunder which shook the church and houses all around. The electric fluid was seen to descend with great velocity and strike the steeple of the church, tearing some of the ornaments off as it descended to the east. It then darted across the churchyard into Mount Lane and entered a house through a door which was open, striking a redolent and ungodly person named Cox (who should've been in church) on the foot, but the force of it being spent, did no damage as it immediately vanished into smoke, leaving a smell of sulphur behind for which Cox sincerely apologised.

6. THE WHEATSHEAF, SLAUGHTERHOUSE LANE:

They always loved their shoes in Newark, once showing their prodigious artistry for the craft by making the largest leather boot in the world at four feet high and six feet long (it was only an ankle boot) which in today's sizes would probably fit a size one hundred and eleven foot. Impressive though it was, there was no buyer for it and records show the left boot was never made. In old-time Newark there was also something of a festival spirit to October, shoe-related, when the Disciples of Crispin came to town for their annual party at The Wheatsheaf, dedicated as they were to the worship of the patron saint of shoemaking.

7. AIR & SPACE INSTITUTE, FRIARY LANE:

Newark has always been at the heart of the space race, ever since Mr. Green the Aeronaut inflated his first balloon at the old gas works nearby and became the first man to fly over the town. The concept of the parachute was also first proposed in Newark when one of Mr. Green the Aeronaut's passengers fell out of his basket at a thousand feet and lived to tell the tale despite severe injury. Mrs. Graham was sustained by a sturdy parasol and several layers of expansive skirts before landing in gardens close to the town centre.

8. ALMS HOUSES, LINCOLN ROAD:

In the listings of proceedings of the town magistrates and the district session courts, inanimate objects and animals deemed responsible for the serious injury or death of a person might be subject to the order of *deo dandum*, that is to say, 'given to God'. For example, a young man died after being run over by his own cart, and since his own incompetence could not be proved in the case, it was declared an accidental death, with a deodand placed upon the specific wheel that crushed his head. Similarly a cat tried for attempted murder of an old widow at the Alms Houses was 'given to God', though whether the outcome was especially pleasing to the cat is not reported.

Downing Tools – A Conversation at The Ram

Speaking of liars:

I took a break from my research to hold a remote-from-work meeting, which is a thing now. Over a much-needed and rather indulgent afternoon cortado[4] at The Ram[5][6], my colleague Tyger Bourne[7] and I were analysing a recent encounter with a bare-faced liar we had not enjoyed so much in the course of a recent working day. Outside of researching historical buildings of the temperance movement, wholly unpaid and therefore more in the realm of 'hobby', as Galloway might dismissively describe my literary pursuits, it is necessary for me to earn an income elsewhere and I am largely occupied by the interminable bureaucracy of the modern secondary education system. Ms.

---

[4] *A Spanish equivalent to the Italian macchiato or French noisette, in which steamed milk is applied to reduce the acidity of the coffee - a welcome smoothing off of the roast after several unadulterated drinks earlier in the day.*

[5] *On Castle Gate, directly opposite the castle itself, The Ram Hotel was frequently cited in contemporaneous local newspaper articles upon commission of The Coffee Palace by Viscountess Ossington as illustrative of the relative iniquities of drink in the town of Newark at the time, a dangerous and rotten tavern at the heart of the ruination of the Victorian working class family. Today you could hardly imagine it - a comfortable and civilised pub-restaurant, the author particularly recommends a light afternoon meal of pole-and-line caught tuna steak with coconut rice and of course their smooth, dark blend Italian coffees (wine is an option of course but it was, after all, a business lunch). Tyger Bourne opted for the risotto con funghi, equally delightful.*

[6] *Public houses do not follow early-closing afternoons, even in Newark.*

[7] *Yes, really. Whether she was christened with it, or whether she chose it to match her fiery mien and combustible personality, I could not say. There was no point asking Tyger Bourne herself, she was another of those unreliable narrators I had a habit of picking up as friends or associates.*

Bourne and I as co-directors of such an establishment had recently not enjoyed an encounter with Mr. Phillips the woodwork teacher. Encounters with Mr. Phillips invariably fall into one of two categories - tedious or exasperating (and sometimes both). As a general rule of thumb all avoidable encounters with Mr. Phillips are rigorously avoided, actual encounters being only the entirely unavoidable. One such encounter was a walk-and-talk in the school gardens, subsequent to a complaint from Miss Gayle, the horticultural teacher.

She had a point. A beloved giant needle palm in the school grounds had been the victim of an inelegant, nay brutal, emasculation - the metre-long leaves of the great bush each severed square across at their widest girth, just beneath where they would taper to a fine, sharp zenith, shortened by half and blunted to impotent flat-ended amputees, poor imitations of their former glory as an array of eye-catching spikes. It was a pointless vandalism: Miss Gayle had cried with the nihilism of it all when she delivered her complaint. (She was also the philosophy cover teacher on standby for the perpetually troubled and often indisposed Mrs. Nallis.)

The evidence against Mr. Phillips was overwhelming, if not conclusive: (i) he often took his most disruptive groups out of the workshop to 'burn off energy' in more useful repair and maintenance activities around the school grounds; (ii) in his brief period as general caretaker he instituted a slash-and-burn policy toward the wilder sections of the gardens for health and safety reasons, proposing to cut down trees to improve line of sight in behaviour management, increasing the application of concrete to as great a surface area as he could reasonably get away with and killing as many insects as possible to prevent bites, stings and flailing panic attacks in lessons; (iii) he didn't like Miss Gayle whom he was fond of dismissing by quoting in two-fingered quotation mark signs and was resentful of for losing garden management to (for reasons see (ii) previous); (iv) he often complained, as a self-proclaimed health and safety expert, that the needle palm was dangerous for over-excited pupils engaged in climbing, leaping and play fighting; and (v) in the lesson before the discovery of egregious pruning he had been seen taking his naughty boys of class 11 to the tool shed before unleashing them in the gardens.

For want of actual video footage the charge could not be upheld without his voluntary admission and on our walk-and-talk with Mr. Phillips, he flatly denied it, felt it unnecessary to speculate on alternative explanations, and - unusually for him, an expansive provider of the minutiae of his fascinating life and thus, a crashing bore - maintained a stoic one-line defence from which he would neither deviate nor expand.

"Well, it wasn't us," he said, "we didn't go near it." He used this line repeatedly to cover the whole of the garden, the tool shed in particular, and the offended needle palm itself. He repeated it until we shook our heads in exasperation and went back to our office to discuss it further without him[8], and then on to The Ram a few days later for more biting reflection over coffee and lunch.

Negotiating the increasingly difficult tightrope of balancing staff satisfaction, productivity and employment law, Tyger Bourne often wished that it was still acceptable to yell at staff to encourage better results and issue disciplinary edicts without conclusive evidence. Common sense, she called it. In the case of

---

[8] *Mr. Phillips excused himself the next day, staying home with a vaguely described and minor-sounding ailment which took eleven months to sufficiently clear in order that he might resume his teaching duties. This put his absence record even below that of Mrs. Nallis and her recurring existential crises. Some staff referred to him as 'a ghost', an epithet we usually reserved for perpetually-absent children.*

Mr. Phillips, I was inclined to agree. I wondered if, in trying to be delicate, we had allowed Mr. Phillips to brush us off too easily. I wondered, as I often did, if we had been working in a more acceptably frank environment - like, say, a building site - whether we might have had a more constructive conversation in which forcefully-made observations on our part might lead to some accommodation of truth.

I recount this here because it does have a bearing on matters of The Ossington folk history:

"Oh, he absolutely wouldn't get away with it there," said Tyger Bourne, referring to our theoretical building site. She went on to describe an incident where a friend of a friend had known of a builder who stole a colleague's angle grinder.

"Absolute flat denial," she said, about the incident when the injured party asked for his grinder back, "bare faced and brazen lying."

Apparently, a round of violence settled the dispute.

"A few of them dragged him off the site," she said, "and dumped him on the road outside. He staggered off, blood all over his face, and never came back. Left all his own gear, refused to come and collect it. Never asked for his pay."

I couldn't see this working on Mr. Phillips without a full employment tribunal and a hefty fine, but Tyger Bourne reflected that summary justice was nonetheless an underrated feature of some nostalgic past she was rather fond of.

"I wonder what he told his friends and family," I said, "about being so roundly spanked."

"He probably lied, of course," said Tyger Bourne, "they always do."

Maybe he told them he saw a ghost, I thought. It was the only acceptable reason, as a burly testosterone-fuelled construction worker, to refuse to go back to pick up your final pay. And maybe, I thought, that was a standard excuse of chastised builders everywhere, a guild secret passed from generation to generation. "I'm never going back there, it's bloody terrifying."

Gin on the Balcony – A Look Inside The Ossington

Rita the truck driver had invited me up to take a look around her apartment at The Ossington. She'd already told me about the hauntings and the cold corners and the 'strange goings-on in the middle of the night' earlier that summer at the Newark Book Festival. I wasn't much interested in the superstitious or the irrational but I didn't tell Rita that because I wanted to go upstairs. That is to say, to the assembly room (also referred to - without any historical accuracy that I could validate - as 'the old ballroom') to get a bit of a feel for the setting. I wanted to understand how what happened at The Ossington could have happened at all, and where, and if not why then certainly how and under what circumstances. I brought her a bottle of expensive-looking gin.

Though the recent history of The Ossington is a rather turbulent matter of one financial ruin after another, the fabric of the building at least has come out with some net gain since being released from government oversight: the shoddy office partitioning and false ceilings have given way to elegant restorations, particularly upstairs where dark oak panelled walls and the full glory of the sculpted cornices and plaster of Paris ceiling roses give Rita's spacious apartment an authentic Victorian luxury we agreed could not be found further south for anyone but the gilded millionaire. Despite the palatial space - I could see why you would call it an old ballroom - and the sensitively integrated open plan contemporary kitchen, the neat bathroom and elegant Country Homes feature bedroom (though surprisingly not with four-poster period bed) what drew most of my attention was the large canvas, three quarters worked in oils in a lush contemporary abstract style which I now recall as mostly lemons, browns and oranges with deft touches in the green spectrum, proud on its easel at the centre of the open room and surrounded by a clutter of jars and bottles, paints and brushes, palettes and palette knives.

I no more knew that Rita was a painter than I did she was a truck driver, before I came upstairs. The painting was astonishing. Rita was thoroughly modest about the whole thing and distracted me with a glass of gin from the bottle I had brought, spoke briefly about her career as an artist and using the apartment as the perfect inspiration for a new series of works, and then changed the subject abruptly as soon as she could.

"You know there is a ghost in the cellars here, don't you?"

We had moved to the balcony overlooking the gardens and the river, where Lady Charlotte herself bestowed the Ossington upon the deserving poor with her speech that they might be happier in their lives, and I turned the conversation back toward the quality of the light by remarking on the sunsets over Tolney Lane encampment, such a scenic setting for the painterly type. I knew a thing or two about that after all, living as I did on the riverside myself just up past the castle. We went inside for another gin, and I hoped not to have to discuss the ghosts of aristocrats past.

"The reason I got in touch with The Writers Group," explained Rita, "was because I want to write a book about what I've done for the last twenty years. People often remark, 'you should write a book', and now I'm here, in this place, I think I will. I just need a bit of help with formatting."

"A book about painting?" - I wondered.

"About my truck," she clarified. This was when I learned Rita was also a famous truck driver.

"You can look me up on the internet," she said, probably because I looked like I might not believe her[9]. She told me all

---

[9] I did believe her but nevertheless did look her up later that evening, and everything was entirely as she said it was.

about her extraordinary adventures, and her famous truck which was now parked in storage down in Carcassonne. We had another gin each and then she told me it was about time for her to be getting on, and therefore it was time for me to go. But she had arranged for an introduction to Jeb, she said, who was her neighbour, and who had an encyclopaedic knowledge of The Ossington.

We knocked on at Jeb's place next door, in what had apparently been 'the other half' of the ballroom. After a long delay, the door opened to an old fellow in a white vest, sliders and lounge pants. He already had two steaming mugs of coffee prepared, though Rita announced she needed to get on and would leave me to it. Jeb was clearly a famous rock and roller of a bygone age who probably toured with a young Dylan before anyone had even heard of him. His long white hair, generous jewellery and the American accent were patent giveaways. I immediately surmised he had retired on modest royalties to lead as close to English Manor House retirement as he could afford. I was quite certain he would have spent the last twenty years accumulating all the key details on what happened at The Ossington at a depth to which I could not hope to do justice.

"You know there is a ghost in the cellars here, right?"

As it happened, Jeb was unable to fill in as many details as I might have hoped but he did give me a guided tour of cold spots in his apartment while I nursed the instant coffee he had kindly furnished. That was boiling hot. He hadn't seen the ghost himself, he told me, but his wife had definitely felt a black mood in the kitchen from time to time, and Little Jeb, a Parson's Terrier who elected not to move from the couch during my tour of the apartment, was highly sensitive to the spirits.

Did Little Jeb look traumatised by hauntings? It was difficult for me to judge, even though I consider myself as having a good understanding of canine body language. He certainly looked a little nervous, or sad maybe.

"One builder downed his tools," said Jeb[10], "walked off site, and never came back."

---

[10] *I often walk by the apartments at The Ossington now and notice on these short winter days that the upper floors remain forever in darkness as if no-one lives there, and Rita has not yet come to The Writers Group as she promised she would. It leads me wonder, did I imagine visiting The Ossington during some autumnal delusion? Have I invented the famous painting truck driver? What if Jeb doesn't really exist? Or Little Jeb for that matter, sitting there, unwilling to dismount the furniture for fear of the Devil knows what? Are they all ghosts? I wonder, sometimes, do I have another story here? Usually, I make a small shuddering motion when I think of it and then banish such nonsense from my mind. Stick to writing about what actually happened at The Ossington, I scornfully remind myself.*

(

Greek Coffee –
An Introduction at The Newark Book Festival

"You know there is a ghost in the cellars there, don't you?"

I first met Rita Hopkirk, the famous Saharan truck driver, at the Newark Book Festival one blazingly hot July afternoon last year.

"I live in the old ballroom at the Ossington," she had told me after introductions.

I was working The Writers Group stall in the Market Square at the time, playing my part in the rotation of members who were there to promote the group, sell our books, contribute to the success of the Book Festival, and do better than the rival writers groups from East Leake and Leicester by selling more books and signing up more members than they did. For my shift at the stall I had been paired with Sam, and as we were both new writers to the group we were a little bit nervous about being put in charge of the stall and the float. It seemed like an awful lot of responsibility for beginners, even if one of the Chief Writers had promised to look in on us frequently (probably to make sure we hadn't somehow accidentally set light to the canopy or grossly offended the Lord Mayor or Duke and Duchess of Newcastle or other dignitaries on their rounds), and the second Chief Writer had given us a demonstration on how to manage the float and how to attract new members to the group with cunning sales patter.

"I usually begin with the line, 'Are you a writer yourself?'" explained Chief Writer Nick, adding further techniques and lines depending on the forks in the conversation, like when a potential customer simply backs away muttering 'just looking' and you have to be extra sharp to reel them in. I first met Chief Writer Nick at the previous year's Book Festival, and I saw this time around, from the other side of the stall, precisely how I'd ended up in The Writers Group myself.

"Are you a writer yourself?" asked my colleague Sam, to the first person who came along that morning. She was a natural. What followed was a lengthy conversation with some hearty laughter that concluded with the sale of two anthologies of work by The Writers Group and an agreeable addition to the float. We decided on the balance of play that she would be the talker and I would handle counting out the change, propping up books that fell down in the wind, and pointing vaguely at anthologies in reference to whatever Sam happened to be telling passers-by at the time. Occasionally I would say 'hello' but I knew in my heart that I was not delivering with her easy aplomb, so I let the arrangement stand and she did most of the voice work. I knew that inevitably Sam would need a break from all the talking at some point though, and I would have to step up. Sure enough, she had just gone to pick up some takeaway coffees from the Green Olive when a glamorously bohemian older woman came to the stall and I was forced to begin a conversation without Sam's more capable assistance.

"Are you interested in writing?" I said, bungling the first line. It was a book festival. Of course she was.

I recovered sufficiently to outline the goings on of The Writers Group and some of the books we had produced over the years. In order to encourage her to sign up I also mentioned that we were presently engaged in the writing of a new collection on the historic buildings of Newark.

"I live in an historic building here myself," she told me, going on to explain that she lived in the precise same building I was researching at the time - the Ossington Coffee Palace.

"What a coincidence!" I said, with my first enthusiasm of the day.

(Was it obvious, in hindsight, that Rita was a famous truck driver and an astounding painter? Perhaps I could be forgiven for not guessing about the heavy goods vehicle. But certainly, she was a person of creative character who took an immediate interest in The Writers Group stall, and it was easy for me to assume she had remarkable powers, probably in the direction of the written word which would be well suited to our fortnightly meetings and the readings at Anthony's café. There was certainly a part of me that was calculating my increased standing with the Chief Writers for bringing such a talent on board, but mostly I was excited to catch a break in my research on what happened at The Ossington, almost from the source, one degree removed. She was immediately generous in offering to help me.)

"I could tell you a thing or two about that place," Rita said, and I picked up my pad and pen to begin some solid note-taking on the subject.

"One builder downed his tools, walked off site, and never came back. Never even collected his wages."

)

Viva Java - Leisure Time at Letsxcape Together Café

I took a break from my research to meet my friend Anthony for a cup of coffee and a game of dice at the LetsXcape Together Café in the Buttermarket. As proprietor, his shop hours are as playful as the theme of his establishment and one never knows quite when to catch him open: he is the platform nine-and-three-quarters of the Market Square, but he defies the town's early-closing afternoons for that rare and precious thing - a coffee after dark[11].

---

[11] *Opening both onto the Market Square and into the atmospheric colonnades under the Town Hall, the café is a cornerstone of the vibrant revival of the historic Buttermarket, a Victorian covered arcade instigated by the town's Urban Sanitary Authority in the 1880s when the former shutts and shambles of the butcher's market became unpalatable to the town's gentleman-councillors in the upper halls during long hot summers, and untenable under the growing understanding of environmental health. It really did stink, by all accounts.*

Despite the impressive arcadian renovations of the time, indicative of the optimism of Victorian market capitalists everywhere and the Newark trading families in particular, the Buttermarket has been thralled to cycles of decline and rejuvenation right through to the present moment and the latest refurbishment - of the mezzanine - in the 2020s. Removing two rows of empty boutique shops in favour of a more open space operated by the county library service toward adult education, it seems - for the time being at least - that the ambitions Viscountess Ossington held for the people of Newark are still alive and actively observed a few hundred metres up the road from her coffee tavern.

I wonder if Anthony's café also fulfils a role Lady Charlotte would have approved of and was in part a precursor to - after all, The Ossington boasted an 'American bowling alley', the first of its kind in the town, and surely the working men of Newark, too poor and too busy or too drunk to otherwise have time for board games, would have been catered for at the sober facility with games of Draughts, Chess, Merels, Hoppity, Taffle, Backgammon and of course Snakes & Ladders as diversionary and developmental activities - the Victorians, after all, loved their board games. (Dice and

Naturally Anthony thrashed me at several quick games including a hand of Viva Java, but a punchy ristretto and a large helping of tap water washed the dizzying effects of the gin away, and before long I was restored and ready for dinner.

---

cards on the other hand, associated with vice and gambling, would certainly not have been available as magistrates listings of the time often featured convictions for both publicans and players leading to fines, closures, and possibly a session in the stocks for recidivist gamblers.) Anthony carries an enormous quantity of board games, card games, dice games, tabletop war games and even vintage video console games of which he is ever happy as custodian to introduce you to and thrash you at over a delightful Stokes of Lincoln-blended americano. The LetsXcape Together Café is Newark's first board game café in an age when such games might be seen in relief to the demon internet and all its unregulated and solitary vices.

Not particularly acquainted with this modern cultural phenomenon, I came to know the café and Anthony because the Writers Group hold their monthly socials there on a certain regular evening - of which you can get full details if you subscribe to the group's newsletter or tap up the Chief Writers. Other groups taking advantage of the space for meetings and activities include the Still Life Drawing Group, the Radio Club, the War Gamers Group, the Future Technology War Gamers Group, the Fantasy War Gamers Group, The Life Drawing Class, The Painters Group (Watercolours and Pastels Division), The Historical Society Civil War Re-Enactment Committee and a Gala of Steam Punks. As a poet, I have been discussing founding a Poetry Group there with Anthony but so far have not been able to overcome my personal dislike of poetry or indeed most poets. Rhyming couplets and navel-gazing notwithstanding, the Viscountess would surely be delighted with the cultural engagement fostered by Anthony and his wonderful team of barista hosts at the LetsXcape Together Café, though what she would make of the Life Drawing Class (or the Steam Punks, for that matter) is anyone's guess.

It was through our meetings of The Writers Group that I also discovered more or less the only opportunity for a coffee in town after Early Closing Weekdays and Weekends. To give my frequent visits to 'the Escape' some semblance of legitimacy during this time of research, I often played Viva Java, a dice and card strategy game in which players attempt to become head of a commercial coffee empire. It is tremendous fun and Anthony is very good at it.

The Pizza Chef – An Italian Thin-Crust Sourdough Recipe

This is a section of the story in which I have failed to source adequate information and so must leave unwritten.

To explain: I wrote to The Zizzi Corporation with a friendly request for some commentary about their time as tenants in the Ossington Coffee Palace, but my email was ignored. Or feasibly my email remains low in a pile of emails forwarded to the company historian, who is a long way from reading it because she has been inundated with requests for information and is struggling to keep on top of demand, especially since she might have only recently returned from a bout of sick leave on account of her condition - her legs perhaps, or her digestion, or her kidneys, or her inner ear and her balance, or her joints: all things which at times have bothered me and cause me to have the utmost sympathy for her, if that is the case. Maybe she'll get round to answering me one day, when it is too late and this essay about what happened at The Ossington is already published and probably lacking a critical detail which she may have furnished, if it weren't for her legs.

As I told my friend Galloway, I had hoped the corporation might've put me in touch with a Zizzi Chef, an eye-witness of sorts who could've told me all about the kitchen and the staff and the customers and the coffee-making appliances they utilised for the restaurant.

"By coincidence," said Galloway, "I do happen to know of a former junior chef who worked down there, had a lot of trouble with Wednesdays."

He was fired, Galloway told me, because he kept missing his midweek shifts on account of coming to believe that Wednesdays were not real. Galloway offered to put us in touch, as soon as he could recall his details. I didn't press him on the matter as it sounded familiar, like a story he had once told me in The Local Tap some miles out of town about an Icelandic fisherman who developed an intolerance of afternoons and began to fear his days were foreshortening. Sensing my reluctance, Galloway came up with a better solution.

"A recipe in the middle of a story sounds like an interesting digression," he said, adding "being only a junior chef he probably wouldn't have had much to say anyway."

I wrote to The Zizzi Corporation with a friendly request for a pizza recipe, but my email was ignored again so here is one of my own:

THE COSTELLO SAUCE SOURDOUGH

Add half a cup of water to half a cup of flour, make sure the water is unchlorinated, stir gently and leave with an air-breathing cap like a coffee filter for one day in a warm place. First thing next morning, add a tablespoon of flour and a tablespoon of water to the mix - this is called feeding. Feed by the same amount four or five times on the first day. Stir well each time. Next day, add about half a cup of each, flour and water, two or three times. Feed two tablespoons of each for the next seven days. When it shows bubbles it is active; remove or gently stir in any liquid gathering on the top. Place a clean cheesecloth over the jar and refrigerate, feed once a month by removing from fridge and placing a tablespoon of flour and one of water twice over the course of the day, and then refrigerate again. Continue to feed monthly for a minimum of two years, and then activate for baking:

Remove from refrigerator and feed, two or three times a day over the next 48 hours. The last feed should be bedtime before kneading day. On kneading day, mix one and a half cups of unbleached flour with a teaspoon of salt. Add one and a half cups of the sourdough (now properly called the sourdough starter) and four tablespoons of olive oil and form into a doughy ball. Knead until soft and drizzle with oil, leave to rest for eight hours, then refrigerate for three days. Make authentic Costello Sauce using sun-dried tomatoes, tomato purée, chopped basil and garlic, one red chilli, a little garlic butter (melted) a dob of black olive pesto and a generous smattering of Henderson's Yorkshire Relish. Grease a pie pan with olive oil and gently flatten out the dough into a thin layer. Apply the Costello Sauce, add thin slices of Welsh goat's cream cheese finished in rosary ash, and cook in a hot oven for 9 minutes. Serve with olives, still water and a double espresso, dark Italian roast.

Later as an afterthought I wrote to The Zizzi Corporation again, requesting information on their procurement policy and specifically where they got their coffee from. I thought it was the least they could do to help, although I didn't say as much for fear of offending or being ignored or filed as junk or labelled as a spammer or an idiot. But as it happened my email was ignored anyway. Or feasibly my email remains low in a pile of emails forwarded to the company coffee buyer, who is a long way from reading it because she always has more important emails to deal with first.

Flat White - A Conversation at The Prince Rupert

I took a break from my research to meet my friend Ade for dinner at The Prince Rupert, where we had a catch up on the progress of our different writing projects.

A favourite on the Civil War History Trail for its apparent connection to the prince who came to the relief of the town during a parliamentarian siege of 1644, the original Tudor building on Stodman Street has been expertly restored to preserve one of the oldest buildings in the town and make it a much appreciated venue for a substantial and high quality English roast dinner. We both went for the pork plate. For all the original wooden beams and sensitive plastering to open up two floors of hostelry, and a delicious apple sauce, what pleases me the most on my visits here is the array of nineteenth and twentieth century signage liberally hung on the lower floor walls to present a fabulous exploration of advertising design for butchers, brewers and cigarette makers and the rich adventure through typography that goes with it.

As always the pork was delicious, and well-fortified by a glass of Chilean Malbec.

I first met Ade at The Writers Group. We'd both joined at a similar time and for similar reasons - somewhere to go where we could talk about our unfinished novels and perhaps get them kick-started again. We found mutual interests in the literature of the American wild west, in air shows and air fields, war planes, The War, stories about The War, nostalgia for a boyhood as the children of people who had lived through The War, the trials and tribulations of our grown-up sons, the variable joys of mediocre football and the constant joy of Malbecs, The Beiderbecke television trilogy, pub quizzes, radio drama, vintage comic books about The War, metal detectors, the villages of

Elton, Shelton, Orston, Syerston, Car Colston and countryside surrounding, the experience of divorce, fragments of industrial machines, coffee, antiques and in particular small and useless artefacts, Putin's War, second-hand books, old maps and diagrams, living in Lewisham in the early Nineties, pub lunches, pub decor, pubs in general and writing. In the short time that I have known him The Writers Group seems to have assisted Ade in finding the spark for his novel, which he reports to be blossoming under the pen. (The Writers Group has assisted me too, in eventually accepting that I had actually abandoned my novel twenty years ago and just hadn't admitted it to myself yet. I have spent the intervening years talking about it with friends or acquaintances over coffee without getting a single word down on the page. Thanks to the generous support of The Writers Group, I have officially given up now.)

After a pleasant meal, I ordered a filter coffee. I'm not sure why.

Ade requested a flat white. The waitress frowned and tried out the sound of it. "A flat white," she ruminated, "flat white". She told us she'd have to check with the kitchen "if they have any of that", and ambled off. I thought she seemed rather irritated with Ade.

While she was gone finding out, Ade told me about The Committee of Adjustment, and his search for a suitable building that may have housed them - for his story of the same name (see page 27). Thinking about what happened at The Ossington, I wondered if the Committee could've operated there when the government adjusted its purpose, since it had been requisitioned for a war effort which did not, apparently, include sitting about drinking coffee whilst listening to lectures by academics, auto-didacts, polemicists, tautologists and the anti-vaccination movement[12]. I thought the whole concept of the Committee was a brilliant foundation for a story, and found myself suddenly quite anxious about my own research, and where it might take me, and just how interesting I could make the temperance movement for a general audience. I was experiencing a sort of writers envy for Ade's good idea but also a nagging insecurity. Galloway loomed large in my imagination just then, and I thought about making the whole thing up, based on one of his many erroneous conceits.

The waitress came back with my coffee.

"We don't do them flat whites," she told Ade, brusquely, again giving off an air of having been offended by the request, "that's a MacDonald's thing apparently - you'll have to go there for one of them.

"I can do you some normal coffee with milk," she said.

Ade had some normal coffee with milk.

---

[12] *The records at the town library show a busy schedule of lectures for many years at the Coffee Palace, something which would no doubt have delighted Lady Charlotte, who died in 1889 only six years after the completion of her 'tavern', as she called it. Listings for the early lecture series include a diverse range of subjects across the sciences, arts, history, philosophy and politics such as would delight even a modern audience had the Coffee Palace remained in the possession of the town, including the relief of women from domestic coercion and violence, the almost limitless potential for hemp farming, and the dangers of vaccination. In this particular field, there seems to have been an ongoing rivalry for several years between two camps - The Anti Vaccination League held their first lecture there within a year of the Coffee Palace opening, and sound like the more hard-line of the rivals supporting a dogmatic and blanket disapproval of this most modern of medical applications, whilst the Society Against Compulsory Vaccination were apparently not wholly opposed to the needle, but just didn't like being pushed around.*
When I described detailed plans for this essay over refreshments at Stray's Café on Middle Gate with my partner, who is neuro-atypically direct, she sipped her mochaccino thoughtfully and said, "it sounds really... boring."

A Thing That Happened Near Here -
A Reading at Letsxcape Together Café

"He never ever came back, not even to collect his wages... and now the fates had caught up with The Lady, and here she was," read Rita from her handwritten paper, dramatically, "in the cellar under the kitchen, in the haunting company of her painted likeness, looking down austerely from the wall. It was a moment when all the shifting sands of her life (and death) were washed smooth by the ebb and flow of time. It was the crux, the culmination, the final whelm of the tide."

After dinner, Ade and I had dropped in on The Writers Group social meeting back at 'the Escape'. The dozen or so listeners around the table at the workshop applauded politely and nodded appreciatively at Rita's haunting recital. She folded her paper and slipped it between the pages of a notebook.

"Well," said Nick, breaking a contemplative silence, "we liked that, didn't we?"

"For sure," agreed several members of the writer's workshop. "Real nice, Rita" said one.

"And look who's back!" said Nick, turning to Martin. "It's Martin! We haven't seen you for a while, Martin."

"Oh, you know," said Martin, "I've been busy, is all."

"We're all glad to have you back, fella!"

"Real nice," said someone.

"Since you've been busy and all," said Nick, "did you get time to write something down for us?"

"Well," said Martin, flicking through his notebook, "I've got this little thing here, it's not much, about - "

As Martin gave a precis of his story, the café owner Anthony brought an extra-shot americano (black, no sugar) to the table, which Martin had ordered when he arrived.

"Oh, that's interesting," said Nick, when Martin finished his summary, "like that thing, y'know... that happened near here, up at The Ossington wasn't it?"

"I know what you mean," said Martin, "yes I suppose that could've inspired me, I guess. Maybe."

"Well then," said Nick, "will you read it for us?"

"I suppose I could," said Martin. "It's not much, you know, not by Rita's standard - but if you're sure?"

"Come on now, Martin," said Nick, "don't be shy, this is an open table - we all like to hear your little stories, don't we, writers?"

"For sure," agreed several members of the writer's workshop. "Real nice," said one.

"Okay then," said Martin, "here it is, I suppose. It's called:

Appendix: "Double Quote Angst" – An Epistolic Punctuation Thread

Hi all

I'm in a minor quandary. Maria & Linda have correctly pointed out that the preferred method of dialogue in the UK is as follows:

'Hello,' said the writer, 'is this one of those "awkward moments" that you've been referring to?'

However, most of us were taught at school that double quotes are how you denote speech. So unsurprisingly that's what we've done:

"Oh, bugger," said the author, "this is definitely going to 'put the cat among the pigeons', as my old gran used to say."

Now the thing is, double quotes are not unknown in UK publishing, they're just rarer. And the rest of the English-speaking world uses doubles. Based on volume, it would be easier to change the singles to doubles than the other way around.

But, this risks the Wrath of the English Department and I don't fancy being a marked man.

Help?

Nick

***

Double-quoter by nature because yes, education. How did it happen that schools taught us all wrong?

Given that "doubles are not unknown" in publishing, it seems to me it's a convention and not a rule. This is the age of disruption! We can do whatever we want! We could identify as International English writers and be damned.

Actually I don't mind either way but if we were to go with singles, does this mean I would have to change to single finger quote actions when I am being annoyingly patronising in an argument with

someone who said something stupid? Somehow that doesn't seem
like it would be passively-aggressively provocative enough?

Martin

***

That's it!! I withdraw the use of my story!!!! I also demand we use
more !!!!!! Throughout!! In fact, I'm leaving this group. I'm sick of the
arguments about doubles and singles!!!
(Maria and Linda's heads have just exploded!!!!!!)
I prefer double quotes but i really don't mind, whatever is easier -
probably neither option in terms of formatting.

Clair

***

I am a little defensive of my single quotes, only because I've had
a fellow British writer *point out* that I'd made the recurring error of
using apostrophes instead of speech marks in my book. :|
No but really, I don't mind. Happy to have my singles swapped
to doubles! :)

Abigail

***

As someone who never notices punctuation, I don't mind what
you decide.

Lynn

***

Morning all!

Well ... I'm glad that my school weren't the only ones teaching doubles for dialogue.

Shall we just not use speech?

In light of committing to one or the other I'd say doubles however ... would you mind sending over the 'law' on this for future considerations going forwards? Especially for my own work. I love some of the humour in your responses but similarly I don't mind either way, I'm just appreciative that you lovely bunch have taken the time to read my waffle. Let alone amend it But no seriously ... use doubles else I'll kill you.

Luke

***

Personal preference is for single speech, double quotes though I was admittedly taught the opposite at school in the prehistoric age. I don't mind either way, so whichever is easiest.

Just checked our other books and although we have always agreed on singles for speech, in the last one, 'Blood, Sweat and Typewriters,' or "Blood, Sweat and Typewriters," there is a mixture in different stories. As the latest book is also a compilation by different writers why not leave each story as preferred by its author?

I now know why I don't write as much as the rest of you. You either rise at the crack of dawn or don't sleep at all.

Linda

***

Just read a book where the author did not use any quote marks! I too at school was brought up on double quotes which I understand is the US way whereas the single quote is the UK way.

I don't mind the outcome. My only thought is that as this is a historical book about Newark in England, should we not be

Americanising it? But as I said, I don't mind. Really appreciate, as Luke states, the time people are putting into this.
Am editing my novel at the moment and 'Dreyer's English' by Benjamin Dreyer has been very helpful and covers some of this.

Mark

***

I like Linda's suggestion of using whichever the author has used for each story. That will really mess with the readers mind which is quite a satisfying thought

Clair

***

Hi all,
As you know, I always notice punctuation.
Please leave mine as it is...single...and I agree with Martin, we can do what we like. So each to his own on this, but if anyone should sometime's misuse an apostrophe, woe betide.

Maria

***

I see what you did there ;-)

Nick

***

Agreed - to each his own but singles for me.

Ade

***

Nick are you getting any closure from this?

'Requiem for a Dream' — no dialogue marks but speech. My other half is currently reading it and it has freaked her out.

I am not precious about it either way. It's a group project so whatever suits the group best!

Luke

***

This came to me through a time vortex:

Historians have uncovered evidence that World War III was not started by the assassination of King Andrew or by events on the remote island of Tagoa where several self-righteous billionaires had been plotting a world takeover. But it had been from the fall out from several writers in the town of Newark discussing double or single quotation marks. Apparently their leader, later to be known as Our Great Leader Nick, had retaliated to mixed information on the matter by savaging the work of several members. Those several members had formed a new group called The Writers of Fosseway. Following multiple nasty emails, a battle had taken place between The Writers of Fosseway and Fosseway Writers in Morrison's carpark. Although no trolleys were harmed the following report in the Newark Advertiser had been the final straw. The Advertiser had simply quoted several observers as stating "It was horrible", 'It was literally a bloodbath, well not literally but...', "I was there with me mam and she's seen a thing or two but this...", and 'It spoilt a really nice breakfast I had had that morning'. The confusing interchange of quote marks made the letters section, was reported on local and then national news. It would seem that things then got out of hand across the world. King Andrew was informed whilst eating pizza and then assassinated. News reached the island of Tagoa where the matter became the main item on the agenda. And the rest became history.

Oh well...

Mark

***

We should add this whole train of messages to Twitter it would go viral... or vile... one or the other.

Clair

***

LOL! I was going to say this could all go at the end of the book as a sort of short story of its own!

Abigail

***

I'm inclined to add this entire thread as an appendix.

Nick

***

And watch me get sued!
If you are going to use the entire thread then can I just remind readers that my new book will be coming out...

Mark

***

Good idea Mark!

My 14th story (i think) was published mid June - it's called *Finding Love*. Please buy it. I'm desperate for money and don't mind begging. Thanks

P.S. my publishers uses single quotes

Thank you for reading

Please buy my books. Also buy all our books. Thanks

Clair

***

About the Authors

Abigail Ted is an author of Regency romance satire whose love for 18th and 19th-century fiction transformed into her telling the stories of dynamite damsels with precarious sanity (see *Oh Dear, Maria!*).

Adrian Bean has worked as a director and writer in theatre, television and radio for over forty years, and is obsessed with British black-and-white films about the war. He is currently writing a book about the death of his uncle in a mid-air collision near Newark in 1941.

C.L. Peache aka Clair... writer, blogger and full time narrowboat adventurer! I enjoy being at the beck and call of my characters and will write anything they tell me to write because I know my place in life! www.clpeache.com

Linda Cooper: Born in the USA (no relation to Bruce) but lived in the U.K. ever since. Retired primary school teacher who moved to Newark six years ago and was delighted to discover the Fosseway Writers who ensure, through projects, competitions and support that writing must take 'top priority' alongside my other interests of reading, knitting, paper crafts, gardening, music, genealogy and walking (which often includes geocaching - a wonderful waste of time). If only sleep and housework were unnecessary.

Luke Settle spent over a decade writing and producing music but decided to go on hiatus in order to embrace his passion in literature. He has produced a short thriller, *A Certain Shade of Lipstick*, and *Forever*, a romantic novella.

Lynn Roulstone is a retired librarian, originally from London. She escaped to the story-filled town of Newark two years ago and hasn't looked back since.

Maria Dziedzan: Drawing on my Ukrainian roots, my first novel, *When Sorrows Come*, was in the top three of the Historical Novel Society Indie Award in 2016. There followed *Driven Into Exile* and later *Bread and Salt* before I turned to Fosseway Writers for a more eclectic range of inspiration. Delighted to be part of another great collection of writing.

Mark Smith: recently retired to spend more time with my wonderful granddaughters. I enjoy sport, music and writing when time allows. Hope to have my first novel, *The Tomato Runner* available shortly, next week, last year, ten years ago, depending on when you are reading this.

Martin Costello is founder and principal of a therapeutic school for trauma-affected teenagers in Nottingham, director of The Urban Worm environmental social enterprise and Churchill Fellow. Performing 'stand-up poetry' as Another Poet, he hosted a regular series of not-for-the-faint-hearted spoken word events including a slam week at the 2018 Nottingham UNESCO poetry festival. The poet has now been retired in favour of the more serene pursuit of the written word.

N.K. Rowe took up blogging by accident and then joined Fosseway Writers in 2016. Three years later he became Chair (also by accident) and accidentally wrote his first novel, *The Ophagy*. He really should pay more attention to what he's doing.

Samantha Hook: writer, photographer, mother, roller-girl, lover, fighter, gypsy, tramp and thief. Vice Admiral, Attorney General, UN Ambassador; winner of Nobel Peace Prize, Purple Heart, Rear of the Year. Compulsive liar.

Printed in Great Britain
by Amazon